# SHADOWS IN OUR BONES

A Novel

## Tamara Merrill

Shadows In Our Bones
Copyright © 2019 by Tamara Merrill

ISBN: 978-1-7338555-0-1 (Hardback Edition)
ISBN: 978-1-7338555-5-6 (Paperback Edition)
ISBN: 978-1-7338555-2-5 (Audio Edition)
ISBN: 978-1-7338555-3-2 (ebook Edition)

Cover Art by Teresa Espaniola
Cover Photo by Park Kitchings
Author Photo by Teresa Espaniola
Editing by Lisa Wolff
Book Design by Integrative Ink

*Shadows In Our Bones* is a work of historical fiction. All incidents and dialogue are products of the author's imagination and are not to be construed as real. Where real-life figures appear, the situations, incidents, and dialogue concerning those persons are entirely fictional and are not intended to change the entirely fictional nature of the work. In all other respects, any resemblance to actual persons, living or dead, events or localities is entirely coincidental.

Published in the United States by CALI Press

# WRITER'S NOTE

In 2016, when I was introduced to the history of Malaga Island, Maine, I knew at once that I wanted to write about the events that took place there in the early 1900s. I was in the middle of writing a different book and I tried not to think too much about the Malagaites; however, the story was so shocking that I couldn't resist reading everything I could find (which wasn't much). What I did find kept me intrigued. I was fortunate to correspond with one of the descendants of Benjamin Darling, and her input send me down a path I hadn't expected.

Over Thanksgiving, 2017, I made a trip to Maine, where Kate O'Brien of the State Historical Society kindly allowed me to view the archives and to read the literature they had collected and displayed during the 2012 retrospective exhibit that was staged at the Maine State Museum in Augusta. My wonderful friends Bobbie and Gary Mahler not only hosted my visit but provided tours of Phippsburg, Malaga Island, and the surrounding communities.

I began researching and writing in earnest. My research centered around anecdotal accounts, newspaper and magazine articles written during the period, and a variety of books, both fiction and nonfiction. I was often appalled by what I learned, sometimes delighted, and always fascinated. The things I studied often differed. Events, dates, and places were reported and recorded in a variety of ways. Names were spelled in multiple ways. The story I have written came out of what I learned. I chose to use the dates and names that best fit the story I wanted to tell.

Characters, whenever possible, are based on actual persons, but some like Cora have been fleshed out to add substance, and some are entirely imaginary. Remember that while this story is about real people who experienced real events, it is not meant to be other than a work of fiction.

The descendants of Malaga Island are scattered throughout the world. The events that took place in the 1900s are a part of their individual, private stories and as such are their stories to tell, not mine.

In 1909, at the National Education Association conference, Charles Bartlett Dyke shared his low expectations of non-whites: "It is absurd to theorize about the propriety of a college education for the mass of Negros, or Indians, or Filipinos, or Hawaiians. They lack the intellect to acquire it." Besides, he said, "for economic reasons, primitive man must be trained on vocations that fit him for life in the white man's world. This is a fundamental requirement in the education of primitive races."

Maya Angelou, American Poet is quoted as saying — "We should all know that diversity makes for a rich tapestry, and we must understand that all the threads of the tapestry are equal in value no matter what their color."

# CHAPTER ONE

## MALAGA
## 1912

Whatever was wrong, Eliza knew that it was serious. Grandfather Jim was never afraid of anything, but something wasn't right. For weeks the adults had been whispering together and she's overheard him speaking to them about fear. Just last night, she'd listened to him tell Grandmother that they needed "to flee to save the children." From the trepidation in Grandfather's voice, she knew he was worried. Something or someone was bothering him. Today Eliza had helped pack their belongings into old grain sacks. But no adult would answer her questions. Now, in the darkest part of the Maine night, the islanders carried their children, and the sacks, to the boats. When this night was over, she vowed that she would insist that Grandfather explain everything.

Eliza scrambled down the steep bank of Malaga Island, shivering in the damp fog that slithered out from the dark pine forest and hovered, low and thick. She shifted her heavy bundle higher on her shoulders, stumbled, and reached out to catch herself. The rough pine bark pierced her palm. Eliza didn't pause. Grandfather had told her to hurry and she knew that she must.

Eliza knew every inch of this island. Whenever her chores would allow it, she had roamed the woods, the two beaches, and been welcome in every home. Born on the island, she had spent every day of her thirteen years surrounded by family and friends. Even the winter her parents had caught a fever and died within hours of one another, Eliza had felt cherished and safe. But now, something terrible was happening.

She slid down the bank and reached the boats. The moon slipped from behind the fog, and for a moment the world seemed less frightening. Already the younger children were huddled together, covered in quilts, and keeping silent. No one cried out or even whimpered. Marcus saw her and started to rise, his big brown eyes shimmering with tears. She longed to pick up her youngest brother and hold him close. He was all she had left in the world. Grandfather's admonition rang in her mind, and instead of reaching for Marcus she placed a finger over her mouth and whispered, "I'll be right back." She tossed her heavy load into the boat and turned back toward the house.

Eliza reached the house and shouldered another heavy sack. "Eliza." Grandfather's voice stopped her. She turned to find him standing on the step, back straight. The moon slid out from behind the clouds again and Eliza thought she saw a tear on his cheek, but the clouds shifted and his face was hidden in the shadows again.

"Yes, Grandfather?"

"When you get to the boats, tell the others that you have the last bundle. They will see you all safely away. I'm counting on you to help your grandmother and the women with the children."

Eliza nodded. "Aren't you coming with us?" Her voice trembled and she tried not to sob.

"I'll be along in a few days. Go now." For a moment his large, rough hand caressed her head. "Hurry, child. You need to catch the tide."

For a moment Eliza thought Grandfather was going to pull her close in a hug, a hug she desperately craved. He squeezed her shoulder and turned her toward the trail. She glanced back only once. Her grandfather was gone.

# CHAPTER TWO

## SEATTLE

Georgia sat in another faculty meeting. To the professors in the room, she seemed alert, as if she were paying close attention to the discussion. In reality her mind was far away. The patter of the rain against the window made her yearn for warm, sunny Hawaiian beaches. How she ended up in Seattle she'd never know. It certainly hadn't been her plan to return there. She hadn't wanted to teach anywhere so cold and wet. Georgia picked up her stylus and began to doodle on her e-ink sketch tablet: a dagger, a zombie, a set of stairs to nowhere, lines and squiggles that had little meaning; just a habit. She added a note to herself: CALL MOM. It'd been a week or more since they talked, which was unusual. Georgia drew a thick line under her note and realized they'd finally finished talking about the need to increase contributions from alumni. She added a few stars to her note.

"Georgia." Mark's voice, as always, was arrogant and slightly patronizing. Georgia felt herself stiffen. "Do you have anything to add?"

"No, Mark. As usual, you have been very informative and articulate." She smiled politely at the Humanities Department head. Linda, her best friend, an English professor, snickered. Georgia managed not to glance in her direction, afraid that if she did, they'd both start laughing. The two women had had many a booze-fueled night where they made fun of Mark Hedrick's less-than-stellar grammar skills, but this wasn't a good time to rile him; she would need his support to achieve her goal of a tenured professorship.

Georgia knew that Mark didn't believe Women's Studies, her field, belonged in the college curriculum. He resented any budget items that weren't what he called "traditional, worthwhile, education." It was quite possible that Mark believed women didn't belong in higher education at all. He'd stated many times that Women's Studies had been included in the curriculum only to make the "do-gooders" happy and that he saw no value in the field.

Martha Schmidt smiled at Mark, and waved her hand like a third grader asking for a bathroom pass. "I have an idea, Mark."

*Suck up*, Georgia thought and wrote SUCK UP on her notepad using balloon letters.

"Excellent, Martha." Mark turned his attention toward the older woman. "I can always count on you."

The rain outside increased. The clock crawled toward 5 p.m. and Randy Kellerman, Dean of Students, finally called the meeting to a close with his usual jovial, "Job well done, folks."

Georgia managed to smile at Mark as she tucked her tablet into her bag. He didn't, she noticed, smile back.

"Smooth move," Linda muttered as they left the room together. "Way to antagonize the Mighty Mark. I thought you had decided to play nice with him."

Georgia shrugged. "I *was* trying. You noticed I smiled."

"See you at kendo," Linda said, draping her cross bag over one shoulder and wrapping a scarf around her throat at the same time.

"Let's skip it. It's pouring outside and I need a cocktail to erase the week," Georgia begged. Her bag slipped and crashed to the floor as she tried to wrap her scarf.

5

Linda grinned and reached for the dropped bag. "Klutz," she said affectionately. "After class I'll buy you a cocktail, but we promised we'd go twice a week and we're going." Linda swung an imaginary sword and strode off.

"Okay, but I hate you!" Georgia shouted at her retreating back.

❦

The kendo class ended. Linda and Georgia bowed to their sensei, placed their wooden swords on the rack, and headed for the locker room. As they stripped off the navy-blue *keikogi* and *hakama*, the traditional kendo top and bottom that they wore for class, Georgia grinned at Linda. "I saw you flirting with that new guy Ken brought to class. I thought we were taking this class to improve our core strength."

"I'll have you know one of my core strengths is flirting!" Linda laughed. "Come on, hurry up. I'm starving."

Georgia slid into her jeans, zipped her boots, and gathered her purse and jacket from the locker. Linda urged her on. "Let's go. How about sushi at that new place on Yesler Way?"

"You're not fooling me. I heard the new guy tell Ken that he'd meet him there. You hope to get to know him, don't you?"

"Not 'know him' so much as check him out. I'm tired of online dating. I want to flirt with a real live person and Ken is always fun, so ..."

"Okay, but you're buying the sake."

By the time Georgia parked her car and entered the restaurant, Linda was already settled in a booth next to the "new guy." Georgia wasn't surprised. What Linda wanted, she always got. Ken waved to her and she joined them. She gave Ken a friendly kiss on the cheek and held out her hand to the stranger. "Hi, I'm Georgia O'Brien."

"Mitch Yamamoto." He smiled, his dark eyes lit up, and he held her hand for a moment. Georgia found herself smiling in return. Linda cleared her throat. Georgia dropped Mitch's hand and reached for a menu.

Ken resumed the conversation Georgia's arrival had interrupted. "I was just explaining that Mitch is my new boss at Microsoft. I talked him into coming to the kendo class tonight, but he's not really a beginner like the rest of us. He's a level-seven *Rokudan*."

"Wow," Linda said, her eyes widening in admiration. "I'm not sure I'll ever even get to level one. You must have been following the way of the sword your whole life."

"Pretty much," Mitch admitted. "My family is quite traditional and my dad is a *Hachidan*, so it was what I did and what I do."

Linda playfully squeezed his bicep. "Yup, you have the muscles for it."

Mitch blushed and Ken saved him by asking, "How are your muscles, Linda? Are you ready to buy your *bogu* and begin the really intense work?"

"Maybe." She turned toward Mitch and flexed her arm as she asked, "What do you think? Am I ready?"

"Perhaps," Mitch said carefully and turned back to Georgia. "Are you interested in advancing?"

Georgia took a swift gulp of her sake and shook her head. "No. I'm only in the exercise class. I can't really see myself actually hitting anyone, even if it's only with a wooden sword."

Linda giggled. "What about Mark Hedrick?" Georgia laughed.

Ken, who had heard many stories about Mark, shook his head. "For two mature, thirty-something college professors, you two sure don't act it."

"Ken Yoshida, I happen to know that you are exactly one day older than I am and that you still like to play the original Pac-Man game every chance you get. When you grow up, I'll know it's time for me to grow up." Linda laughed at the look on his face. "Don't worry, Ken, I won't tell all your secrets to your new boss." She turned toward Mitch in the narrow booth.

"Ken and I grew up next door to each other. He's the closest thing to a brother that I'll ever have. He had to tutor me from kindergarten through my master's. Without his ability to share his math skills, I would have failed."

Mitch laughed. "Somehow, I doubt that." Mitch caught Georgia's eye and grinned. "What about you? How are your math skills?"

"Excellent, thank you." She pulled her eyes away and quickly picked up her paper-wrapped chopsticks. She busied herself cracking the sticks apart and smoothing their edges by rubbing them together. *He has beautiful eyes,* she thought, *and a very nice smile, but Linda has first dibs.*

Her phone rang and she pulled it out to look at it. "Sorry," she said, excusing herself, "it's my mom."

Georgia swiped the answer button as she stood and walked away from the booth. "Hi, Mom. Sorry I didn't call back. The meeting ran long and then I had kendo. I was going to call you when I got home tonight."

"Are you still out and about?" Her mother's voice was as calm and as cultured as always, but something alerted Georgia.

Her steps slowed. "I am. Linda and I are having sushi with Ken and a friend of his. Is everything okay, Mom?"

"I was hoping to talk to you about a few things."

"Sure, what's on your mind?"

"I really don't want to interrupt your dinner." Susan O'Brien hesitated and Georgia started to speak, but her mother continued, "Let's talk tomorrow. Can you come by?"

"It's my short day. How about meeting me downtown for a late lunch?" Georgia offered.

"I'll fix lunch here. Can I expect you by two?"

"Sounds fun. How about if I bring Linda? It's been a while since we had a 'girls' lunch."

"Not this time, sweetie. I really need to talk to you alone."

"Mom, what's wrong? I'll be there, but give me a hint so I don't have to worry all night. Is Dad okay?"

Susan chuckled softly. "Don't be silly. Your father's fine. Now go enjoy your friends and I'll see you tomorrow. Love you."

Georgia slipped the phone into her pocket and returned to the table. Linda asked, "How's Susan? Any good gossip?"

"Mom just wants me to come for lunch tomorrow. She says she wants to talk to me about something."

Linda looked concerned. "Is Henry okay?"

"I asked about Dad, but she says he's fine. She probably just wants to make Christmas plans.

"My dad had a heart attack about a month ago," Georgia explained to Mitch and Ken.

"Have you and Linda been friends since kindergarten, too?" Mitch asked.

"No. College. We were roommates freshman year."

"And they've been bonded at the hip ever since." Ken raised his glass in a mock toast.

"Sisters from a different mother," Linda and Georgia said at the same time and clicked their glasses together.

"I'm not exactly sure what that means," Mitch admitted. "But," he, too, raised his glass, "here's to friendship."

# CHAPTER THREE

## SEATTLE

Queen Anne's downtown is a mishmash of restaurants, clubs, and gyms tucked into a wide variety of old and new buildings. As the hill climbs, the urban center drops away and the neighborhood's historic houses, upscale boutiques, elegant restaurants, and spectacular views change the landscape. Georgia turned off Denny Way and headed north through Lower Queen Anne and then up the steep hill to Upper Queen Anne. She preferred to reach her parents' home this way to the quicker route around the bottom of the hill.

She turned west on McGraw and then north again on 8th Avenue, and smiled when she found a space open directly in front of the large Craftsman-style home her parents had lovingly restored. "All is right with the world," Georgia murmured, hearing her grandmother's voice in her head. Granny O'Brien had passed her belief in fairies, mantras, and magical thinking to Georgia and she often found herself repeating them.

Slamming the car door, Georgia looked up the twenty-one steps that led to the wide front porch just as her mother stepped out the cherry-red door and waved to her. "Hi, Mama," Georgia called, and started up the stairs. She took in the glorious riot of color that exploded on either side. "The rhododendrons are gorgeous this year."

Her mother beamed. "They are, aren't they. It must be all the rain."

Georgia reached the top and hugged her mother. "Or perhaps it's your tender, loving care. Have you lost weight? You know you need to take care of yourself, not just Dad."

"Maybe a little." Susan O'Brien pushed the door wide open and drew her daughter into the large square entrance hall. A fire burned in the fireplace and was reflected in a large gilt-framed mirror. Georgia slipped out of her coat, hung it and her purse on the hallrack, glanced in the mirror, and ran a hand over her tousled, dark curls in an attempt to control their unruly behavior.

"It smells great in here. Is that twenty bean soup? Linda is going to be so jealous. You know it's her favorite."

"Don't worry, I made enough so you can take some home and share. Come on into the kitchen and I'll just pop the bread into the oven to warm."

"Where's Daddy? I'll go say hi."

"It's Thursday. He's having lunch with his friends at Betty's Restaurant." Georgia cocked her head as if listening to a student spouting a crazy theory. "Don't look at me like that," Susan continued. "Your father had a very mild heart attack more than a month ago, and the doctor wants him to get out and about and live his life."

"I know. I'm sure you're right. I just can't help worrying about him."

"I do, too. But he hates us to hover. And, I want to talk to you about something else."

"You sound serious. What's up?"

The timer on the oven dinged. Susan turned away to remove the bread. "Sit. We can talk while we eat."

As always, the cheery kitchen and the smell of her mother's excellent cooking soothed Georgia. She might have created a busy, independent life, but she loved her family and hoped she'd also have a husband and children someday. She buttered a piece of the warm baguette and dipped it into her soup. "Ummm, this is so good."

Susan smiled at her daughter. "You look so much like my mother."

"Old and wrinkled?"

Susan laughed. "Of course not, young and beautiful. But you certainly have your father's sense of humor." She picked up her spoon and thoughtfully stirred her bowl of soup. She laid the spoon back down carefully placing it next her bowl. "Georgia," she started. Georgia stopped eating. Susan reached across the table and took her hand. "Do you remember me mentioning that I was having a bit of trouble with back pain?"

Georgia nodded. "From too much gardening, right?"

"That's what I thought, but I went to the doctor and he seems to think it may be more than a muscle strain. He wants to do a bunch of tests."

"Mom, you're kind of scaring me. What does he think it is?"

Susan's eyes filled with tears. She tried to blink them away and squeezed Georgia's hand. "He's worried that it may be some kind of bone cancer, I think. He was vague but he wants me to see an oncologist, as soon as possible."

"Wow!" Georgia exhaled loudly. "Okay." She sat for a second accepting the news, and then stood and hugged her mother. "It'll be okay. Even if it *is* cancer, they have lots of new treatments. We'll get through this. Does Daddy know?"

"Yes, of course. I was going to wait to tell you until after the tests so that you wouldn't have to worry, but he convinced me to talk to you, and your brother, now."

"He's right, Mom. I'll go with you for the tests, and when you get a clean bill of health we'll celebrate together." She wiped a tear from her mother's cheek and hugged her again. "Now, eat some soup—you really are too thin. I can feel all your bones. Tell me everything. What test have you already had? Have you scheduled the visit to the oncologist?"

Georgia pulled apart a piece of bread, making smaller and smaller pieces, as she listened to her mother recount the progress of her pain from what she'd self-diagnosed as a muscle strain, through muscle relaxants, then X-rays and a CT scan, and finally a number of blood tests. "Dr. Hendricks assured me that the blood work was inconclusive, but he insisted that I see a specialist. So, I have an appointment at Swedish Hospital with a Dr. Ramirez on Tuesday."

"I'll come with you." Georgia began mentally rearranging her week to be there for her mother. "What time is the appointment?"

"You don't need to come, Georgia. Your father will be with me, and I'm sure this doctor is just going to order more tests." Susan stood and removed the bowls from the table. She swept Georgia's torn bread into her hand and laughed. "My mother used to tear things whenever something troubled her. I guess you have her 'rip-it-up' gene."

Georgia forced herself to smile back. "I guess I do. If I can't doodle on something, I tear things into pieces. You should see what I can do to a Styrofoam cup. It's funny what we inherit from our ancestors, isn't it? Dad doodles, Grandmother McKinney ripped things, and I have your green eyes."

"And, my intelligence," Henry O'Brien boomed, as he swept into the kitchen and kissed first his wife and then his daughter. "So," he pulled out a chair and sat down at the table, "did your mom fill you in?"

"I did, Henry. I told her everything will be fine. Neither one of you needs to worry about me." Susan changed the subject. "Did you stay on your diet?"

"Yes, dear." Henry pulled a sad face and winked at Georgia. "I ate nothing but rabbit food. Georgie Girl, tell us what's new at that college of yours. What kind of trouble have you and Linda gotten into lately?"

⟡

Susan and Henry stood on the stairs watching Georgia leave. She unlocked her car door and forced herself to smile and wave gaily to her parents. She pulled out, turned the corner, and parked in the first open space. Her hand trembled as she found her phone, scrolled down her favorites list, and pressed the call icon next to her brother's name. The tinny sound of the international connection plinked in her ear. She waited impatiently for the ringing to begin. Georgia calculated the time difference. It was about 1 a.m. in Barcelona. She hoped Jeff would be home. People ate so late in Spain he might still be at dinner, and if he was, she knew he'd have his phone turned off.

"Hey, Sis."

"Hey, Jeff." She couldn't go on. The tears she'd been holding back spilled over, and Jeff heard her small sob.

"What's the matter, Sissy?" Usually Georgia hated it when Jeff used her childhood nickname, but today she heard only his love. "Did Mom tell you her news?" Georgia nodded and then realized he couldn't see her, but his voice continued. "She called me a few hours ago and said she was having tests. I don't think we need to panic. Even if it is cancer, they really have a lot of new treatments. It isn't always a death sentence, not anymore."

"But she's so thin. And, I don't know, she just doesn't look right."

Jeff laughed gently. "She's been taking care of Dad and she probably hasn't been eating right. I'm going to call Dad. I'll get his take on how she's doing. Then I'll call you back, okay?"

"Okay." Georgia gulped back her tears. "Thanks, Jeff."

"Don't worry, Baby Sister, everything will be okay."

Georgia knew it might not be true, but Jeff's familiar, calm voice soothed her fears. Five years older, he'd always been her rock, keeping her secrets and helping her figure things out. "I love you to the moon and back."

"To infinity and beyond," he responded.

"Forever and always," they finished together. The goodbye tradition from her childhood made them both feel better. Georgia disconnected and drove home.

# CHAPTER FOUR

## SEATTLE

Georgia stayed busy and tried not to dwell on her mother's plight, but when her father called, she knew as soon as she heard his voice that the news would not be good. The diagnosis was, in fact, swift and brutal. All the tests revealed the same result: stage two multiple myeloma. Susan needed to begin treatment at once.

Georgia struggled to hold back her tears. Her Google searches had shown her that multiple myeloma was a scary diagnosis. "How's Mom doing?"

"You know your mother—she's more worried about all of us than she is about herself," Henry said. "She called Jeff and assured him that there was no need for him to come home. And, I promised her that I'd tell you everything will be all right."

"Oh, Dad." Georgia heard the tears in her voice and tried to get herself under control. "I'll be over after work. Tell Mom I love her."

They hung up and Georgia hurried to find Linda. She needed to tell her best friend the terrible news.

⧼

The next day, both Georgia and Henry went with Susan to her appointment. Dr. Ramirez greeted the family. His calm manner allowed Georgia to take the first deep breath she'd managed since Henry's call. He assured them that, while the diagnosis was frightening, new treatments were being developed all the time. And, that Hutchinson Cancer Research Center had the best, most experienced team of medical professionals.

"I'm sure that at least some of you have been on the Internet reading about this cancer." Georgia felt herself blush and she looked down at her shoes. Dr. Ramirez continued, "Multiple myeloma is also called Kahler's disease. It is a cancer of the bone marrow, not a bone cancer. That means it begins in the blood plasma cells in your bone marrow. This is a relatively rare cancer and it, like most cancers, varies from patient to patient. We do know that it develops slowly over time, and many persons are totally asymptomatic until the cancer is quite advanced. As it is in your case, Mrs. O'Brien."

Susan shifted uncomfortably in her chair and wiped away a tear. Henry slid closer to her and placed his arm around her shoulders. Georgia wondered if she should have noticed something, anything at all. *Mom is never sick,* she thought.

"Your cancer has been staged at stage two based on the amount of albumin and beta-2-microglobin that was found in your blood. Our next step in your treatment will be to conduct another series of tests that help us determine the levels of monoclonal immunoglobin, calcium, and hemoglobin in your blood, as well as the number of bone lesions you have developed. I'll see that these tests are scheduled immediately and then you can begin treatment."

The family sat stunned by the foreign words they were hearing. Everything sounded awful, dismal and scary.

Dr. Ramirez kept talking. "The back pain you have experienced lately is a symptom of the cancer. Your red blood cell count is quite low and is, no doubt, causing your fatigue, general weakness, and bruising. Susan, I'd like you to meet with

Marybeth Jackson today. She is a patient care coordinator and will be your personal advocate here at Hutch."

He pressed a button on his phone and straightened his pen so that it lined up perfectly with the edge of his blotter. The office door opened and a tall, raw-boned black woman entered. Dr. Ramirez didn't pause. "I will give you something today that will help with the anemia and something for the back pain. Our first step is to determine, as exactly as possible, the extent of the damage to your plasma cells. Marybeth will explain her role in your treatment and can answer any additional questions. In the future your appointments may be with me or with other members of our team." He stood and held out his hand to Susan. "Cancer is a life-changing event, but our team is here for you." He dropped Susan's hand and reached for Henry's. "I'll see you again soon."

Dismissed, the family shuffled out the door Marybeth was holding open. She smiled warmly at them all. "That was a lot to take in, wasn't it?" Not waiting for an answer, she added, "My office is right down here. Follow me." Silently, holding hands, they trailed her around the corner and into a large, sunny office. A sofa and several chairs were arranged around a coffee table, and a desk was pushed off to the side of the room. It felt warm and cozy. "Let's take a break before we get started. Make yourselves comfortable. The restrooms are just down the hall. I'm going to pop out and get us all something to drink. Who wants what—coffee, tea, soda, water, juice?" She took their coffee requests and disappeared, closing the door gently behind herself.

Susan sank onto the sofa. She didn't say a word, but tears overflowed and ran down her cheeks. Henry extracted a Kleenex from the strategically placed box on the side table. He gently wiped his wife's face as he whispered to her. Georgia excused herself and stepped into the hall. Her parents didn't notice. She leaned against the wall, her knees weak and her hands shaking. *My mother is going to die,* she thought. She tried to stop the thought; the doctor hadn't said it was a death sentence, had he? She tried to recall his exact words. She blinked away tears, pulled herself away from the wall, and forced herself to move down the hall. She passed an open doorway and glanced in. Marybeth was arranging a coffee tray. "Need any help?" Georgia asked.

Marybeth smiled at her. "Sure. The coffee will be done in a minute and you can carry the carafe. Grab that box of cookies and put some on a plate. Our clients keep us supplied with goodies." Georgia choked back a sob, but Marybeth just touched her arm and didn't comment. Georgia was relieved. If one more person told her everything was going to be all right, she would explode.

∽

Georgia let herself into her apartment and found Linda grading papers at the dining table. "Hey," Linda said, and Georgia burst into tears. The emotion she'd been blocking all day erupted. Covering her face with her hands, she sobbed like a child. Linda wrapped her arms around Georgia and led her to the sofa, gently forcing her to sit. "I think my mom is going to die," she managed to say at last.

Linda handed her a wad of tissues. "Blow." She waited a minute. "Better?" Georgia gave a hiccup, nodded, and blew her nose again. "Sit right there. I have a bottle of Pinot breathing in the kitchen and I think you need a glass."

She returned with the bottle, two glasses, and a plate of cheese, poured the wine generously, and lifted her glass in a salute. "Okay, tell me."

Quickly Georgia recounted the doctor's words and explained the needed tests, ending with, "But after that we met with a really nice woman. She's our main contact during treatment, some kind of social worker I think. Marybeth Jackson. She was very kind and we all liked her."

"So that's good, right?"

"Right. This cancer thing is like stepping into a whole different dimension. My mom is never sick, we all rely on her, and now ..." Georgia's voice trailed off.

"Don't get ahead of yourself, girl. Your mom is still Susan McKinney O'Brien and I've seen her work miracles before." Linda refilled their glasses, and this time when she raised her glass she said, "To the wonderful, amazing Susan."

They clinked and drank deeply. "I think we should make a plan."

Georgia grinned. "You want to put my mom's cancer on a spreadsheet?"

"No. Well, not exactly, but I want to help. If she has to have chemo, or some other gross treatment, we could take turns sitting with her, we could cook for them, maybe clean the house or do the shopping." Georgia giggled. "Well, maybe not cook or clean, neither one of us could ever meet Susan's standards, but I must be able to do something."

"You did just do something. You made me laugh on what has to be the worst day of my life, so far."

# CHAPTER FIVE

## SEATTLE

It was amazing how quickly Susan's cancer treatment became the new normal. While the cancer was definitely stage two, Susan's condition remained stable. She started a series of corticosteroids to strengthen her immune system and reduce the inflammation and responded well, exhibiting none of the side effects they'd been warned about. Some days it was almost possible to forget that she was ill.

On a warm afternoon in May, Georgia sat in her tiny office, grading papers and trying to ignore the sunshine that was beckoning her to come out and play. When a tap sounded on her open door, she didn't even glance up. "Come on in, Linda. I'll be done in a minute."

"I'm not Linda," a man's voice answered.

Georgia dropped her pen and looked up. "Mitch." She smiled. "Hi, come in."

"I hope I'm not disturbing you."

"Definitely not. I was just finishing up here. What are you doing on campus?"

"Actually," Mitch dropped his gaze, "I was at a meeting and I thought, maybe, if you had time, we could get a cup of coffee." When Georgia didn't answer immediately, Mitch added, "If you're busy ..."

"No," Georgia shook her head, "a cup of coffee sounds like a good idea. I need some fresh air and a jolt of caffeine will make it easier to finish these papers." She stood up and stretched. "There's a great coffee place just across the quad."

Walking beside Mitch, Georgia felt her mood lift and she smiled. Her shoulders relaxed. She took a deep breath and felt the stress of the last few weeks recede. Mitch smiled down at her. "Have you dropped out of kendo?" he asked.

"No, not really. Life has been hectic. Are you still taking the beginners class?" Georgia's surprise showed in her voice. "You're way too advanced for our group."

"I was hoping to see you again," Mitch admitted, "and I didn't have your number." Georgia stopped on the sidewalk and turned to look into his eyes. He seemed sincere. "This was the only way I could think to find you. I asked for your office location at the admin office."

"I thought you'd be dating Linda by now."

"Why would I be dating Linda?" Mitch was perplexed. "She's very nice, but ..."

Georgia laughed. "I guess I just jumped to the conclusion. Whenever Linda flirts with someone they get together."

"When did I ever flirt with Linda? I see her at the gym, but ..."

"Don't worry about it." Georgia began walking again. She changed the subject. "If it's not a secret, what was your meeting about?"

Mitch blushed. "No secret; I didn't have a meeting. I know it makes me sound like a stalker, which I assure you I'm not, but I just wanted to see you again."

"You could have asked Ken for my number."

"Yes, but I'm his boss and it didn't seem right." Georgia nodded. That made a certain kind of sense, and it was flattering that he'd gone to so much trouble after only spending one brief evening in her company. She wasn't sure what to say and was relieved when they entered the coffee shop.

Mitch suggested she hold a table for them while he went to the counter to place their order. Georgia fiddled with her phone as she waited. She'd been attracted to Mitch the night they met, but between her mom's diagnosis and her belief that Linda wanted to date him, she'd completely put Mitch out of her mind. And yet here they were, and it felt right. When he set the cups on the table and slid into his chair, she smiled at him. "I thought it over and I believe you aren't a stalker. So, tell me who you are."

"Mitch Yamamoto, computer nerd."

Georgia laughed. "That much I know. Where did you go to college?"

Within minutes the discomfort between them vanished, and soon they were talking and laughing like old friends. When Mitch again asked why she hadn't been to the kendo class, Georgia hesitated only a moment before telling him of Susan's diagnosis and her need to spend more time with her parents. Mitch covered her hand with his. "I'm so sorry for your troubles." The words were old-fashioned and from someone else Georgia would have found them strange, but she had no doubt of Mitch's sincerity.

Georgia's phone vibrated and she glanced down to see a message from Linda. "Oops," she said, running her thumb across the screen to open the app, "I completely forgot that I was supposed to meet Linda at my Mom's house, at five. I need to get going. They're wondering where I am." She quickly typed, SORRY ON MY WAY.

"I'll walk you to your car." Mitch rose gracefully and held out his hand. Georgia took it without thinking. They walked quickly to the parking lot. Mitch held the driver's door as she got in and smiled down at her. "May I have your number now?" he asked.

"Absolutely." Georgia dug a card out of her bag and gave it to him. "This was fun. Thanks for stalking me."

Mitch laughed and closed the door. "Drive carefully. I'll call you later."

*♫*

"You look happy," Susan commented as she hugged her daughter. "What's going on?"

"Can't I just be happy to see you guys?"

"You can, and you should, but I know you have a secret. I'm your mom. I know stuff." Susan waited, her arms crossed, pretending to be stern. "Tell us where you were."

"Do I get a glass of wine first?" Georgia appealed to her dad. He shook his head.

"Susan's right," Linda agreed. "I'd know that look anywhere. You've met someone."

"I was just talking to a friend and we lost track of the time. That's all," Georgia declared.

"What friend?" Linda demanded

"Mitch," Georgia admitted as she felt a grin spread across her face.

"Mitch?" Linda looked at Susan. "Mitch who?" Susan shrugged.

"Mitch Yamamoto," Georgia said.

"Ken's friend?" Linda asked.

Georgia nodded.

Linda continued. "I didn't know you two were seeing each other."

Henry caught the tone of Linda's question and busied himself pouring wine. Susan kept her eyes on her daughter and saw her blush.

"We aren't. He came by my office this afternoon and we went for coffee."

Linda grinned and hugged Georgia. "He totally stalked you. And you liked it."

Henry handed them each a glass of wine. "Who is this guy? I'm not sure I like the sound of a stalker."

Linda accepted her glass and tilted it toward Georgia in a friendly salute. "Don't worry, Henry. Mitch is an extremely good-looking, perfectly respectable Microsoft nerd."

23

"Do we get to meet this young man?"

"Dad, for heaven's sake. I'm an adult, remember? I had coffee with him once." She glared at Linda. "He may never call again."

"Oh, he'll call," Linda declared. "I saw his reaction to you when he met you and he did take the time to stalk you. And, you'd better say yes when he calls. You need to get back on that horse and start dating again. You broke up with Charlie ages ago."

"Could we please stop discussing my love life in front of my parents?" Georgia took a gulp of her wine. "Mom, what's new with you?"

Susan took pity on her blushing daughter and changed the subject. "I'm feeling stronger, and your dad and I thought we'd take a little trip." She waved away the protest that was forming on Georgia's lips. "Just over to Ocean Shores for a few days. I think a few days walking the beach is exactly what I need."

# CHAPTER SIX

## SEATTLE

Seattle can be cold and rainy in the spring, but when the weather is warm and sunny the city is beautiful. The dogwood trees burst into bloom and the lilacs fill the air with their delicate scent. The days begin to lengthen and everyone seems to be smiling. Mitch and Georgia, who had quickly become a couple, took full advantage of the weather and spent as much time as possible outdoors, wandering the city and getting to know each other.

As spring term drew to a close, the invitation to Dean Kellerman's end-of-the-year party appeared in faculty mailboxes. The professors who were not teaching summer sessions talked incessantly about vacation plans. Finals were given and graded. Students cleared out of the dorms and houses.

At the last minute, Georgia invited Mitch to the Kellerman party.

"This is getting serious," Linda declared when told that Mitch had accepted. "Guess I'd better find a date, too. I don't want to look like your ugly stepsister."

"Ask Ken. We can go together."

"Yah, like that won't look weird if we both show up with Asian dates. I think one mixed-race couple at a time is all the faculty can handle."

Georgia turned to Linda, surprised by her comment. "You're kidding, right?"

"Sort of, but not really. You know that neither my family nor Ken's approves of us being more then friends." Linda hesitated and continued, "Mitch told us that first night that his family is very traditional. Has he introduced you to his parents yet?"

"Of course not," Georgia protested, "we've only been dating a couple of months."

"And have you introduced him to *your* parents?"

"No, but they know I'm dating him."

"And do they know he's Japanese?"

Georgia stammered, "It never came up. It's not like it matters."

Linda nodded, saying nothing.

"My family isn't prejudiced. They have lots of friends from a variety of races." Linda stayed silent. "My brother is living with a Spanish woman, for heaven's sake, and we all like her."

"Lola is blond and blue-eyed. She speaks with a charming accent, but she looks as Caucasian as you do. I'm just saying, you might be surprised how many people still have a problem with interracial couples." Linda held up her hand to stop Georgia's protest. "I think Mitch is a great guy, and most likely your parents will agree."

"Well, I like him and I've invited him to the party. So, that's all that matters. Right?"

Linda nodded and changed the subject.

❦

As they drove toward the Madrona Park neighborhood on the shores of Lake Washington, Georgia remembered Linda's words. Surely, she thought, no one from the college would be rude.

They found a parking spot and walked toward the Kellerman house. Following the sounds of the party, they entered through the open side gate. Lake Washington glittered in the setting

26

sun, and a few sailboats moved across the water toward Mercer Island. Party lanterns hung in the trees. It was a perfect setting for a party. Randy Kellerman saw them and hurried across the grass to greet Georgia. "Welcome," he said, holding out his hand to Mitch. Introductions were made and Randy moved them along toward the bar. Georgia let out the breath she hadn't realized she was holding.

"Hey, guys." Linda swept in and gave them each a kiss. "Nice to see you, Mitch. How's everything at Microsoft?"

"Microsoft?" Mark Hedrick approached with his hand held out to Mitch. "What do you do at Microsoft? I'm Mark, head of the department, Georgia's boss. She's been keeping you a secret." He winked at Georgia.

Georgia thought about slapping him but instead took Mitch's arm. "Mitch is the head of a department, too, Mark. And, I don't believe he would ever wink at anyone working in his department."

Mark frowned at her. "Lighten up, Georgia. This is a party. I just wanted to meet your boyfriend." He turned back to Mitch. "Seriously, are you one of those geniuses they hire from foreign countries?"

Georgia stiffened. She could feel Mitch's arm tense under her hand, but he said smoothly, "No, I'm one of those American geniuses." He turned away from Mark. "Linda, what do you have planned for the summer?" Mitch moved past Mark and continued talking to Linda.

Georgia noticed Martha sidle up to Mark and whisper something. She could feel them both watching. Georgia reached for Mitch's hand and felt his light squeeze. She smiled up at him. He grinned. "So, now I'm officially your 'boyfriend'?" He waggled his eyebrows at her and joined the women in their laughter.

Driving home, Georgia apologized for Mark's behavior. Mitch shrugged it off. "The guy's a rude jerk. When you look like a 'person of color' you grow up hearing all sorts of things. I was delighted that you didn't let him get away with that wink."

"He is arrogant and I'm not sure why he has tenure, but, I admit that I don't like him, so I'm not a good judge of his teaching ability."

"I was raised to believe that one should not make judgments hastily, or impulsively, but that said, some judgments are based on reality."

Georgia laughed. "Is that a Buddhist belief?"

"Well, sort of. I may have simplified it a bit. He did act like a jerk not only to me, but also to you. I might have judged him myself."

"Are you a Buddhist?"

"If you were to ask my father, I think he would say that I'm not, but I was raised in a Buddhist family. I'm more a Buddhist than anything else. How about you?"

Georgia considered the question carefully before she answered. "I guess I'm a Christian. My family doesn't go to church, but both my parents did when they were kids. I took a World Religion class for a humanities credit and nothing really grabbed me. It wasn't something my family talked about. Is your family religious?"

"They wouldn't call themselves religious. We don't consider Buddhism a religion; it's more a way to live and understand life. Each person practices in their own way and that way changes over time. It's a path, not a destination, as my grandfather used to say."

Georgia wanted to ask how his family would feel about their relationship, but it seemed too soon. They hadn't actually declared any relationship, despite Mitch's comment tonight. As Mitch parked in front of her building, she thought about asking him up for a cup of coffee or a nightcap. Mitch jumped out of the car and came around to open her door.

He took her hand as she stepped out. "Thanks for inviting me to be your date tonight. I enjoyed meeting the people you work with." He kissed her cheek. "I have an early meeting in the morning. I'll call you after, okay?"

"Sure," she managed, surprised by his abrupt departure. "Sleep well."

"You too." And he was gone. Georgia let herself into the building and climbed the stairs to her apartment. *That was kind of weird,* she thought.

# CHAPTER SEVEN

## MALAGA
## 1903

Christian missionary and Civil War veteran Captain George W. Lane prided himself on caring for his fellow man. It was, he felt, his duty to assure that others were brought to an understanding of the Lord. During the winter months he and his wife, Lucy, taught Sunday school at their church in Malden, Massachusetts, and participated in charitable works. They enjoyed and entertained persons who were their intellectual equals. It had been their pleasure to meet many dynamic scientists, reformers, and professionals engaged in the national eugenics projects.

Ensconced now at their summer home on Horse Island, Maine, Captain Lane pondered the arguments that had been made by his eminent guests last winter, arguments that affirmed his beliefs that the lower classes were inferior to the educated upper and middle classes. *It is certainly true,* he told himself, *that we must pay attention and do whatever is necessary to assure that the human race is not weakened by the underclass.* Why, only last night his dinner guests had spoken of the residents on Malaga Island. Something had to be done to correct the blight that this degenerate community of half-breeds was casting on the fine city of Phippsburg, in fact, on the state of Maine, perhaps even on the whole of the United States.

"Lucy," he declared, "I have decided that we will establish a summer mission on Malaga." He held up his hand to stop her protest. "I know, it is quite possible that the inhabitants are inca-pable of learning to read or write, but it is our Christian duty to bring the poor, ignorant bas-tards the word of God." He paced the floor for a few steps, stirred the fire, and then continued. "They must be shown the error of their ways. The good Lord does not intend for his races to intermarry. On Sunday mornings I shall row to the island and preach to the inhabitants. I shall show them the way to redemption."

Lucy dropped her needlework back into its bas-ket and beamed up at her husband. "An excellent idea, Captain. I believe the good women of our church in Malden would be willing to support us in this endeavor."

"That is fine thinking, my dear. But before we approach our home church, I will assess the abilities of the natives and determine if they are capable of learning. Our first priority will be to save their immortal souls. I will go alone, this first Sunday, to assure that you and Cora will not suffer from exposure to these…," he hesitated, searching for the right word, "these sinners."

"I'm sure you know best, dear." Lucy dropped her eyes and resumed her needlework.

31

The following Sunday, July 5, 1903, Captain Lane rowed across the mile of choppy water to the shore of Malaga Island. He hailed the group of young boys playing on the shore. Two of them dashed out and pulled his boat onto the rocky beach. Taking his Bible from the oilskin his wife had wrapped it in, he stepped ashore and asked the gaping boys, "Who is in charge here?"

Both boys ducked their heads and didn't speak. "Are you both deaf?" he demanded. "How can the Lord expect me to save sinners who can neither hear nor speak?"

The older of the two straightened his spine but kept his eyes downcast. "We can hear and talk, sir."

"Well then, answer the question. Where is your leader, the man they call the King of Malaga?"

"We ain't got no king, mister. We Americans."

"Barely," Captain Lane muttered. "Where do I find Jim? Jim McKenny?"

"That be his house there, sir. Up that path in the trees."

"Go fetch him." The boys hesitated. "Go, now!" He pointed in the direction the boy had indicated. The boys rushed away. Captain Lane straightened his spine and assumed the at-ease stance of a former soldier.

Soon a tall, rugged-looking Caucasian man, dressed in overalls and wearing a fedora, ambled down the path. He seemed completely at ease as he approached the visitor. "Morning, mister," he said, holding out his hand. "What brung you to Malaga this fine morning?"

Lane drew himself up as straight as possible and did not extend his hand. "I'm Captain George W. Lane from Malden, Massachusetts, and I've been called by the Lord to bring you, and the other natives, the word of God."

Jim McKenny smiled. "Well, I reckon the missus will be glad to hear that. Come on up to the house and sit a while." He turned and started up the hill. Lane, having no choice but to follow or turn back, followed. Several children, including the boys from the beach, fell in behind them. Captain Lane did not look back to see the oldest boy imitating his walk, posture straight and chest puffed out. McKenny didn't turn around but ordered, "Mind your manners, Joshua." The boy dropped his pose and fell back a few paces.

∽

Over dinner, Captain Lane told his wife and daughter about his day. "The island itself is quite beautiful," he began. "But the people," he shook his head sadly, "they are as we were told, an abomination. They are living like savages, cohabiting, and procreating like animals."

"Captain!" Lucy raised her napkin and covered her mouth in surprise.

"I'm sorry, my dear. Please forgive my strong language." He nodded to both Lucy and his daughter, Cora. They smiled their forgiveness.

"Go on, Father," Cora said. "I fear if we are to help these people find the Lord, my mother and I will need to know the worst. If you intend to return next Sunday, perhaps we should go with you." Captain Lane raised his eyebrows at the

33

suggestion and Cora hurried on, turning toward her mother as she finished, "If the women and children are ignorant of the ways of the Lord, Mother and I can show them the way that God-fearing women comport themselves."

Captain Lane pursed his lip and slowly gave a nod. He beamed at his daughter and wife. "You are a good girl, Cora. I think that is an excellent idea. A woman's touch may be just the thing."

Lucy shuddered at the thought of unwashed natives, but she nodded her acquiescence and they began to make plans for their ministry.

Cora smiled to herself and thought, *At last something interesting to do.*

# CHAPTER EIGHT

## SEATTLE

Georgia and Linda sat on the dock of the Carson house. They dangled their feet in the cold, clear water of Lake Tapps. Mount Rainier loomed to the south, its slopes just beginning to turn pink from the setting sun. Georgia leaned back on her elbows and sighed in contentment. "This must have been a great place to grow up," she commented.

"You know I didn't grow up here." Linda nudged her, causing Georgia to collapse.

"Hey," Georgia protested and sat back up. She shaded her eyes to locate Jeff and Lola, who were paddleboarding toward the dock. "I know this was your grandparents' summer house, so yes, spending summers here counts as growing up here."

Linda laughed. "I guess. But I really didn't spend that much time out here. Maybe just a few weeks every year."

"Poor little rich girl," Georgia teased.

Linda turned serious. "It really wasn't that great here. My grandfather had very strong opinions on everything and there was always a lot of tension."

"Opinions? Like what?"

"Well, for starters, he complained all the time about how and where my parents lived. He called our house the shack in the ghetto."

Georgia was stunned. "You lived in Wallingford, didn't you?"

Linda nodded. "Grandfather said the houses were too small and too close together. He was angry because our next-door neighbors were Asian, and he always called my mom "that hippy you married." He hated the fact that Dad chose to be a teacher."

"He sounds like a real charmer."

Georgia tried to think of a way to change the subject, but Linda continued, "Most of the year my grandparents lived in Manhattan, so we didn't see them except in the summer. Then Grandmother died when I was in high school and Grandfather never came back out here. We were all surprised that when he died, Dad inherited this house."

The sky brightened into a riot of pink, coral, and deep purple. Mount Rainier turned a bright gold. "And," Linda finished her thoughts, "with a sunset like this I now love this place, and I'm glad my parents decided to retire out here and make it a year-round house. Come on." She jumped to her feet and stretched out a hand to pull Georgia up. "The paddleboarders have returned and it's time to open the wine."

They linked arms and walked toward the patio.

☙

"Thanks for inviting Lola and me to stay out here with you and Sissy." Jeff tilted his glass toward Linda in a salute.

"Don't call me that!" Georgia frowned at her brother. He grinned back at her. Linda excused herself to open more wine, leaving the siblings to quibble.

Jeff sobered and spoke seriously. "So, how is Mom, really?"

Georgia quickly told Jeff everything she'd learned by watching her parents and going along on appointments with their mother. "I'm really glad you were able to come over for a visit. When they get back from Ocean Shores tomorrow, you'll see for yourself. She says she's fine, but," she shook her head, "I just don't know."

Jeff reached over and squeezed her hand. Georgia managed a weak smile. "I do know that she'll be really happy to see you and Lola. You're the best present anyone could give Mom right now."

"Thanks. Lola and I decided to grab a cheap flight and come for a surprise visit. I didn't expect them to be out of town, but I'm glad it gives me a chance to get over my jet lag and for us to talk. I want to do whatever is best for Mom. Do you think I should take a leave of absence and come home for a few months?"

Georgia considered the idea and shook her head. "I don't really know. Mom would certainly be against the idea."

"Yeah, I know, but if I can help in any way, I want to be available."

"I think we need to take things one step at a time. Mom is holding her own right now."

Linda and Lola reappeared with trays of food and the wine. "I thought we'd just eat dinner out here. It's such a beautiful evening. Jeff, could you light the fire pit?"

"Excellent idea," Jeff agreed.

Glasses were refilled and they all settled in with plates of food. Jeff took Lola's hand and smiled first at her and then at Georgia. "Lola and I would like to make an announcement." Georgia set her plate down. "If you think you can keep a secret, Sis, I'll tell you."

"Secret? A secret from Mom and Dad?"

"We plan to tell them, too, but I want to tell them myself, and you're such a blabbermouth, I don't want you to give them even a hint."

"I swear." Georgia hooked her pinky finger with his and pretended to spit.

Jeff looked questioningly at Lola, who nodded back. "We are going to have a baby!" He grinned broadly and brought Lola's hand up to his lips.

Linda applauded and Georgia leapt up to hug the happy couple. After the excited congratulations calmed down, Georgia asked when the big event would take place.

"Not until Christmas, but," his grin grew even larger, "first we'd like to get married."

"Oh my God!" Georgia squealed, and hugs, toasts, and congratulations were exchanged again. With everyone settled back and their glasses refilled, Georgia asked about their plans.

"If you think it wouldn't be too much of a strain on Mom, we'd like to do it at their house, as soon as possible. Then we will be married again by a priest at our church in Barcelona."

"I think she'd love it. I promise not to say a word until you do—but you'd better do it right away, because you know I can't keep a secret."

⁂

The next afternoon Georgia, Jeff, and Lola let themselves into the house on Queen Anne. They kept on eye on the driveway. When their parents pulled into the garage, Jeff and Lola quickly hid in the laundry room. Georgia sat at the kitchen table pretending to drink a cup of tea, a book open in front of her. Susan entered first. She smiled warmly and hugged Georgia as she sank down in the opposite chair.

"What a lovely surprise. I didn't expect to see you until tomorrow. Everything okay?"

Georgia grinned. "Everything's fine. How was the coast?"

"Windy. A little cold. Absolutely beautiful," Henry answered as he dropped their luggage on the kitchen floor and regarded his daughter. "What are you grinning about? You look like the cat that swallowed the canary."

"Nothing, Dad. I'm just happy to see you guys."

"Georgia," Susan said firmly, "you're up to something. I'd know that look anywhere. What are you hiding?"

Georgia laughed. "Let me get you a cup of tea, Mom. Do you want one, Dad?"

Susan picked up a duffel bag. "In a minute. I want to put our wet clothes into the wash. We got caught by a wave this morning."

"Are you going into the laundry room, Mom?" Georgia spoke loudly, hoping to warn Jeff.

Susan looked baffled. "Yes, Georgia. That's where the washer was last time I checked."

She hesitated a moment, looked back at her daughter, turned the knob, opened the door, and started to laugh. "Oh my God, Henry. Look who's here!" She pulled Jeff and Lola into a hug. "I knew something was up the moment I saw that look on your sister's face. She never could tell a lie or keep a secret."

Georgia laughed. The sound of her family together and teasing just like always made her believe that everything would be all right. Her mother looked so happy and rested, it was impossible to believe she was sick. The laundry was forgotten in the pleasure of their reunion.

Later, after Jeff and Lola had shared their news and expressed their desire to be wed at the house, a desire that Susan embraced wholeheartedly, they sat together making plans. "So, it's decided," she said. "The wedding will be two weeks from today. First things first, we need to make a guest list and send out invitations. Can you kids have your lists ready tomorrow? Maybe we can just use that Evite thing, Georgia. You know how to do that, don't you?"

Jeff and Georgia exchanged a smile, happy to watch their mother in what they used to call full battle mode. Susan stopped her list-making for a moment and turned to Georgia. "Will you be inviting your young man?"

"He's not my young man, Mom. We've only been dating a couple of months. I don't know if he's ready for a family wedding."

"Oh, I thought it was getting serious. Linda mentioned that you invited him to that faculty thing." She looked down at the list she'd started. "Lola, do you want any special flowers? And, unless you brought a dress with you, we need to go shopping right away."

Jeff watched Georgia as his mother steamed ahead with the plans. He pulled her up. "Come on, Sis. Let's take a walk around the old neighborhood while they discuss flowers and girly stuff."

⁂

They left the house and turned, automatically, toward the Willcox Wall. Since childhood it had been their place to talk. They chatted casually about changes to the neighborhood and what friends were doing until they reached the Betty Bowen Viewpoint. The Olympic Range spread out in the distance, the sun lighting the snow that was still present on the peaks. Jeff sighed. "I love Spain, but sometimes I dream about this view."

Georgia laughed. "It is spectacular on a day like today."

For a moment they stayed silent. Boats were visible on the Puget Sound and in the distance, a ferry whistle blew. Jeff turned his back to the wall and looked at his sister. "So, new boyfriend, huh. Why is he a secret?"

Georgia avoided his eyes and began walking slowly. "He's not a secret," she protested.

Jeff waited, knowing there was something more. When Georgia stayed silent, he prompted. "Does he have a name?"

"Of course. Mitch," she hesitated and then said quickly, "Mitch Yamamoto. He's Japanese."

"Good thing with a name like that." Jeff grinned. "And, is he a nice guy? Do you like him?"

"He is and I do."

"So, what's the problem?"

"I don't know. It's just something Linda said about mixed-race couples." She stopped and looked over the wall. "Remember when we used to play tag up and down these stairs?" Jeff nodded and waited until she finished her thought. "I don't think Mom and Dad would mind me dating an Asian. Do you?"

"I don't think our parents would mind at all. They always welcomed all of our friends."

"I know, but dating is different. With Mom sick, and everything, I don't want to give them anything to worry about."

"If you are happy, they will be happy. You know that, right?" Georgia nodded.

"What did Linda say, anyway? Did it have anything to do with the fact that she's in love with Ken Yoshida?"

"Linda's not in love with Ken!" Georgia protested.

"Of course she is. She's been in love with him her whole life."

"You don't know that. You've only known her since my freshman year of college."

"Duh, how can you not know it? It's always Ken this and Ken that."

"But they've never even been out on a date. Their families are friends. Linda told me neither family would approve of them being more than friends. I like Ken, too, but I never considered them as a couple."

"Exactly my point: why not?"

"He's Japanese."

"Actually, he's an American."

"Well, yeah, but..."

"So, little sister, what are you really worried about? If you like this guy, why not introduce him to the family?"

⌒♊⌒

Georgia stared at herself in the bathroom mirror, toothpaste foaming from her mouth. *I wasn't worried about introducing*

*Mitch to my colleagues; why not introduce him to my family?* She spit out the toothpaste and rinsed her mouth. *I'm an idiot,* she concluded as she reached for the phone.

"Hi, Mom. Hope it's not too late to call."

"Of course not, sweetie. I was just looking at a bridal magazine." Susan laughed. "That sounds a little weird, doesn't it? I'm having so much fun helping Lola with the wedding plans. We're going dress shopping tomorrow. Lola was going to call you in the morning and invite you to come along."

"That sounds like fun, Mom, but I was calling to invite you all over tomorrow night for dinner. Mitch will be here and I'd like you all to meet him before I invite him to the wedding."

"What a lovely idea." Susan didn't miss a beat; no surprise showed in her quick acceptance of the invite. "I'll accept for all of us. May I bring something?"

"Absolutely not. Just come around six and we'll have a glass of wine before dinner."

Georgia ended the call to her mother and quickly tapped on Mitch's picture to call him. She needed to do it before she lost her nerve.

"Hey." Mitch answered on the first ring. "I was just reaching for the phone to call you. Was your mom happy to see your brother?"

"She was, but she was even more delighted when they told her they want to be married next week, at Mom's house."

Mitch laughed. "Wow! That must have been a surprise. My mother would kill me if I sprang something like that on her."

"There's nothing my mother likes better than a party. She's great at planning events." Georgia took a deep breath. "I invited the family over here for dinner tomorrow and I'd like you to come, too." Mitch didn't say anything and she hurried on. "I thought, if I was going to cook anyway, it might be time for you to find out that my skills in the kitchen are limited."

Mitch chuckled. "I don't scare easy. I'd love to meet your family." Georgia blushed, aware that he'd seen through her excuse. She was glad he couldn't see through the phone. "What time are they coming and what can I do to help?"

"About six, and you really don't need to do anything."

"I'll bring the wine and I'll be there early. My mother taught me to set a perfect table." They chatted a few minutes and said good night. Georgia hung up thinking about how easy it was to be with, and talk to, Mitch.

༄

Promptly at five the next afternoon Georgia's doorbell rang and there was Mitch, wearing perfectly pressed khakis and a blue button-down shirt. His arms were burdened with a wine carrier, a large bouquet of flowers, and a blue sport coat. Georgia smiled at him and kissed him quickly.

"It smells great in here. I thought you said you couldn't cook."

"It's chicken cacciatore. I hope you like Italian, because it is the only food I do know how to cook."

"Perfect. I bought both red and white wine because I forgot to ask. Flowers for you and a jacket for me in case your father or brother will be wearing one. I didn't know how formal your family might be."

Georgia laughed. "I like a man that is always prepared. Dad will probably have on a jacket, but Jeff will be wearing whatever he has in his luggage. Trust me, my family is not formal."

"I just want to make a good first impression. Now let me help."

They worked well together. He chatted with her as he opened cupboards and found what he needed to set the table. She felt herself relaxing. *I really like this man,* she thought.

# CHAPTER NINE

MALAGA
1903

All week the weather had been cold and foggy. With Sunday morning approaching, Lucy, who had reconsidered her agreement to minister to the natives, decided to use the weather to bow out of the trip across the water. "The weather is quite inclement, dear," she said to Captain Lane. "You know Cora has a weak chest and I don't think it would be wise for her to go out on the water. I do believe it would be best if Cora and I stay home this morning."

Captain Lane glanced between his wife and daughter. "She does look flushed. No need to expose her to the elements." He patted his wife's arm. "Yes, you two should stay indoors today. Perhaps you should dose her with a mustard plaster."

"I'm fine, Father," Cora protested. She'd been thinking all week about the opportunity to do something different, have an adventure, even if it was with her father.

"Cora, your mother knows best. You do as she says and I'll be home by dinner."

Cora watched from the window as her father rowed across Casco Bay and disappeared into the mist. "I feel fine, Mother," she said, turning to look at Lucy.

"I'm sure you do, dear. But…" Lucy laid her knitting down and considered her daughter. "You sixteen years old now, Cora. We need to consider your future. If you intend to attract a suitable husband you must always be seen as a worthy, God-fearing woman."

"But, Mother," Cora argued, "certainly doing charity work among the poor is a respectable occupation for a lady."

"For a married woman, yes. But a young woman or a girl, such as yourself, should not be exposed to the rougher elements of society." Lucy resumed her needlework and avoided her daughter's eyes as she continued, "At tea on Thursday, Mrs. Ellison was saying that the living conditions on Malaga are deplorable. Their houses are miserable hovels. The children are filthy and," Lucy took a deep breath, gathered her courage, and finished, "the parents are not married."

Cora almost giggled. She lifted her embroidery to her face to cover her smile. She was determined to get permission to join her father on the island next week. Certainly, one parent was all the protection her reputation would need. The idea of meeting persons who lived "in sin" was very appealing.

Last winter, one of her classmates at Girls' High School in Roxbury had returned from the Christmas break with a copy of Kate Chopin's book *The Awakening and Selected Short Stories*. Cora and her friends had pored over the pages, gasping and giggling as they read about Edna's pursuit of an affair. Cora longed to know if it was possible to live as an independent woman, a woman who made her own decisions and controlled her own life the way the women in Chopin's stories did. She knew that her parents would be scandalized if they discovered her thoughts.

"I only want to be of assistance to Father," Cora said. "His work as a missionary is admirable and very brave, don't you agree?"

"It is," Lucy murmured, avoiding her daughter's gaze.

For a few minutes the two worked in silence. Lucy laid her knitting aside and said, "Cora, if you will promise me that you will stay near your father at all times, and that you will not touch any of those people with your ungloved hand, you may go to the island next Sunday, weather permitting."

Cora's eyes glowed with excitement and she smiled broadly. "I promise, Mother. I'll be very careful." She wanted to jump for joy, but that would never do. Instead she laid her hoop aside and asked, "May I make you a cup of tea?"

✍

The following Sunday dawned bright and clear. Lucy plead a headache but raised no objection to her daughter rowing across the bay with her father. Cora sat in the bow of the boat watching Captain Lane pull hard on the oars. The small craft skipped quickly across the mile of open water. Cora quivered with excitement. She wanted to turn and watch the approaching shore, hoping to catch a glimpse of the natives, but she stayed quiet following her father's rules about remaining still in a boat.

At last, a man's voice hailed them from the shores of Malaga and Cora felt safe to turn her head and take a look. A tall man stood on a rock waiting for the Captain to toss him the painter. Cora dropped her gaze. He was not at all what she'd expected. He looked like any other fisherman. True, his skin was weathered, but she was sure this man was Caucasian. His beard was groomed and his overalls were patched and seemed clean. She felt a tinge of disappointment. She'd been led to believe that everyone on this island would be Negro or mixed blood. *But at least,* she thought, *I'm on an adventure.*

Captain Lane clambered onto the rocks and turned back to help Cora. Her long, heavy skirt made it difficult to climb over the gunwale without exposing her ankles. Cora hoped her father wouldn't notice. If Mother knew she hadn't even been introduced before her first faux pas, she'd never be allowed to come again. She saw a small child watching from behind a tree and winked. The child darted away. Cora realized the little boy was naked and felt herself blush.

Captain Lane did not extend his hand to the tall man, but he did dip his head as he said, "Morning, McKenny."

"Mornin', Sir. We was wonderin' if you'd be by today."

"I'm a man of my word, McKenny. When I say every Sunday, you can set your watch by me." Captain Lane gestured toward Cora. "My daughter, Cora, is with me today. She will hold a Sunday school for the children while I preach to the adults."

McKenny tugged his hair and nodded. "The children will enjoy that. Come on up to the house. We all be gathered there for the preaching." He turned and strode away. Captain Lane followed rapidly and Cora was left to scramble over the rocks by herself.

*Sunday school,* Cora sputtered silently. It would have been nice if someone had mentioned that she would be expected to provide entertainment. "I hope the children are wearing clothes," she muttered, as she struggled to climb the steep path with her long skirts twisting about her legs and her thin boots sliding on the loose rocks.

Having reached the clearing, Cora looked around at the cluster of small, ramshackle frame houses. Lobster traps, nets, fishing gear, and piles of discarded shells surrounded each house. It smelled strongly of the fishing docks Cora had experienced in Boston. She raised her handkerchief to her nose in an attempt to block the odor. She looked around. A larger house was set off to the side of the others and commanded the best view. It, too, was unpainted, but somehow it seemed less slovenly. *That must be King McKenny's house,* Cora thought as Mr. McKenny opened the door and waved her father forward.

Captain Lane looked back, as if remembering he'd left his daughter behind. He gestured impatiently for her to hurry. She picked up the pace. They stepped through the doorway into a square room with a large fireplace. The room was crowded with people of all colors. Children sprawled on the floor and the adults sat on rough benches that appeared to have been gathered just for this occasion. The men rose to their feet when they caught a glimpse of Cora standing behind the Captain. *So,* Cora thought, *not savages after all.*

Jim McKenny raised a hand and everyone settled down. "This here is the Captain's girl." He gestured toward Cora. "She's going to take the children into the yard for Sunday school while the Captain preaches to us. You go along now, children, and behave yourselves. I don't want to hear about no talking out."

Parents urged their children to follow Cora. Captain Lane seemed to want them gone. Cora had no idea what to do, but she turned to the door and stepped out into the yard. The children tumbled out after her and followed as she started uncertainly across the broken shells. She looked about, hoping to spy a place that would be appropriate to worship the Lord. Someone tugged at her arm. Cora looked down into the face of a very thin girl. Bright blue eyes shown out of her olive complexion. A heavy sprinkling of freckles covered her nose and cheeks. She nodded to the child in way that she hoped would encourage the child to state her need but allow herself to maintain her dignity.

"We can go over yonder. There's a good sitting space past that tree."

"Excellent. Lead the way, please."

∽

The small clearing was surrounded by ragged pine trees and littered with boulders of various sizes. Cora settled herself onto one of the

49

larger boulders as she watched her self-appointed helper direct the other children. At last, the girl turned to Cora and said, "We ready now, Miss." She sat down herself and pulled one of the smallest children onto her lap.

Cora looked over her group. She was relieved to see that they were all fully clothed and appeared to be quite clean. Cora smiled. She hoped she looked like a teacher. She still had no idea what she was going to say. She took a deep breath and began the way she had heard other teachers begin. "I'm Miss Cora Lane and I am delighted to be here today. Before we commence our lessons, I'd like to get to know you. If you would each just tell me your name and how old you are, I think that would help."

The skinny girl spoke up first; she seemed to be the natural leader of this ragtag and bobtail group. "I be Sarah McKenny. I eleven. This," she patted the child in her lap, "be my sister Eliza. She three."

The children followed her lead. By the time the fourteen children had finished, Cora was much calmer. "I will tell you a story, but first, let us pray." Fourteen heads bowed obediently and Cora began, "Thank you, Lord, for bringing the Captain and me to this beautiful place..."

The children sat rapt and attentive as Cora told them the first Bible story that came to mind, the story of the loaves and the fishes. One little boy said to his neighbor, "How that work? Ain't no way that little fishes feed that many." Cora knew she should respond and explain, the way she'd learned: how believing in God could work miracles.

Instead she smiled at the child and finished the story.

Cora struggled for something more to keep their attention. The adults were still inside the house and she knew her father would be angry if they played a game on Sunday. Sarah came to her rescue again. "Can we sing, Miss Lane?"

"Indeed we can." Cora's relief made her smile broadly. "This is my favorite Sunday school song." She began:

*"Jesus loves me—this I know, For the Bible tells me so*
*Little ones to Him belong— They are weak, but He is strong.*

*"Yes, Jesus loves me!*
*Yes, Jesus loves me!*
*Yes, Jesus loves me!*
*The Bible tells me so."*

Cora sang the second verse.

*"Jesus loves me—He who died Heaven's gate to open wide*
*He will wash away my sin, Let His little child come in."*

This time the children joined on the refrain and their joyous enthusiasm filled the air.

*"Yes, Jesus loves me!*
*Yes, Jesus loves me!*
*Yes, Jesus loves me!*
*The Bible tells me so."*

Cora began the third verse as the adult service ended. They spilled into the yard. Someone's sweet soprano voice joined with Cora's, and soon the entire group of islanders were singing together.

⁓

Sarah walked beside Cora as she and Captain Lane returned to the boat. Cora felt a small hand slip into her own and tug. She stooped down to hear Sarah's whispered question, "Will you come again next preaching?"

"I will," Cora promised, and squeezed the hand that was not much darker then her own.

Settled in the boat, Cora listened to her father recount his sermon and then was surprised to hear him say, "You did a good job today, Cora. The Lord will be pleased, but perhaps there should be less singing next time."

"Thank you, Father." Cora clasped her hands together to keep from protesting the rightness of blessing the Lord with song. She realized that she had never put on her gloves. *Not only did I touch a native,* she thought, *I did it ungloved. I won't mention that to Mother.*

# CHAPTER TEN

## SEATTLE

Georgia let out a breath she hadn't been aware she was holding and let herself relax. She looked around the table. Everyone was talking and eating; it all seemed perfectly normal. She caught Jeff's eye. He gave her a grin and a thumbs-up. She grinned back and passed the open wine bottle to her brother.

She wasn't exactly sure what she'd expected, but this was great. "Does anyone want coffee with dessert?" she asked, rising to clear the table. Lola and Mitch both stood to help. She waved Mitch back down. "The kitchen is too small for more than two."

"He's very nice," Lola said softly as soon as they were safely away from the diners. "And very good-looking."

Georgia almost giggled. "He is, isn't he?" Laughter rose from the table; she could hear her dad telling a story and hoped it wasn't about some embarrassing incident from her childhood. They quickly sliced and plated the tiramisu and returned to the table.

"Your cooking has certainly taken a turn for the better," her dad teased as she placed his serving in front of him. "This looks much better than the coffee cake you made with coffee grounds."

"I was seven, Dad." Mitch laughed along with everyone else, and Georgia continued, "You're all safe to eat this. I bought it at Terra Bella this afternoon."

The family chatted and gossiped for another hour. Mitch was included in every conversation. Georgia watched her mother closely but could see no sign that she was tired or ill. Jeff's visit and the upcoming wedding seemed to have made her very happy.

◦∽◦

Mitch stood next to Georgia as the family hugged and kissed each other good night. Henry shook his hand and smiled warmly. "It was a pleasure to meet you, Mitch." Turning to Georgia, he pulled her into a bear hug and whispered in her ear, "We need to talk." He stepped back, and in a normal tone said, "How about going for a walk with your old man tomorrow. The doctor says I need exercise."

"Ah, great." Georgia stumbled a bit with her answer.

"Eight a.m. I'll pick you up and we'll do Green Lake." Georgia nodded. "Okay, I'll see you in morning. Come on, everyone, let's get out of here so Georgia can do the dishes." He herded the family down the hall, waving as the elevator door closed.

◦∽◦

"Your family is very nice," Mitch said, pulling her into a hug. He kissed her forehead. "Let's get these dishes done. It sounds like you have an early-morning date."

Georgia washed and Mitch dried. He carefully returned the plates and glasses to their proper cupboards without asking. "How do you know where everything goes?" Georgia asked.

"I took most of it out to set the table. And," he cocked an eyebrow at her, "I am an engineer; we know things."

Georgia snapped a damp towel at him. "Want a nightcap?" she asked.

"I'd love one, but I have an early day tomorrow, too." He pulled her back into his arms. "Do you and your dad get together often?"

"Maybe once or twice a month."

"I've never gone for a walk with my father," Mitch mused.

"Never?"

"I don't think so. He's pretty reserved. My family is very different from yours."

"Well," Georgia said carefully, unsure of how to respond, "Irish families are talkers and touchers." She remembered her dad's whisper and thought, *I hope Mom is okay.* She shook off that thought. *More likely he just wants my opinion on a wedding gift for Jeff and Lola.*

☙

Knowing that Henry was always on time for everything, Georgia was waiting on the curb in front of her building at 7:55 a.m. At exactly 8:00, Henry pulled into the drop-off area. Georgia hopped into the car. She leaned over the console and kissed her father's cheek. The smell of good coffee filled the car and she gratefully picked up the cup closest to her seat.

"Vanilla latte, right?"

"Absolutely. Thanks, Dad."

"My pleasure." Henry kept his eyes on the traffic as he pulled out, turned toward Green Lake, and then picked up his own cup.

"I thought the doctor told you to cut out coffee."

"He suggested it," Henry acknowledged as he took another swig. "I've cut back, but I need a cup in the morning. It just makes my day begin in the right way."

They stayed quiet the rest of the way to the parking lot. Georgia was thinking about her mother. If Dad had bad news to tell her, she wanted to put it off as long as possible.

Green Lake shone in the sun. Canada geese strolled through the bright green grass that stretched down to the shore, pecking and honking at one another. The joggers and bikers circled the water, keeping to their respective lanes, waving occasionally if they spotted a friend. The playground was empty at this early hour.

"It's so peaceful here in the morning." Georgia looked around. "Remember when we used to come to this playground? You could always push me higher and faster than anyone else."

Henry chuckled. "Not sure your mom thought that was a good idea. Let's walk." He strode off quickly. Georgia did a quick hop-step to catch up. She waited, knowing that he'd spill whatever was troubling him when he was ready.

"Mom seems good," she ventured.

Henry nodded.

"It sounds like she is really enjoying planning Jeff's wedding. I hope it won't be too much for her." Henry glanced down at his daughter. *He looks upset,* Georgia thought.

They walked in silence for a minute, and then Henry motioned to a bench. "Let's sit."

Georgia refrained from making a comment on how little exercise they'd had so far and waited for him to tell her what was on his mind. Henry gazed at the lake, his eyes following a canoe. He sighed. *Here it comes,* George thought, steeling herself.

"Georgie Girl," he began, still not looking at her, "you know your mother and I want you to be happy more than anything else, right?" Georgia nodded silently. "We are very proud of you and your brother." He seemed at a loss to continue.

"I know, Dad. Jeff and I feel very lucky to have parents like you guys."

Henry began again. "Even when you were very young we allowed you to make your own decisions. We tried not to interfere unless it was really important. But..." He cleared his throat. "Mitch is a very nice man. We were both impressed by him last night."

*Huh?* Georgia thought. Aloud she said, "Yes, he is. He enjoyed meeting you, too."

56

"Have you considered what it means if your relationship becomes serious? Marriage is difficult enough when the couple shares the same background."

Georgia wanted to lash out; she was thirty-four, not fifteen. She struggled to stay silent and see where Henry was going with this.

"Mitch is certainly smart, but he is not like us. He is a foreigner, a practicing Buddhist."

"Mitch is as American as I am, Dad. He was born in San Francisco. I never would have expected you to be racist."

"Calm down, Georgia." Henry reached over and placed his hands over her shaking ones. "I love you and I want what's best for you. Have you thought about what you are getting into? Before you get your heart broken, you need to realize that his parents may not approve of a relationship with you. And what if you decide to have children together? What about your children? What will it be like for them to grow up biracial? I just want to know that you are looking at this from all sides before you rush into a life with a Japanese man."

"I need to move." Georgia jumped up and strode quickly down the path and away from Henry. Linda's words of caution about Mitch's traditional family echoed in her mind. She wanted to forget them. If she was falling in love with Mitch, and she wasn't absolutely sure she was, race just wasn't that important, was it? Every couple had obstacles to overcome. Her thoughts flew around in circles. She wanted to scream, or cry, or pound something.

Henry caught up with Georgia and they walked in silence until, at last, Georgia slowed and caught his hand. "I know you mean well, Dad, but I'm an adult."

"I know, darling girl. But you are also my baby daughter and I don't want to see you hurt. Your mother and I like Mitch. I just want to be sure you know what you are getting into. Just take your time, okay?"

Georgia's heart twisted with love for her Dad. She tried to stay mad at him. "I really like Mitch. He's good and kind, smart and funny, and we have a great time together. But, I know there would be some people who would never approve of us as a couple. At the end-of-the-year party for the faculty there were a couple of jerks who said really stupid things."

Henry pulled her hand through the crook of his arm. "Get to know him, Georgie. Don't rush into anything. But if he's what you want, we'll adjust."

*I suppose that's the best I can hope for,* she thought. Aloud she said, "I really just want Mom to get well."

# CHAPTER ELEVEN

## MALAGA
## 1903 - 1904

In late August 1903, the Lane family returned to their home in Malden, Massachusetts. Cora began classes at the Horace Mann Normal School in Lexington and vigorously championed the idea of establishing a school on Malaga, when they returned to Maine the next summer. "I believe the Lord wants me to teach those children to read and write," she declared.

"What makes you think they are capable of learning?" Lucy asked. "It is well-known that the black child does not have the same capabilities as the white child. And, these people have inbred. I've been told that many of them are actually imbeciles, some are even morons."

Cora thought about the bright faces of the fourteen children who'd regularly attended her Sunday school classes. True, they were poor, and most of them were quite thin, but their faces had been scrubbed and, for the most part, their clothes were clean. They'd seemed interested in the Bible stories and had been able to follow her instructions. They might not know how to read and write or do sums, but she didn't think they were imbeciles. Sarah McKenny was certainly no dunce and the oldest boy in the group, twelve-year-old Joshua, had been very interested in looking at her Bible. She actually thought he might be able to read a few words.

"Mrs. McKenny is quite taken with the idea that a school could be established for the children," Cora said. She heard the quick intake of her mother's breath and realized her mistake.

"Captain," Lucy said sternly, "our understanding was that Cora would interact only with the youngest children."

"The children have parents, Lucy. Parents who do not live the way polite society does, but parents who love their children. Certainly Cora talks to the mothers. Seloma McKenny is a decent woman. She keeps a clean house."

Lucy huffed, but she refrained from arguing with her husband. *Decent woman, my eye,* she thought.

Captain Lane turned back to Cora. "I believe you may be onto something. The Malagaites will never amount to much, but teaching the children basic skills seems appropriate. The church has sent missionaries to China who are teaching the yellow devils, and this is not so different. I will speak to the Foreign Mission Society."

Cora smiled, pleased with the way the discussion had gone. "May I pour you another cup of tea?" she asked.

<br>

ℳ

Captain Lane met with the Women's Missionary League. He explained how he rowed his small boat across the water each Sunday morning, stopping at the scattered islands to preach the gospel to those who came out on the water to listen. He spoke of his daughter's Sunday school class and of her willingness to function as a summer teacher. He thanked his wife, Lucy, for her support and asked that the League lend their backing to the cause.

"We require no monetary support. Doing the Lord's work is a blessing. But if the League could request that our congregation donate books and slates and chalk, I would like to see Cora be given a chance to teach the children of Malaga to read a few words, to sign their names, and, perhaps, even do simple sums."

❧

The good women of Malden responded to the Captain's request and by May 1904, they had collected a variety of beginning readers, slates, chalk, two Bibles, a few story books including *Pilgrim's Progress,* and a book of poetry by Samuel Coleridge. From her own library, Cora chose *Black Beauty* and *Five Little Peppers and How They Grew*. She admitted to her classmates at the Normal School that she was a bit frightened. To her mother, she declared only that the Lord was supporting her.

"Your father has spoken to that 'King of the Island' person and he has agreed that the school will be held in his home."

Cora nodded. The McKenny home was the largest home on the island. If the school had Mr. McKenny's support, she was sure the children would attend. "I believe that will be adequate."

"I'm proud of you for taking this on, Cora. I intend to visit the schoolroom and speak to Mrs. McKenny before you begin. Your father is busy with his own work and I do not want him to row you to that island each day." Cora started to speak, but Lucy stopped her. "I know many teachers board, but you certainly cannot board with those people. You must consider your reputation at all times. They will need to provide you daily transportation."

Cora nodded. She hoped that was possible. "The islanders need their boats for fishing, but some of the women work in Phippsburg. Perhaps whoever rows them across could also provide transport for me."

Captain Lane folded his newspaper and sipped from his tea. His eyes rested on his wife and daughter. "Your mother mentioned her concerns about safety, reputation, and transport. I have just completed a trip during which I spoke to McKenny about the arrangements and examined the room where the school will be held. The children who are not working will attend each forenoon from ten and a half until twelve. Unless, of course, their parents have chores that need to be done.

"I've decided," he declared, "that we will go to our summer home on June fourth. Cora, you may help your mother settle into the cottage, and, if all goes well, school on Malaga will begin June eleventh. That boy Joshua will provide you with transport."

"Thank you, Father." Cora managed not to allow her smile to turn to a grin. "Joshua was in the Sunday school class last year. He seemed strong," she said, acknowledging her father's choice. *And very smart,* she added to herself.

"I expect that your class will include the teachings of the Lord."

"Of course, Father. The children will begin each day with a Bible reading and a prayer."

"While the people in Phippsburg are not opposed to our school, there is concern over the rising cost of supporting the residents. Only last winter, the legislature spent forty-eight dollars on care of the islanders. An outbreak of measles required that the good citizens of the state of Maine were obliged to send food and other articles, or practically all would have perished."

"Measles!" Lucy looked worried. "If the measles are still about, Cora will be exposed."

"I believe that problem has corrected itself." Captain Lane waved her to silence. "I will need to discuss the school with the mayor of Phippsburg, however. The dispute over the ownership of Malaga has been settled by the Maine legislature. In February, they ruled that the persons of mixed race living on Malaga had no claim to the land, and awarded ownership to the Perry family. In addition, they placed Malaga within the Phippsburg limits. The townspeople are angry and do not want to accept responsibility for the wastrels on the island."

"But …" Cora began, and was silenced by the Captain's look of reproof.

"Perhaps the establishment of our school will make the town's responsibility more palatable."

∽

Cora stood on the dock, straightened her hat, and clenched the hold-all that contained her carefully printed lesson plans. "I can do this," she spoke aloud, summoning her courage to face her first day of teaching.

Joshua cast a line over the dock cleat and pulled the tiny rowboat tight to the dock. Cora smiled down at him. "Good morning, Joshua." She held out her gloved hand for help stepping over the gunwale. Without hesitation, Joshua pulled her aboard and waved to the center seat. *There,* she thought, *that wasn't so hard.* He carefully loaded her box of school supplies and they set out.

Joshua pulled hard on the oars. The boat seemed to fly across the water. Almost too quickly, Cora found herself stepping onto the Malaga shore. She straightened her shoulders and marched up the path to the McKenny house. Lined up in a row, she found eight scholars, all grinning and excited to see her.

Sarah stepped forward. "Mornin', Ma'm. We be ready. Grandpa Jim say we should all behave and learn. He set up our school in the front room." She pushed the door open and Cora stepped through quickly. She looked around. The house had two rooms downstairs. The larger room had been given over for the classroom. A table, placed at the front, faced the students and would serve as her desk. She saw no chair, but supposed she could stand to teach. The rough benches that had been used for church were now in two straight rows.

"Joshua," Cora turned back to her oarsman, "please place the box on my desk. Children, find a place to sit and we will begin."

After a brief prayer asking the Lord's blessing on the Malaga School, Cora began the task of sorting out the children, discovering their names, reading and writing abilities, and ages. The morning flew past, and she was sad to find that it was time to return home.

Joshua led the way to the boat. The other children trooped along and, as the boat pulled away, they waved and cheered. *This is going to be an interesting summer,* Cora thought.

The Malaga children progressed much more quickly than Cora's instructors at the Normal School had led her to believe they would. The older children learned the alphabet, how to write and how to say the letters, and began sounding out simple words. The youngest children drew pictures on their slates and waited patiently to hear a chapter of the story she read aloud every day.

On Sundays, Lucy began accompanying her husband and daughter to the island. She watched Cora as she led her Sunday school class and noted no improprieties. In the middle of July, Lucy volunteered to join Cora at the school. "I can spend time with the youngest, and you will be able to work longer with the ones who are learning to read."

Cora had to admit that this was a good plan and welcomed her mother's help. By the first of August, every Malagaite who was not off-island working gathered to listen as Cora read aloud from

*Black Beauty*. Some days, her students ranged from age six to age twenty-five. Cora made no comment on anyone's attendance, but simply passed each student a slate and helped them sound out letters and words. With summer quickly drawing to a close, Cora added simple addition, using pebbles, pine cones, and fingers, to her curriculum.

On the mainland, newspaper reports continued to instigate ferocious hysteria against the Malagaites. The *Bath Enterprise* called them "a heathen mix of races genetically inclined toward crime, laziness, poverty, mental deficiency, immorality, and a fear of soap." Cora and her mother were much disturbed by these reports and invited the ladies of their home church to visit the island.

On Tuesday, August 2, after rowing the teachers home, Joshua returned to the island and found a magnificent yacht at anchor off the coast. He sounded out the name USONA, but had no idea what it meant. With his knife, he scratched the letters on the mast thwart so that he would remember to ask Miss Lane tomorrow. He pulled the skiff onto the rocky shore and tied it to his usual tree. Pushing his cap back on his head, he gaped, open mouthed, at the well-dressed strangers who strolled among the cluster of buildings he called home. "Who are these people?" he asked Sarah. She shrugged. "What do they want?"

"I think they want to talk to Grandpa." She pointed toward the McKenny house. "Or, maybe they be friends of Miss Lane, dat want to see the school."

Joshua grunted. "They look like trouble to me."

∽

The following morning, Joshua told Cora and Lucy about the visitors. "There be bunch of ladies and a couple of men wearing those preacher collars. This one lady, name of Stevens, asked a lot of questions. She weren't very nice."

"*Wasn't* very nice," Lucy corrected.

"Why do you say that?" Cora asked.

"She had dat 'I smell something bad' look on her face."

Cora tried not to smile, but she knew exactly what Joshua meant. "Did she speak to the children?"

"Jus' Sarah, I think. She want her to spell her name, but Sarah be too scared to do it. After a while, they all go back to the boat and we could see them eating and talking. Some mens from the boat. They brung da leavings to the island and they sail away."

Cora considered this. She wondered if the visit had accomplished what she and her mother had hoped for: that people would see the islanders as poor, but worthy.

"The chillums gobble up the leavings, most s'specially the sweet stuff." Joshua changed the subject. "Hey, Miss Cora," he asked, "what that word mean?" He pointed to the letters he'd scratched on the seat.

"It's an acronym. A group of letters that stand for other words, a way to say or write things quickly. In this case it means United States of North America. Where did you see it?"

"It be the name of the boat." Joshua slipped the oars and leapt out, ready to pull the skiff onto the rocks and help the teachers disembark.

If the owner of the boat were amenable to the use of USONA, perhaps he was not as close-minded as others, Cora thought.

⁓

Captain Lane took a quick trip down to Massachusetts to assure that the Lanes' winter home was ready. When he returned, Cora's hopes, that the islanders would be seen in a new light, were dashed. He brought with him a copy of the *Boston Journal* that containing an article date-lined Portland, Maine, August 11. The headline screamed "Monarch Rules Maine's Most Lawless Colony." Captain Lane handed the paper to Cora. She turned pale as she read the account that Mrs. L. M. N. Stevens had provided the reporter.

"We saw first an old negro that seemed to lack all intelligence … [the Malagaites] were sitting about on the rocks aimlessly, and there were no signs of work or industry on the whole island … their filth was as repelling as that of the lowest slums of New York or London. We talked to a very bright looking girl, who appeared white. Her mother said was 13 years old. I asked her if she could spell her name, but she was unable to do so."

*Poor Sarah*, Cora thought as she continued to read the harsh judgment set forth in the paper. Finished, she folded the paper and returned it to her father.

"The article does praise the cleanliness of the schoolroom and your efforts to provide a rudi-mentary education," Captain Lane said, trying to soothe his daughter.

"It is not enough," Cora declared. "The people on Malaga are no more ignorant or poor or dirty than other residents up and down the coast. They work hard at any job they can find. Mr. McKenny is a good leader. I'd wager he is more honest than the mayor of Boston."

"Cora!" Lucy remonstrated.

"Sorry, Mother. It just makes me so mad to hear such evil things about anyone."

"They are mostly unmarried and of mixed race," Lucy reminded her.

Cora bit her tongue, excused herself, and went to her room to pack for the journey back to Malden. *Somehow, some way, I'll make people understand,* she thought. *I'll start by speaking out to whomever will listen. These people are just as bright as I am.*

# CHAPTER TWELVE

## SEATTLE

The happiness surrounding Jeff and Lola's wedding kept Georgia from thinking about Susan's cancer, but not from brooding about her dad's admonitions concerning Mitch. She had assumed he was welcome at the wedding, and now she wasn't sure. With the wedding date quickly approaching, she went to Costco with Jeff to pick up the champagne.

"Lola tells me you haven't confirmed that Mitch is coming to the wedding. What's up with that?" Jeff asked as they walked through the huge parking lot.

Georgia stumbled over her words as she tried to explain. "I don't know. I can't seem to make up my mind. One minute I think I want him to be there, and then the next I think it's not such a great idea."

"Why not?" Jeff stopped in the parking lot and turned to face her. "Lola and I like Mitch. You like Mitch. Mom likes Mitch. Dad—"

"Dad," Georgia interrupted, "is not so sure about Mitch. Or, I should say, not so sure if Mitch and I are a good match."

"Ahh," Jeff started walking again, "he had one of his talks with you, didn't he? Dad can be a little harsh, but he's just looking out for you."

"I'm old enough to look out for myself and it wasn't a nice talk. He said he's not sure that what he referred to as a 'mixed marriage' is a good idea."

Jeff remembered that his father had voiced the same kind of concerns when he first found out that Jeff was serious about Lola. But, after meeting Lola over Skype, his concerns had vanished. Jeff had assumed that it was because Lola was so sweet and charming. *Perhaps,* he admitted to himself, *it was more because she had blond hair and blue eyes.* "You know how proud he's always been about our Irish heritage. Remember how he used to always introduce Mom as his Irish bride and tell everyone that we were Irish babies, through and through?" Georgia nodded. "You'll always be Irish no matter who you marry, so don't worry about Dad—he'll come around. Invite Mitch."

They finished the shopping. Jeff loaded the last of the champagne into the car and Georgia declared, "Okay, I'm calling Mitch right now." She pulled her phone out of her pocket.

✑

The clouds hung low and thick, threatening to burst into rain at any moment. Lola cast a wary eye on the sky. The buffet table was set up inside, but the ceremony itself was scheduled to take place in the garden. Susan adjusted the veil and caught Lola's eye in the bedroom mirror. "Happy the bride the rain kisses," she said. "Don't worry, it will hold off until your vows have been read."

Susan took Lola's hand. "I'm so happy you are joining our family. When I can travel again, Henry and I will come over and meet your family." Susan stepped back and admired her soon-to-be daughter-in-law. "Thank you for allowing me to see Jeff marry." Lola started to speak. Susan held up her hand and continued, "You are a warm and generous woman. Our Jeff is lucky to have found you. I am sure that you will be there for him no matter what this next year brings."

A soft knock sounded and Georgia pushed the door open. "Wow!" she exclaimed. "You are one beautiful bride. I'm not sure my ugly big brother deserves to marry you." The tension that had built up in the dressing room was broken as the three women laughed together.

Susan squeezed Lola's hand and kissed her cheek. She took a deep breath to push away her fears and refused to let the thought that she might never see her grandchildren into her mind. "You both look very beautiful." For a moment the women stood, their reflections framed together in the antique mirror. Susan smiled and said, "I'd better get downstairs." She fluttered her fingers and hurried out of the room. Out in the hall, she leaned against the wall and wiped away the tears that were threatening to ruin her makeup.

Mitch appeared at her side and offered his arm. He didn't ask any questions, just escorted Susan to the porch. Once there, she took a deep breath and smiled her thanks. Mitch moved away toward the garden, following the other guests. Linda waved to him and gestured at an empty chair next to her. He waved back and joined her.

"Thanks," he said, giving Linda a quick hug as he seated himself.

"I figured you might want a friend to sit with, and," she shrugged, "I don't have a date."

Mitch laughed. The wedding began.

&#8450;

Later, when her maid-of-honor duties were complete, Georgia joined Mitch and Linda. The rain, which had begun just as the ceremony ended, pattered against the windows but was ignored by the guests. Laughter, the tinkling of glass and silver, and the smell of roses combined to provide the perfect party background. "Let's fill our plates and go sit on the stairs,"

Georgia suggested. She took Mitch's hand and led him to the buffet that was spread out in the dining room.

"Jeff and I used to sit on these stairs and watch my parents' parties," she explained to Mitch as they settled in and began to eat. "If you lie down on your stomach, you can see the dining room and all the way to the fireplace. On Christmas Eve we'd lie up here, hoping to see Santa come down the chimney." She sighed. "I really like Lola and I know they'll be happy, but I miss having my big brother around."

"I always thought it would be great to have a sibling," Mitch said.

"Me, too," Linda agreed. They watched as Susan and Henry waltzed together in the entry. "Your mom looks really happy today."

Georgia nodded. Jeff and Henry exchanged dance partners. Jeff swirled his mother and pulled her close. "She also looks really thin," Georgia said thoughtfully. Linda nodded in agreement.

With the house clear of guests and the caterers packing away the last of the food, the family sat, shoes off, relaxing in front of a fire. Jeff and Lola had only one more day in Seattle before their flight back to Barcelona. Susan rested her head against the sofa back and closed her eyes. "Tired, sweetheart?" Henry asked. "Do you need a pill?"

"I'm fine, Henry." Susan sat up and looked at the newlyweds. "I know your wedding in Spain will be lovely and I would have liked to be there. You must tell your mother how sorry we are."

"My family understands." Lola smiled warmly. "My mother lights a candle for you every day. When you are strong again, you will come to visit."

Georgia and Jeff exchanged a look. Susan suddenly seemed very frail.

"I'd better go up to bed." Susan stood slowly. "I have a doctor's appointment tomorrow." At the door, she stopped and turned back to Georgia. "I'm so glad Mitch came. He really is a nice man. You could do worse."

Georgia saw her dad's lips move and she was sure he whispered, "Or better."

"Whoa, Mom. I'm not ready to get married yet."

"I know. It's just that I'd like to see you settled and happy. Good night, everyone."

❦

The following afternoon, Jeff called Georgia and told her the evening's good-bye dinner had been shifted from a restaurant to the house. "Dad says we need to help eat up the leftovers."

"That doesn't sound like Mom. Is everything okay? How did her doctor's appointment go?"

"Slow down, Sissy. Let's not jump to conclusions. They're still at the doctor's. Dad said they'd be here around five."

Georgia took a deep breath and forced herself to slow down. "You're right. Mom was kind of tired last night and things must have been backed up at the doctor's office. She's probably just tired. I'll be there before five, and you and I can figure out what to serve."

When Georgia arrived at the house, she was surprised at how few leftovers from the wedding were actually in the refrigerator. Certainly not enough to feed five adults. "I don't know what Dad was thinking. I'll call Olympia and order salad and pizza to be delivered. You go find some wine." Jeff saluted. Georgia picked up the phone and dialed. "It'll be fun to have family pizza night, just like when we were kids."

Susan and Henry arrived and approved the pizza idea. Jeff poured the wine, and the family gathered in the family room to wait for the delivery. Henry gazed at his family and smiled.

"You and Jeff aren't going to start fighting over which movie to watch, are you?"

"Dad." Georgia rolled her eyes. "So, Mom, what did Doctor Ramirez have to say?"

Susan reached for Henry's hand. Jeff stretched one hand to his new wife and the other to his sister. Everyone seemed to hold their breath for a long moment. "The cancer is progressing more rapidly than expected." Susan sounded calm, but her fingers turned white as she gripped Henry's hand. "The last tests show that the tumors have increased and my calcium count is much higher. They want me to consider a bone marrow transplant."

"You can have mine," Jeff said instantly. He crossed the room to sit next to his mother.

"Thank you, honey. But they will do an autologous transplant. That means they use my own stem cells. I've begun taking medicine that will make the stem cells move into my bloodstream. Then they will be harvested. After that I will have to go into the hospital, and stay in isolation, while I have more chemo. They'll transplant my cells, and then I will continue to stay until the transplant works."

Georgia was too stunned to speak. Somehow, she'd never believed that her mom wouldn't beat this cancer.

Lola spoke first. "What can we do to help, Susan? We can stay as long as you need us."

Jeff pulled out his phone. "I'll call right now and change our tickets."

"No, no, no," Susan said as she shook her head. "Lola's family is expecting you. The wedding is planned, the church is reserved. People have already made plans to attend. You must go home."

"We have two weeks. Mama will take care of the final details. So, we will stay another week," Lola stated firmly. She reached out and clasped Susan's hand. "I'm sure your cells will be strong and plentiful, but Jeff and I will both be tested in case you need a donor." She kissed Susan's cheek as Jeff nodded vigorously.

"I'll be tested, too," Georgia said. "It's always good to have a backup plan."

"It's just a simple swab and some blood," Henry added. "I was swabbed and stabbed today." He pulled up his sleeve to show the bandage.

⁂

Friday night, Georgia and Mitch met Linda and Ken at Duke's Chowder House on Lake Union. They ordered drinks and appetizers. Ken teased Linda, the way he always did. But tonight, there seemed to be an undertone that Georgia had never noticed before. She caught Linda's eye and raised an eyebrow, the secret "what's wrong" code they'd developed in college. Linda shrugged, but a few minutes later she excused herself from the table and added, "Come with me, Georgia."

*We aren't usually the kind of women that go to the ladies' room together*, Georgia thought as she followed Linda. As soon as they were safely away from the table, she asked, "What's up? Why are you guys acting weird?"

"Ken's mother saw him kiss me."

"Kiss kiss or friend kiss?" Linda's face gave her away. "Whoa, how long has this been going on? Why didn't you tell me?"

Linda pushed open the door to the bathroom and leaned against the wall. "Just this summer, but you know I've always liked him."

"So, what's the problem?"

"I told you, she saw us kissing."

"Last time I checked, you were both old enough to kiss without permission." Georgia looked puzzled. "Oh, I get it. It's that thing about his parents wanting him to marry a Japanese woman. Is it really that big a deal?"

"I guess so." Linda sounded miserable. "We've talked about it and Ken said he'd tell them we were dating, but ..."

"He didn't, right?"

"He didn't and he still hasn't. He admitted on our way over here that he let his mom think that it was just a silly, friend kiss, that it didn't mean anything." Linda wiped away a stray tear. "I feel like an old fool. I thought we were getting serious."

"Ken's an idiot!" Georgia hugged her best friend. "Come on, let's go out there and kill him."

Linda giggled. "Not a bad idea, but I think I'll just demand that we talk about it instead. That'll teach him."

❧

Back at the table, Linda got right to it. "Ken and I are dating and his family is upset because I'm Caucasian." She turned to Mitch. "How does your family feel about you dating Georgia?"

Mitch was caught completely off guard and he stammered a bit as he said, "They don't know who I'm dating." Georgia stiffened. "I was waiting to tell them until the time was right."

"And," Linda asked, "exactly how will you know when the time is right?" Ken and Mitch looked at each other. Neither one had any idea how to respond. Linda turned back to Ken. "Your parents have known me my entire life. I have been in and out of your house a million times. Your mom and my mom used to serve on the same school committees. Why is it so terrible that we are in love with one another?"

"It's not terrible. It's wonderful." Ken tried to take Linda's hand. She dropped her hands into her lap and stared at him defiantly. "You know they have this thing about our culture. Remember how I had to go to Japanese school every weekend and in the summer? My mom was just surprised when she saw us kiss. I'm sure she didn't mean the things she said."

"Said? What exactly did she say?"

"Linda, she was just upset. They'll come around."

"Ken," Linda turned to face him directly, "I will never be Japanese. If it's a problem for you, tell me now and we'll go back to being friends."

"You know how I feel about you. I've wanted to marry you since I was ten years old. If you'll marry me, I'll be the happiest man in the world."

"Was that a proposal?" Linda whispered.

"I guess it was, is, whatever, yes. Will you marry me, Linda Carson?"

Linda sat perfectly still, her eyes wide. Slowly she began to grin. "Ken Yoshida, that was the most awful proposal ever. Our children are never going to believe I said yes."

Georgia and Mitch clapped as Ken kissed Linda. Mitch waved a waiter over and ordered champagne. The mood lifted as toasts were made and the question of family acceptance was dropped.

Hours later, after final hugs and congratulations had been exchanged and Mitch had gone home, Georgia paced the floor. *Perhaps my father is right,* she thought. *Maybe a mixed-race marriage is too hard.* She forced herself to stop thinking and crawled into bed.

❧

The family members received their test results and were disappointed to learn that none of them were compatible enough to be considered appropriate. They met with Marybeth, their social worker from the oncologist's office. She explained that it wasn't unusual for children and spouses to not be the best donors. "Your mother's mother or father, or a sibling, even an aunt or cousin from her side of the family is more likely to match. But remember, only about thirty percent of patients can find a fully matched donor among their family members."

"I was an only child and my parents are both gone," Susan said. "I don't think I ever had any aunts or uncles, or cousins. My mother and father never talked about their childhoods. It was kind of a forbidden topic." She frowned slightly, remembering how her mother had always shushed her when she asked questions.

"Both Jeff and Georgia have some markers that match, and, if it becomes necessary, the doctors will evaluate the risk of using cells from one of you. Lola and Henry are not compatible. I would encourage all of you to consider placing your names on the donor registry." Marybeth turned to look Susan in the eye. "Susan, you are responding to the medication that will move your own cells to your blood. However, Dr. Ramirez would like to place your name on the list for matching."

"If I'm going to use my own cells, why is that necessary?"

Marybeth continued, "It is merely a precaution. At this time, the odds that two random individuals are HLA matched exceeds one in twenty thousand. If you should need a donor, in the future, it would be wise to have you on the recipient list now. Then if a match is found and you don't need it, we can reject it."

"That makes sense," Henry said. "Let's do it, honey."

# CHAPTER THIRTEEN

## MALAGA
## 1904-1905

As the cold winter of 1904 dragged on and turned into 1905 the people of Malaga Island, and other coastal communities, struggled to survive. Phippsburg residents were asked to contribute clothing and food to the starving Malagaites.

"This must not continue," declared the mayor. "Those rogues in the legislature will not be allowed to bamboozle the good people of Phippsburg. By assigning Malaga Island to our fine town they have attempted to shirk their responsibility. The Malagaites are lazy and shiftless. Our resources are not best spent on such as these. We shall, this winter, do our Christian duty and provide food supplies and such clothing as my good people can spare. But the legislature must correct this wrong."

Cora learned of the mayor's statement when her mother read aloud a letter from her friend, Mrs. Ellison. "They are not shiftless and lazy," Cora declared. "Everyone on the island works all the time."

"Cora," Lucy said. "Calm yourself. You know they live like heathens."

"Mother, how can you say that? You see how clean the schoolroom is, how the children always arrive with clean hands and faces."

"Perhaps, but their clothing is practically rags, the yards are not swept, and the smell of fish is everywhere."

"Of course it smells of fish! The men make their living fishing, clamming, and lobstering. Fish processing smells."

"Cora, a lady never raises her voice, nor does she argue with her elders."

"I'm sorry, Mother." Cora clenched her hand into a fist. *It's so unfair,* she thought. *The people on Malaga are poor, but so are many other fishermen and their families.* She drew in a deep breath. "I think we should appeal to the ladies in our church on Sunday. They are quite taken with your teaching the youngest children their letters and numbers. I believe they would find it in their hearts to send a few pieces of warm clothing."

"They have enjoyed my tales," Lucy agreed. "I'll ask the Captain what he thinks."

Cora picked up the copy of Jack London's *Call of the Wild* that she'd received for Christmas and found her place. *This book really is quite thrilling,* she thought. *I wonder if Father will allow me to read it to the islanders next summer. The men and boys would love it.* She glanced at her mother, who seemed completely absorbed in her needlework, but her fingers moved slower than usual. The seed had been planted. Mother would see that warm clothing was sent to the island.

❦

Without school to attend or teach, the winter seemed endless to Cora, but finally spring arrived, and with it the knowledge that the family would move to Maine for the summer. She began to pack the school supplies they had collected over the winter.

Lucy noted the trunk standing open in Cora's room. "The good people of Malden have been quite generous. We are returning with an abundance of supplies." She counted the chalk sticks and said again, "Very generous indeed."

"Would that the population were as generous in their attitude toward the Malagaites as they are with their used chalk and broken slates."

"Cora! How dare you speak that way! This winter the islanders have received not only support from the city of Phippsburg, but our church sent the children coats and shoes."

"Old coats and mended shoes."

"Well, of course. What would persons living in squalor do with new coats and shoes?"

"Perhaps they would stay warm and dry."

"Enough. It's time you found yourself a husband. A home of your own and children to tend will set your mind on more important things than those beggar children on Malaga."

Cora dropped her eyes so that her mother would not see her look of rebellious anger.

❦

Captain Lane pushed back from the dinner table and pulled a cigar from his chest pocket. Lucy frowned as he clipped the end. "Not to worry, my dear, I'm going to the parlor to smoke." He rose and then turned back. "It was in the news today that the city of Phippsburg is petitioning the legislature to rescind the order that placed Malaga in their jurisdiction. The financial burden of caring for the Malagaites is too great." He looked at Cora. "I hope you were not planning to request church funds for those people. If you are to teach, you must make do with what you have."

"Our church here has been most generous," Lucy said. "I believe we have everything we need."

Cora bit her tongue and asked to be excused, pleading a headache.

From her room, Cora could hear her parents conversing. She walked quietly to the top of the stairs, avoiding the squeaky board just outside her room, the board that always gave her fair warning so that she knew when her mother was about to open the door. The parlor door was ajar and Cora could hear quite clearly.

"Marry?" The Captain sounded surprised. "The girl won't be eighteen until this fall."

"I fear she has had too much education."

"Balderdash, education is a good thing. She is doing a fine job teaching."

"I agree, Captain. But do you want her to be a spinster?"

"Cora is an attractive girl; suitors will appear."

"She is a young woman, Captain. We need to assure that her head is not turned by the wrong man, or by the wrong ideas. Just the other day I overheard her discussing the suffragettes with her friend Olivia."

"Good God!"

"Captain!"

"Sorry, Lucy. I didn't mean to swear. No daughter of mine will ever need to vote. Find her a suitable husband quickly."

"I'll find my own husband," Cora whispered. *That is, if I even want one,* she thought. *And, I'll vote, too, Captain. Just wait and see.*

⁂

Lucy approached the task of finding a suitable husband for Cora the way most gentlewomen would plan a major party. She made a list of all the single men in her acquaintance. There were not many, and most were too young or too old. *Cora would need a firm hand,* she reasoned to herself. The Captain showed little to no interest in this process and declared that he knew no one to add to her list.

"If you truly know no one, then I believe our best candidate is Jonathan Smithson. His wife has been gone a year or more now and his children need a mother."

"Smithson? Isn't he too old?"

"I don't believe he's much more then thirty-two or three. He's well established in business and his home is large and well maintained. I'll speak to him on Sunday next and determine if he is appropriate."

⁂

Sunday morning, Lucy looked over the ensemble that Cora had chosen to wear. The deep blue of the gown accented her daughter's coloring and eyes. "You look lovely, dear." Lucy adjusted the tilt of Cora's hat.

"Thank you, Mother." Cora pushed her hat back to the angle she preferred. Lucy sighed but said nothing. She didn't want to alert Cora to her scheming.

The Lanes were seated in their usual pew at the front of the sanctuary. Lucy wanted to see where Smithson and his family were sitting, but she didn't dare turn around and look. Instead she dropped her bulletin on the floor and bent to retrieve it, glancing about as she did so. Captain Lane frowned. *If only someone would tap me on the shoulder,* Lucy thought. But no one did.

Usually, Lucy enjoyed the majesty of Sunday services, but today she didn't really listen. She rose for the singing, bowed her head for the prayers, and pretended to be entranced by the sermon. Her thoughts were entirely consumed with how she could approach Mr. Smithson. *A lady can't just start talking,* she mused. *If only the Captain would play his part in this husband search.* Her husband looked down at Lucy and glared. He seemed to know that she wasn't paying attention.

When the service ended, Lucy rose quickly and turned to survey the congregants in the pews behind them. Smithson was only three rows back. Lucy caught his eye and smiled slightly. He tipped his head in return. Lucy tweaked the bow on Cora's dress and followed her daughter into the aisle.

Captain Lane shook hands with Reverend Clark, and began his usual long discussion about the message that had been presented. Lucy saw her friend Helen Grayson talking to Mr. Smithson. She moved quickly across the courtyard and was gratified to see that Cora followed her. "Mrs. Grayson. Mr. Smithson. Isn't it a lovely morning?"

"Indeed, it is," Jonathan Smithson said as he tipped his hat. "I believe spring in Boston may be the loveliest time of the year."

Lucy beamed enthusiastically. "I so agree. Have you met my daughter, Cora?" She pulled Cora forward.

"I don't believe I've had the pleasure. Charmed I'm sure." Smithson doffed his hat and bowed slightly to Cora.

Cora smiled and inclined her head in return. Lucy said, "How are your children? A boy and a girl, is that correct?"

Smithson's face lit up. "Yes, Jack is four, and my Elizabeth will be six in a few weeks. They keep me busy."

"I'm certain they do. Cora loves children. Did you know that she has been teaching the impover-ished children on Malaga Island for the past two summers?"

"I did not." Smithson seemed to look at Cora with more interest. "Do you enjoy teaching, Miss Lane?"

"I do. The children are so excited to learn that it is a pleasure to spend my time with them."

"The teaching of children is an important voca-tion," Helen Grayson chimed into the conversation. "It is good of Cora and Lucy to give so much to those miserable waifs."

"All children, of any circumstance, are deserv-ing of attention and learning," Smithson stated firmly. "And, speaking of children, I'd best col-lect mine from the Sunday school lest they believe

I have abandoned them. Good day, ladies." His eyes lingered on Cora as he tipped his hat again and strode away.

"He needs to remarry," Helen said. "Children need a mother."

"I'm sure he will. His wife has been gone at least a year, and it must be a burden to care for such young children. Even with help," Lucy agreed.

"He doesn't seem to mind caring for his children," Cora said without thinking. Lucy smiled to herself.

Lucy immediately began to plan a dinner party that could take place before the family departed for Maine. She enlisted Cora's help with the guest list. "The Reverend Clark and his wife and the Graysons, of course," Lucy stated and then asked, "What about Mr. Smithson? He seemed quite pleasant after services. He has no spouse, but you could partner him in a game of whist after dinner, couldn't you? That would give us two tables, and I would dearly love to play one more time against the Graysons before we leave."

"Of course, Mother. Although you know I'm not very skilled." Cora remembered Smithson's remark about "all children deserving" and thought, *This may be a rather interesting dinner party.*

"The reverend isn't very skillful either. You'll be fine, dear. I hope you haven't packed your green silk. I think that would be perfect for a spring dinner party."

Cora laughed. "I certainly don't plan to take my green silk to Maine. It's hardly appropriate for the life we life there. I've packed the usual twill skirts, serviceable shirtwaists, sturdy shoes, and warm sweaters and shawls, and I was considering adding one of those split skirts Mrs. Pankhurst is wearing."

"No need to make fun, Cora. I'm sure you've packed appropriately and you are not a suffragette."

"Wouldn't you like to vote, Mama?"

"Absolutely not. The Captain is much better at all that than I am. Now, do you think we should serve Lady Baltimore cake with custard or cottage pudding with nutmeg sauce?"

∽

Cora found herself enjoying dinner. Most often at her parents' dinner parties she waited for an excuse to escape. This evening the conversation had centered around art. A recent exhibit of Claude Monet's work evoked strong opinions. The reverend and his wife were firmly against the work and refused to see it. Lucy and Helen Grayson admitted they had been a "bit overwhelmed." The Captain and Mr. Grayson said that they had had no time to view the exhibit.

"And you, Miss Lane?" Jonathan Smithson turned to his right and smiled at Cora.

She noted the twinkle in his eye and stated firmly, "I adored it. The paintings are alive with color and emotion."

"I quite agree."

"The docent I spoke with told me of other paintings Monet has done. I would so enjoy seeing more of his work."

"My daughter, Elizabeth, was taken by his work also and has declared that she will become a painter."

"A fine hobby for a woman," Captain Lane interrupted. "I certainly hope she will be able to paint a tree that looks like a tree. From what I've read, that is a skill this Monet fellow has not mastered."

The gathering, with the exception of Cora and Smithson, chuckled. The table conversation changed to the planned move by the Museum of Fine Arts of Boston from its location in Copley Square to the proposed location in the Fenway-Kenmore.

Smithson said softly to Cora, "Do you teach drawing and painting to your students?"

"How lovely that would be! Our school is only in session half a day, and only in summer months. I fear the children have no time for more than simple reading, writing, and arithmetic."

Lucy noticed their conversation and was pleased. Ordinarily she would have reminded Cora of her responsibility to include everyone at the table. *He likes her,* she thought. *They do make a lovely couple.*

"Do you often take your children to the museum, Mr. Smithson?" Cora asked.

"I take my children everywhere," he declared. "This is a most unusual night for me. My sister-in-law insisted that I attend." He smiled, and again Cora noted the twinkle in his eye. "And, I believe I'm glad I did."

*He's flirting with me.* Cora felt a giggle rise and fought it back. "I am looking forward to returning to Maine next week. It will be lovely to see the students."

"Do you intend to continue teaching?"

"I'm certain I shall marry. But, until then, teaching on Malaga Island is most fulfilling."

"And have you chosen the lucky man who is to be your husband?"

Cora blushed and shook her head. Lucy called for the women to leave the table and Cora was saved from answering. As Smithson pulled her chair back, allowing her to rise, he spoke again. "I believe we are paired for whist. I look forward to joining you and the other ladies." Cora nodded slightly.

❦

Reluctantly, the evening drew to a close. Lucy maneuvered the other guests away from the young couple. She wanted to eavesdrop on their farewell but knew that Cora would be angry if she believed her mother had arranged their meeting.

Cora handed Smithson his hat and gloves. "May I write to you this summer, Miss Lane? I would like to hear about this island and the people that live there."

"I would look forward to your letters, Mr. Smithson. But perhaps you should call me Cora if we are to be friends."

"And you must call me Jonathan." Cora looked directly back and smiled widely.

She inclined her head. "Good night, Jonathan."

"Good night, Cora. Until we meet again." He stepped into the night and the Captain closed the door firmly.

"That went well, Lucy." Captain Lane locked the door. "Smithson seems like a nice enough chap. I'm going to my study. Please, have someone bring me a nightcap."

⁓

The summer move to the cabin in Maine was accomplished with dispatch, and the Lanes rapidly settled in. The Captain, who had recently reached his seventy-second birthday, showed no signs of slowing down. Each Sunday morning, he left early and rowed between the small islands of Casco Bay, preaching at any island and to anyone who rowed out to meet him. On Malaga, the McKenny family made their home available so that he could come ashore. Cora and Lucy spent Sundays with the ladies in Phippsburg, but Monday through Friday, Joshua arrived to row them to Malaga and their eager students.

Sarah, thirteen now, was working full-time at a resort in Phippsburg. Cora missed her. One Saturday, while shopping at the market in Phippsburg, she saw Sarah carrying a large basket of produce and called out to her.

Sarah turned quickly and grinned broadly. "Miss Cora." She gave a brief curtsy.

"Sarah, I'm so happy to see you." Cora hugged the girl. "I miss you at the school."

"I miss it, too," Sarah admitted. "But I keep reading and figuring my sums." She rubbed her foot in the road dust. "I want to be a teacher someday, Miss Cora."

"Oh, Sarah. That's wonderful. I'll lend you some of my books and when you turn sixteen, you can take the test for Normal School."

"I be appreciating …" Sarah paused and corrected herself. "I would appreciate the books, Miss."

"The children told me you read to them all winter."

"Yes, Miss."

"And, you made them practice reading, writing, and arithmetic." Sarah nodded. "See, you are a teacher already."

An older woman called to Sarah and she scurried away. Cora smiled. *I will tell the ladies' society about Sarah and perhaps they will increase their donations. I wonder if we could have a real school on Malaga one day?*

Two or three times a week, a letter arrived from Jonathan. Each one was filled with questions about her students, comments about the minutia of life, and, almost always, proud stories about something his children had said or done. Cora responded in kind. Late in the summer she wrote, "I do so admire Mrs. Pankhurst. Just this day I read of her speech in which she extolled the need for 'deeds not words.' I fear that, without extreme action, women will never be allowed the vote."

She waited for his reply, anticipating his disapproval but hoping for his concurrence. When the letter arrived, she seized it eagerly from her father's hand and hurried away to read far from her parents' prying eyes. She lifted the flap carefully and took a deep breath. Her eyes scanned quickly down the contents, searching for a mention of Mrs. Pankhurst and/or the right to vote. On the second page she found his reply. "I pray that there will be no need for extreme measures to ensure the rights of women, but, like you, I fear that it may become necessary. Rich and powerful white men have, for too long, decided what was allowed for others. I hold a strong belief that all citizens, property owner or not, should have an equal voice in our government. Neither race nor gender should be considered a barrier." Cora pressed the letter to her heart.

Captain Lane and Lucy watched their daughter as she sat in the garden, reading Smithson's letter. Lucy smiled and nodded. "I do believe that Cora has a serious beau."

The Captain frowned. "How old is that Smithson?"

"Mr. Smithson is thirty-six, just eighteen years older than our Cora."

"Eighteen years!"

"Might I remind you, Captain, you are eighteen years older than myself."

# CHAPTER FOURTEEN

## SEATTLE

By November, Susan's blood cells were ready for the procedures that would complete the autologous implant. It was difficult for the family to accept that she would be in the hospital over Thanksgiving. Marybeth explained again that Susan would first have her own blood cells removed and frozen, then receive a massive dose of chemo and/or radiation. When it was determined that her cancer cells were killed, the harvested cells would be reinfused into her bloodstream. "After all of that," Marybeth said, smiling at Susan, "your blood counts will begin to recover."

"I'd rather miss Thanksgiving and be home for Christmas and the birth of Jeff's baby," Susan declared.

"How long will she be in the hospital?" Henry asked.

"There are a number of factors involved. But plan on about thirty days. The length of time is different for every patient."

"It will give me a chance to read and watch some silly movies." Susan patted Henry's arm. Georgia tried not to cry. "I'll be in isolation, but you can visit me. You just have to wash your hands and wear gloves, gowns, and masks."

"Two visitors at a time are allowed. But, never visit if you have a cold, the flu, an upset stomach, anything at all," Marybeth said sternly.

"I'll come every day," Georgia said. "Daddy and I can take turns."

"We've got this. Everything is going to be okay." Henry's eyes were filled with tears. He blinked them away. "You'll see."

∽

Susan spent the evening doing laundry and packing for her stay. She took her favorite family pictures from the walls and the top of the piano and carefully stowed them with a few books and a knitting project. Henry watched and tried bravely to keep smiling. "At least you can visit." Susan paused to hug him. "The time will go by quickly and Lola's baby boy will be here by Christmas. I wonder if they chose a name yet? Last time we talked, they were discussing naming him after the two grandfathers."

"Poor kid. I hated being a Henry when I was young. They called my dad Hank, so I got stuck with the whole name."

"I remember you saying the same thing when I was pregnant with Jeff." She folded a pair of soft yoga pants and a warm sweater. "We've had a wonderful life, haven't we?"

"We have, sweetheart. And we will have many more wonderful years. When you beat this thing, we'll go see our grandson." Henry wiped away the tears that had trickled from his wife's eyes. "You finish up and I'll make us a cup of tea."

Susan sighed. "What I need is a stiff drink."

Henry chuckled. "The only other time I heard you say that was when Jeff broke his arm."

"Oh, I think I've said it a few more times than that. Neither of our children were angels. Put a fire in the fireplace. I'll be down in a minute, but I want a cup of real tea—Earl Grey—not that awful herbal stuff that is supposed to be so good for me."

∽

The first ten days in the hospital dragged. Henry spent every day with Susan. Georgia arrived after work. The family ate dinner together in Susan's room, and then Henry went home. Their evenings were spent with Susan knitting or reading while Georgia read and graded papers. Jeff called every night at 9 p.m.—6 a.m. Barcelona time. Georgia stayed until her mother threw her out each night.

Most nights when she left the hospital, Georgia went straight home to bed. Her relationship with Mitch had been reduced to text messages. On the second Saturday, as she drove toward home only a bit after 9:00, Georgia called Linda.

"Hey, sweet thing." Linda's happy greeting made Georgia smile. "What's up?"

"Is Ken over at your house?"

"Nope. He went to some game with Mitch. Do you want to come by? I've got wine."

"How do you always know what I need?"

"I told you I was a witch. Are you on your way?"

"I am. Pour the wine. I'll be at your door in five minutes."

"The door will be on the latch."

⁓

Georgia kicked off her shoes and curled up on the deep sofa. She sighed and took a large gulp of wine. "Mom is so sick." She wiped away a tear. "I wish Jeff were here. Dad looks exhausted. This is all so hard, and I'm sitting here whining yet Mom never complains about any of this."

"You aren't whining, you're venting. Venting is good." Linda refilled Georgia's glass. "I'm going to grab us some snacks. You sit here and try not to think too hard. You look exhausted yourself. I'll be right back."

Georgia leaned her head back and closed her eyes. The chemo had begun to take a toll on Susan. Her hair, which had started to grow back, was falling out again. *I need to bring some pretty scarfs to the hospital, maybe a warm beanie,* she thought. A tray clattered on the coffee table and she opened her eyes and sat up again. "You're an angel. I didn't get a chance to eat tonight, and this looks great." She took a cracker and spread it thickly with goat cheese and honey. "Mmm, this is so good." She added a slice of apple and took another bite.

"Why no dinner? I thought you guys were eating with your mom."

"We were, but the last few days, the smell of food has been making her nauseous. I was going to grab something on my way to the hospital, but I was running late." Georgia spread cheese on another cracker.

"Mitch asked how you were doing. He's such a sweet guy."

Suddenly Georgia's phone began shouting, "Your brother's on the phone! Your brother's calling you! Waiting patiently so he can tell you something new." Georgia pulled the phone from her pocket and pushed the answer button.

"Hi, Jeff. Didn't I just talk to you at the hospital?"

"You did. But I want to tell you something."

"Are Lola and the baby okay?"

"The doctor says everything is normal and right on track." Georgia gave Linda the okay sign and waited for Jeff to continue. He did. "Are you with Mitch right now?"

"No, why? I stopped at Linda's to have a glass of wine and some dinner."

Linda leaned into the phone. "Hi, Jeff."

"I guess that's okay. You'd probably tell her anyway." Jeff seemed unsure that he should continue.

"Spit it out, big brother. Linda is your other sister, remember?"

There was a long pause and then Jeff spoke. "Do you remember when Marybeth told us that we didn't match?"

"Of course, but she said that children are not usually the best matches, siblings are."

"Well, I didn't match because I'm adopted. I wouldn't match you either."

"Jeff, what the hell are you talking about?" Georgia waved her hand at Linda to be sure she was following the conversation. "You're not adopted. There are about ten million baby pictures of you. If anyone is adopted, it's me. I think there are two pictures of me as an infant."

"Pictures don't tell the whole story. Have you ever seen a picture of Mom pregnant?" Jeff asked.

"No, but lots of pregnant woman don't want their picture taken. What gave you this crazy idea?"

"After all the stuff Marybeth told us about genetics, I was curious. So I had my DNA tested. And I'm not much Irish at all."

"Just because your hair is red and I have dark hair doesn't mean we aren't related, or Irish. Mom had dark hair, too, before it all fell out."

"My tests show I'm almost twenty-five percent African American." Jeff stopped talking and waited for Georgia's reaction.

Georgia was stunned. Linda whispered, "What's up? What did he say?"

"Jeff says his DNA shows that he is a quarter African American."

"Wow, cool! How did that happen?"

A whistle came from the phone. Georgia turned on the speaker phone and said, "I don't care if you're green, Jeff. You're my big brother."

"You think I'm adopted, too?" Jeff asked.

"I think the test must be wrong," Linda said firmly. "Have it done again."

"I did," Jeff admitted. "Same results."

"Well, I know Susan, and if you were adopted, she would have told you," Linda declared. "She doesn't keep secrets. And, how do you account for the fact that you and Georgia look alike? You remember when she was born, you told me so."

"Maybe I don't remember. I was only five. Maybe I'm just repeating stories."

"And maybe," Georgia spoke firmly, "the test was wrong. Jeff, you know Mom loves us. She needs you to keep calling her and giving her updates on Lola's pregnancy."

"You know that I will. I love Mom and Dad. If I'm adopted, there is some reason they didn't tell me."

"I don't think you're adopted, but we'll figure this out. Marybeth keeps stressing how important it is that the patient is taken care of emotionally as well as physically during this implant process. Mom has to be our priority." Georgia bit her lip and held back her concerns. "Did you talk to Lola about your test results?"

"Yes. She doesn't care, nor does her family. When we told her parents, they acted like it was no big deal. Her dad actually said every family tree holds people of every color and creed."

"Okay then. Let's keep this to ourselves." Georgia smiled. "Remember how Granny O'Brien always said 'it will all come out in the wash'?"

"She also said that black men are shiftless and worthless."

"You don't believe that and neither do I."

"I don't either," Linda chimed in. "Jeff, you are worrying too much about this. Just take care of Lola." She glanced at Georgia, who still looked stunned. *We need a change of subject,* she thought. "Did you decide on a name?"

"That seems to be much harder than I would have expected." Jeff laughed a bit. "We still have almost three weeks. I'm sure Lola won't bring him home from the hospital with a Baby Boy O'Brien sign around his neck."

They talked a few more minutes and hung up. Georgia and Linda reached for their forgotten wine and took large drinks. "Wow," Georgia sighed, "that was totally not what I expected. I think I'll be tested, too. There must be a reason his test came back so strange. Do you think he is adopted?"

"No ..." Linda considered carefully. "You two look and act so much alike that you must be born of the same parents. Anyone can see the resemblance you have to your mom and dad. If your test results are the same as Jeff's, I think one of your parents has a bloodline that they aren't telling you about."

꩜

Georgia went the next day and provided her spit for the DNA test. The results could take up to a month, so she put it out of her mind and concentrated on her work. She saw Mitch for a few minutes whenever their schedules allowed. Mark Hedrick asked at every department meeting if she was okay and if she needed to take a leave of absence. His oily, over-solicitous tone made Georgia cringe, but she managed to smile and say thanks, but no thanks. Linda had taken it upon herself to keep Georgia's refrigerator stocked with easy-to-fix meals and often had something prepared when Georgia returned from the hospital.

Susan's friends were doing much the same for Henry, so Georgia was able to quit worrying about her dad's care and comfort. She still thought he looked tired, though. When she asked, he admitted that he didn't sleep well without Susan by his side. Jeff suggested he sleep in one of the guest rooms, but Henry refused.

Finally, on December 15, the test showed that all of Susan's cancer cells were killed and the infusion of her own cells could take place. "If all goes well, you may be home for Christmas," Dr. Ramirez reassured her. "I'm going to give you two days to regain your strength and we'll schedule the infusion for the eighteenth."

The infusion was much like any other intravenous procedure. The port that had been placed for chemo now carried Susan's blood cells back into her body. An hour into the infusion, Susan squeezed Henry's hand. "I swear I can feel my cells going into my bone marrow and beginning to make healthy new, cancer-free cells."

Henry grinned. "Exactly what they should be doing." Susan drifted off to sleep. Henry stared down at his wife. She was so thin and pale. Her bald head was uncovered and he felt like he could see through her skin. *It will break my heart if you die*, he thought.

⁂

Jeff had promised to call when Lola went into labor no matter what time of day or night it happened. Every morning, when Henry arrived to keep her company, Susan asked if he'd called in the night. "Honey, I told you that if Jeff calls me at home, I'll call you right away. But he knows you are sleeping with your cell phone. He'll call you first."

"Is the Skype working? I want to see the baby as soon as I can."

"Relax, Granny," Henry teased. "Stewing over it won't hurry things up. You know babies appear when they are good and ready."

Susan sighed. She was too weak to knit or even read. The daily laps around the hall wore her out.

On December 23, Dr. Ramirez made his rounds as usual, but this time he seemed happier. "You handled the infusion very well, with almost no side effects. We will monitor you very closely for the next one hundred days. During that time, you will need to undergo tests to determine the status of your disease and how it is responding to your treatment. But for now, I'm discharging you. Go home and enjoy the holidays."

"Really?"

"Yes, really. You need to take it easy. Rest a lot and follow all the instructions the nurse will give you. A hospital is no place to spend Christmas. My office will set up an appointment for you on the twenty-sixth. Recovery from an infusion is gradual.

It will take about one year for your immune system to return to normal and for your bone marrow to begin producing blood cells normally again. But don't worry about that now. However, if you develop any side effects, a fever or any other complication, you need to return to the hospital at once."

Carefully, Henry hugged Susan and wiped the tears from her face. "I'll call Georgia and let her know, and then I'll help you get dressed. The paperwork will take a while. You'll probably be able to take a little nap."

"I'm much too excited to nap," Susan declared. But after dressing in yoga pants and a sweater, she lay back against the pillows and dozed off.

⁂

Henry helped Susan out of the car. The trip home for the hospital had exhausted her and she was almost too frail to stand. Georgia had heard the car pull into the garage. She emerged from the kitchen and hurried to help her mother. "Dad, the wheelchair is just inside the kitchen."

"I don't need a wheelchair," Susan protested. Georgia felt her mother's legs quiver and slid an arm more securely around her.

"Just for a couple of days, Mom. Then you'll be up and walking around."

Susan acquiesced. She knew that she wouldn't be able to walk more than a few steps on her own. Settled in the chair, her coat off but with her beanie on her head, Susan looked around. "It's lovely to be home."

"Mitch and I decorated the Christmas tree when we heard you'd be home today. You and Dad go into the living room and I'll make us all some hot chocolate."

The sound of Susan's favorite Christmas album drifted into the kitchen as Georgia stirred the chocolate. Reaching for the Santa mugs they always used on Christmas Eve, she heard her father's phone ringing. "Georgia, get out here. Hurry!" Henry called.

Georgia spun and ran to the living room. "Jeff's on the phone. The baby's here." Henry was grinning from ear to ear and Susan's wan look had disappeared. "He's FaceTiming us. Okay, Jeff. Go ahead. We're all here."

The image moved from Jeff's grinning face to Lola's calm smile, and then down to the tiny bundle in her arms. "Meet your new grandson, Gabriel Enrique O'Brien. All six pounds, four ounces of him." Lola turned the baby to the camera and everyone exclaimed at once, declaring him to be the most beautiful baby ever.

When they had calmed down, Henry asked, "I thought you were going to call us when Lola went into labor. What happened?"

"Gabe was in too big a hurry. Everything happened so fast, I never got the chance."

Lola chimed in, "My mama said it would be that way. I felt the first pain four hours ago and here we are already."

# CHAPTER FIFTEEN

## MALAGA
## 1905–1906

Much to Lucy's delight, Jonathan Smithson courted Cora throughout the fall and winter of 1905-1906. They attended the symphony and a performance at the Bijou Theater. Lucy arranged for the couple to be together as often as possible. *It is obvious,* Lucy reasoned, *that they like each other. Every time they are together, they do nothing but talk.*

As Thanksgiving neared, Lucy suggested that Jonathan and his children might enjoy eating dinner with the Lanes. However, her plan was thwarted when Jonathan declined, saying he and the children would be traveling to Atlanta to spend time with his late wife's family.

"I had no idea you were from the South," Cora said.

"I'm not. My wife was. I promised I would raise Jack and Elizabeth to know her family."

"Children can never have too many loving adults in their lives," Cora said. "I'm sure they will have a marvelous time."

"They will, but I think I would prefer to spend the day with you and your family."

Cora blushed.

*Ah,* Lucy thought, *progress.* "We would love to entertain you and the children on another day. Perhaps for a luncheon, or tea, whichever you feel would fit the children's schedule best. Are you free Saturday, December second?"

"I will arrange to be, and a luncheon would be perfect. We will look forward to it. I would like the children to meet you." Jonathan tipped his hat to Lucy and lifted Cora's gloved hand to his lips. "Until Saturday, then."

✧

Cora dressed carefully for the luncheon. *How silly,* she thought, *I'm nervous about meeting two children. But what if they don't like me?* She surveyed herself in the mirror, pinched her cheeks to add color, and hurried downstairs.

Jack and Elizabeth were introduced and displayed perfect manners. They played quietly together until it was time to go into the dining room. Jonathan held Elizabeth's chair, helped Jack up onto a high cushion that had been placed on his chair, and adjusted their napkins before taking his seat next to Cora.

Lucy noted this and marveled at his parenting skills. *Not many men would know how to help a child.* "Do you employ a nanny, Mr. Smithson?" Lucy asked.

"Please, Mrs. Lane, call me Jonathan. We do. Dinah has been with us since Elizabeth was born." He smiled at his daughter, who was helping her brother eat his soup. "I am trying to decide if we should employ a governess or send the children to public school. Elizabeth is currently attending a church school, and she has begun to teach Jack his letters." He turned toward Cora. "As a teacher, Cora, what is your opinion?"

Captain Lane, who had been about to speak and expound upon his own aversion to public schools, was startled to hear his daughter's opinion sought over his own.

Cora placed her fork carefully on her plate and spoke firmly. "I, myself, attended a boarding school, but Boston has a fine public school system. I believe children benefit from attending classes with a group of their peers and returning to their homes each evening. School is a place for much more than book learning, and in a public school they learn about the world." She smiled at Elizabeth, who was listening intently. "Would you like to attend school, Elizabeth?"

Elizabeth looked at her father and then back at Cora. "Yes, Miss Cora. But Jack is used to me being there to take care of him. He would miss me."

"I believe he would be able to attend the same school, at least until it is time for you to move on to high school," Cora explained. "You would be in different classrooms and learn different things, but you could walk to and from school together, couldn't they, Jonathan?" She turned to her dinner companion and noted that he was watching this interaction with a slight smile. *Oh, dear,* she thought. *Did I overstep?*

"I'm sure that could be arranged," Jonathan said. Then he turned toward her mother. "The meal is delicious, Mrs. Lane."

"If I'm to call you Jonathan, you must call me Lucy. I'm glad you are enjoying the food. Cora helped with the cooking."

"I peeled a few potatoes and stirred what I was told to stir. I'm not sure one should call that helping with the cooking. I did set the table, however." Cora winked at Elizabeth and was rewarded with a giggle. "Do you cook, Jonathan?"

"Heavens, no!" He seemed shocked at the idea. "I have a housekeeper, of course."

For the first time, Jack spoke up. "Father told us to eat whatever you put on our plates, but I like this wiggly stuff."

Everyone laughed. "The wiggly stuff is creamed cabbage, Jack."

He nodded and took another bite.

Cora contemplated the table. The gleaming white cloth was covered with dishes: roast pork, apple sauce, mashed potatoes, creamed cabbage, stewed corn, beet pickles, and two types of bread. All of this had been preceded by a meat soup, and in the kitchen an apple cake waited to be served with whipped cream, cheese, and coffee. Her face clouded, and she said without considering the impact of her words, "I wonder what the children on Malaga are eating today."

"Don't the children have food, Miss Lane?" Elizabeth looked worried.

On Malaga, Thanksgiving had not been mentioned. There was no spare money for feasting. Jim McKenny was a master fisherman, and therefore the McKenny family had more than some. Seloma worried that if they shared their meager stores, her own family would suffer, but her generous heart did not allow her to hold back.

Whenever the weather permitted, Jim, his son Simon, and a few of the older boys walked across the frozen bay to Phippsburg. They offered to do work of any kind. At many homes and businesses, they were turned down. A few families allowed them to chop wood, muck out animal pens, and repair broken fences. In return for their labor they received canned food, a few potatoes, old cabbages, and carrots. With this, Seloma and the other women managed to concoct thin soups using bits of dry fish. Occasionally, someone would snare a rabbit or a fox that had ventured out of hibernation, and the Malagaites would share the bounty.

In December, the church people, inspired by a pleading letter from Cora Lane, prepared a bundle of used clothing, added a little food, and sent it across to the island.

❦

New Year's Day, Cora opened the *Boston Daily Globe* and read with dismay another article maligning the Malagaites. When next Jonathan came to call, she directed his attention to the article. "Just listen to this, Jonathan. This reporter has written that 'they work only when it is necessary, and gain a living by fishing and make but little preparation for the winter.' That just isn't true! I've never seen such hardworking people. This article makes it seem that they are wastrels and beggars just because they received a bundle of clothing and food. Here in Boston, churches prepare food and clothing for the poor. Why aren't they called to task for being unprepared for the winter?"

"Charity is injurious unless it helps the recipient become independent of it," Captain Lane interrupted. "Daughter, you need to consider that the Malagaites are a burden on the state of Maine and on the city of Phippsburg in particular. When a group doesn't learn from past experiences, it is to be expected that others will tire of providing for them."

Jonathan considered the Captain's words carefully before he spoke. "If you plan to teach again next summer, Cora, perhaps you could incorporate accepting responsibility into your lessons."

"Of course I intend to teach. And," she struggled to express herself without anger, "these are good people. They are decent, hardworking, and take care of themselves. They are not the only persons in Maine that require assistance to survive the winters."

"They live in sin and squalor, Cora. You and your mother are making a difference, but it cannot be ignored that the black person is inferior to the white. When they breed together, the result is always inferior." Captain Lane's words caused Cora to flush, but she held her tongue, knowing that arguing with her father could come to no good.

"I have read Mr. Darwin's work, *The Descent of Man*, and he does make some interesting points. His understanding of the need to selectively breed to type may have some value," Jonathan said.

Cora could contain herself no longer. "People are not animals. If given the opportunity, even the poorest can raise above his birth circumstances."

"I'm afraid that is not true, Cora." Captain Lane spoke firmly. "This summer I will preach to the Malagaites using Proverbs 6:6-8, 'Go to the ant, O sluggard; consider her ways, and be wise. Without having any chief, officer, or ruler, she prepares her bread in summer and gathers her food in harvest.' I will show them the Lord's way is right and that if they plan ahead, they will not need to suffer each winter."

Jonathan seemed to agree. Cora fumed silently. She picked up her knitting and refused to meet Jonathan's gaze. When he departed, she walked him to the door and only said, "Perhaps," when he spoke of seeing her on Sunday.

Cora avoided Jonathan for several weeks. She pleaded fatigue when he offered an afternoon stroll, and she used any excuse she could find for turning down dinner invitations where she knew he would be among the guests. To Lucy's dismay, Cora seemed to have lost all interest in Jonathan's courtship.

Then on a bitter cold day in late March, as she stepped out of the public library on Boylston Street, she met Jonathan face-to-face.

"Cora!" He smiled broadly.

"Jonathan," Cora replied, acknowledging his presence. *He's so handsome,* she thought, *but that isn't enough.*

"It's a bitter cold day. Might I persuade you to join me in a cup of tea?"

Cora started to shake her head no, but reconsidered. She lifted her chin and looked him squarely in the eye. "All right. Shall we go next door?"

Jonathan offered his arm. Cora ignored the gesture and walked down the wide granite steps. "At least let me carry your books. The steps are quite slick today."

Cora handed over the books. *Pride goeth before a fall*, she thought and almost giggled, *but without the books my feet are less likely to slide out from under me.*

Without speaking, they hurried to the tearoom, removed their outerwear, and were seated at a table. Jonathan spoke first. "I fear you have been avoiding my company, Cora. If I've done something to offend you, I did it quite unintentionally, and I do sincerely apologize."

Cora considered equivocating. She knew that a polite woman would make an excuse. "Jonathan, I found your callous disregard for the humanity of the Malagaites very upsetting." She squared her shoulders and continued. "I, too, have read *The Descent of Man* and I do not subscribe to Mr. Darwin's theories. All persons, if given the opportunity to overcome the circumstances of their birth, can add value to our society."

Jonathan took a sip from his tea. He set the delicate cup back on the saucer and began to fiddle with his spoon, turning it over and over between his long fingers. Cora waited, clenching and unclenching her hands beneath the table. Finally, she could stand the silence no longer and lifted her eyes to Jonathan. She found him watching her.

"You are a most unusual young woman. I envy the children who attend your school." He put down the spoon and leaned slightly forward. "Tell me, why do you find teaching fulfilling?"

111

"I take great pleasure in seeing the look in a child's, or for that matter, an adult's eye, when suddenly the letters make sense and begin to form words on the page. At first, I was simply looking for something to fill my summer, but now I find that I miss it in the winter months."

"Have you considered applying for a full-time position?"

"Of course, but Father would never allow it. And, even if I could convince him, Mother would be mortified if I were to become a spinster." Cora took a bite of scone. "The children on Malaga deserve a real school. I will continue there as long as they will have me."

Jonathan nodded. "I agree, Cora. All children deserve an education and, whenever possible, a real school. You can count on my support in the future. I realize that in attempting to give no offense to your father, I failed to support your position. That will not happen again."

With the air cleared between them, Cora began accepting Jonathan's company again. Lucy waited, impatiently, for Jonathan to request Cora's hand in marriage. With summer drawing near, Lucy considered suggesting that the family remain in Massachusetts. Cora was busy collecting school supplies for the children. Jonathan seemed to enjoy helping. *If,* Lucy thought, *he is this supportive of her teaching, perhaps he did only enjoy her company, and has no interest in marrying again.*

"Cora," Lucy said, as her daughter knelt on the floor sorting a pile of used books, "have you no interest in marriage and a family of your own?"

Cora rocked back on her heels. She laughed and pushed her hair off her forehead. "I'm actually much more interested in getting the vote for women, Mother." Lucy paled. "Don't faint—I do care about the vote, but I was only teasing. I'm sure I'll get married and have children someday, but now, I'm only nineteen."

"Motherhood is a woman's natural state." Cora chose not to argue and returned to sorting the books. Lucy continued, "Your father is getting older. He would like to have grandchildren before he dies."

Cora's hand trembled. "Is father ill?"

"No. No, of course not. I only meant that he would like to see you happily settled with a good man. A man like Jonathan."

"Jonathan is a good friend," Cora said firmly. "I have told him that I will teach on Malaga as long as they have need."

*Then,* Lucy thought as she reached out to Cora and tucked a hairpin firmly into place, *it is up to me to see that they no longer need you.*

The first week the Lane family was settled in their cottage on Horse Island, Lucy began her campaign. She attended a tea at the church in Phippsburg, and after the usual pleasantries she said, "I do believe that the Malagaites have progressed to the point where the children might benefit from attending school with others."

"Goodness, Mrs. Lane. You surely don't mean that they would attend the school here in Phippsburg. Those children are half-breeds. Why, some of them have Indian blood."

Lucy realized her blunder. "Most assuredly not. I was thinking that perhaps the state of Maine would be willing to build a school on the island and supply a year-round teacher."

"I believe," the mayor's wife spoke with authority, "that the state, and our city, have better things to do then throw good money away on imbeciles. Whatever you feel they have learned is, I fear, no different than a monkey mimicking a man."

Mrs. Albrecht spoke up. "They are not all imbeciles. The girl Sarah, who works at our resort, does sums, reads, and even writes a legible hand."

"The exception proves the rule. Lucy, do tell us the recent news from Boston. What are ladies wearing?"

⁓

Lucy was not to be deterred. Without disclosing her motive, she enlisted Cora in her drive to provide a "real" schoolhouse on Malaga. Together they approached the Captain, who agreed to support their effort. After deciding that the way they were most likely to raise money was to approach their home church in Malden, Massachusetts, they began mentioning the school in letters to their friends.

Cora wrote enthusiastically to Jonathan, "My father has agreed that a year-round school on Malaga Island would be of great value to my students. When we return at the end of August, I shall pursue the funding of this endeavor. I plan to be quite persistent. I pray you do not tire of hearing me discuss this."

Jonathan's reply came at once: "I do not believe that I would ever tire of hearing you speak on a topic of concern to you. I find that your intelligent ideas are, sometimes, a challenge to my own, but on this I quite agree and will do whatever I can to assist you in this matter."

The Captain was pleased with Jonathan's support. "It may be wise to formalize your fund-raising for this school," he told Lucy. "I will consult with Smithson. His experience as an attorney may be quite useful. If there is to be a school, someone will need to address the plan with the State Superintendent of Schools. I would do it myself, but Smithson is well known in the statehouse."

Lucy watched her husband lift his legs onto the hassock. He seemed more tired than usual, and his feet and legs often pained him. *I wonder if this will be the last summer he can preach to the islanders,* she thought. "May I pour you a whiskey, Captain?" she asked.

# CHAPTER SIXTEEN

## SEATTLE

Georgia's test results arrived in January. They were a perfect match to Jeff's. She called to tell him. "I think this proves you really are my brother."

"I remember when Mom was pregnant with you and when you were born, so I guess that means neither one of us was adopted."

"Exactly. Should we talk to Mom?"

"I don't think so. She has enough to worry about right now."

"I agree. But ... do you think the African-American heritage could come from Dad's family?"

There was a long pause while they considered the idea. "I guess that's possible," Jeff said. "I just assumed it came from my birth family, but if we have the same birth parents, I suppose it could come from either side."

"Weird, isn't it?" Georgia ran her fingers through her curly, dark hair. "Your hair is as red as Dad's and mine is dark. Mom's was kind of dark brown. We all have fair skin, and light eyes."

"And, you and I both have big feet." Jeff's comment broke the tension and they laughed together.

"So, who does Gabriel look like?"

"Everyone here thinks he looks like Lola. But I think he looks like Granny O'Brien. When we FaceTimed with Mom yesterday, she said he looks like me. Genetically speaking, the only thing I can say for sure is he has big feet."

⌘

Georgia brooded over her results. "I never would have thought I'd care," she told Linda. "But I think I do. It's weird to think that instead of Irish American, or mixed Northern European American, I might be all that plus African American. And, the most disturbing thing is that Mom and/or Dad never said anything. It's like they are ashamed or something."

"Are you ashamed?"

"I don't know. Maybe a little. But that makes me racist, and I really don't think I am."

Linda hugged Georgia. "I think it makes you confused. I don't believe you have changed and I've never considered you racist in any way. What does Mitch think about all of this?"

"I haven't told him," Georgia admitted. "I want to, but ... the time just hasn't been right."

"Well, sweetie, if you aren't serious about Mitch you don't need to say anything, but if you are, don't start by keeping secrets."

"I know, you're right. Do you think the test could be wrong?"

"Sure, but what are the chances that you and Jeff would both have the same 'wrong' results? Why don't you and Jeff just talk to your parents?"

"That seems like the simple thing to do, but we think we should wait until Mom is better."

⌘

All through the dreary Seattle winter, and into spring, Susan's health had improved. She'd gained back some of her strength. Henry and Susan began to make plans for a summer trip to Spain. On a warm, late May evening, the family sat outside on the patio. The scent of lilacs filled the air. Against the back fence, the peonies bobbed their heavy heads. A robin perched in the wisteria and sang his evening song. "Everything is so beautiful this year." Susan tilted her head back to watch the robin. "Don't you think the lilacs are especially beautiful, Henry?"

"You say the same thing every year."

"And every year, it is true." Susan rose from her chair. She stumbled a bit and steadied herself by reaching out to the trellis. The robin flew away, his song interrupted by her movement.

"You okay, Mom?"

"I'm fine, Georgia. Don't fret. I'm just a little tired. I think I'll make a cup of tea and crawl into bed with a book." She dropped a kiss on Georgia's head. "Don't you have a date with Mitch tonight? You'd better get going."

Georgia watched her mother leave the patio and enter the house. "When does Mom see Dr. Ramirez again?"

"Soon; they follow your mother very closely."

"I know, but ..."

"Try not to fret. Your mom is hanging in. But, yes, I'm worried, too. She seems more tired this week but she insists that she wants to be out and about, and I do whatever will make her happy."

"I know you do, Dad." Georgia and Henry headed into the house. "You guys are the best parents ever. Jeff and I were very lucky to have you. But, now, you need to ask us for help. Tell us what we can do."

"Just do what you are doing. Come by often, but live your life. All your mom wants is for you to be happy."

&

Susan sat very straight, her hands folded in her lap. She was determined not to show how afraid she felt. She'd known last week, when Dr. Ramirez had ordered all those tests, that he suspected something. And now, the look in his eyes told her everything she needed to know. "The infusion isn't working, is it?"

"Your results are not what we had hoped, Susan. You initially showed a good response, but your tests show that your body is no longer creating healthy cells and we see an increase in the cancer cells. We should begin treatment at once. I'd like to try you on a drug that stimulates your immune system. You need to be aware that you may need to have additional chemotherapy and perhaps a donor infusion."

Henry held Susan's hand tightly. They both nodded but were unable to speak.

Dr. Ramirez continued, "Even though multiple myeloma is more prevalent in African Americans, there are only a few black donors on the list. It may take some time to find an HLA match for you."

Henry exploded. "What the hell does that have to do with anything?"

"When it comes to matching human leukocyte antigen–HLA types, a patient's ethnic background is an important predictor of the likelihood of finding a match," Ramirez explained patiently. "HLA markers are inherited. Each ethnic group is complex in its own way. So, in Susan's case, her best chance of finding a donor will be to find an African-American donor."

"But, I'm not African American."

"Your genes say you are."

"There must have been a mistake," Henry declared. "Do that cheek-swab thing again. Susan is Scotch-Irish. There's not a drop of African American in her."

☙

Susan's thoughts ran in circles. She had no idea what she felt. *If I'm African American, was I adopted and never told? Or, were my parents not who they told me they were? Of course, they were who they were, but they might have been a different race than I've always believed.* She stared at herself in the bathroom mirror. Her hair was growing back silver-white and very wispy. It had never been anything but plain dark brown and straight as a stick. Her eyes were still green; her skin still burned in the sun. *If I'm African American, why do I look so Irish?*

Dr. Ramirez had ordered a rush on her cheek swab, and the results would be back in just a few days. Henry refused to discuss the possibility that the first results had been correct. "No need to worry over nothing, honey," he declared, and then changed the subject.

Susan worried anyway.

The cheek swab returned the same results: 48.125% Mixed African, 48.75% Mixed Northern European, 3% American Indian. Henry held Susan's hand tightly. She was afraid to look at him. *What if he doesn't love me anymore?* "Do you think I should call the kids?" she asked.

"Yes, of course, but first we need to talk about this." He rubbed his hand over his head, a gesture Susan knew meant he was upset. "I knew your parents, you knew your grandparents. How is it possible that no one ever talked about your racial background?"

"They did. Dad used to say he had a little Indian blood, but that his Scotch nature overruled it. Mom just said she was a bit of everything, mostly Scotch and Irish. Dad used to tease me about having my mom's 'Irish temper.' I don't remember anything else."

Henry took a deep breath. "This really doesn't matter. You are exactly the same woman. The woman I love. A little glitch in your genes doesn't matter."

*I wonder if that's true*, Susan thought. "I'm going to ask Georgia to come over this evening, and then we'll call Jeff and I'll tell them both at the same time."

Henry nodded. He was tapping away at his phone and didn't pause.

Susan sent Georgia a text and received a prompt reply. "Georgia will be over about seven p.m."

"Huh," Henry grunted. "Do you realize that, if your swab is correct, one of your parents was one hundred percent black or else both of them had some black blood?"

"I suppose that's true." Susan studied her hands. She felt like with this new knowledge, she should see a change. "It just doesn't seem fair that they would keep such a big secret. My dad was a doctor and my mom was the best mom ever. Why would they be ashamed?"

Henry didn't answer.

⁂

Late that evening, Georgia returned home and immediately called Jeff again. "That has to have been the weirdest conversation we've ever had with our parents."

"I agree. Do you think Mom is okay?"

"I think she will be. This has all been a big surprise. I think that because you and I already knew, it made it easier for her. I'm actually more concerned about Dad's reaction. He was awful quiet."

"Yeah. But right now, the only thing that really matters is finding a donor. And if the donor has to be black, who cares?"

"When you sent in your spit sample, did you check that that box about finding relatives?"

"I didn't, but I was thinking I might go back and do it. Maybe, if there is a close relative in the database, it would help with the donor search. Did you do it?"

"No, but I agree. Finding a donor is the most important thing and, obviously, Mom isn't sure about her family history. As soon as we get off the phone, I'll change my account."

"I will, too. Hope you come up as my sibling."

Georgia laughed. "No matter what, you're stuck with me for life."

"Love you to the moon and back, Sissy."

"To infinity and beyond."

"Forever and always," they finished together and said good night.

# CHAPTER SEVENTEEN

## MALAGA
## 1906–1907

Miss Lane's annual departure from Maine created a void in the lives of the families living on Malaga Island. Sarah spoke to her grandparents. They agreed that the schoolroom could be used for a classroom whenever she had a day off.

"You're a good girl, Sarah." Grandfather Jim McKinney never gave out hugs, but his warm smile was enough. "If you can help these young ones learn to read and write, maybe they'll have an easier life."

Sarah borrowed an envelope and piece of paper from the inn. With a pencil stub, she wrote a note to Cora, apologizing for her skill and asking how to help the children. Using two carefully saved pennies, she posted the note and waited for a reply.

Cora responded quickly. On embossed stationery in bold black ink, she wrote:

*Dear Sarah,*

*I read with delight your letter of October 21. If you are able to continue the education of the younger children, in any way, it will be to their benefit and, I believe, to your benefit as well.*

*While I am not worthy of giving advice, I will, at your request, do so. The learning of letters and how they sound is primary to learning to read and write. All but Tommy have mastered this skill. So, for him, continue using a slate to encourage his recognition of the letters. Your sister, Eliza, is quite proficient even at her very young age and she might be able to assist you in this. For the others, I left readers in the schoolroom. Use them to encourage reading sections aloud. Writing should be practiced. Your own hand is quite lovely. And, of course, the learning of numbers and sums. I find that it is best to show sums using everyday objects (two pine cones, take away one, leaves one pine cone, etc.). The children respond to this as if it were a game.*

*You will be doing a great service to your community by working with the children. If I can be of assistance, I remain at your service.*

*Cora Lane*
*October 29, 1906*
*Malden, Massachusetts*

Sarah checked at the post office in Phippsburg and was thrilled to receive the letter. She held it gently in her hands. *This is*, she thought, *the most beautiful gift.* She pressed it to her lips and caught the faint whiff of Cora's perfume. She lifted the flap with great care, determined not to spoil the crisp paper. Reading Miss Lane's copperplate handwriting was not easy. Sarah had begun practicing the Palmer Method of writing with Miss Lane but still found it difficult to read. But as the words became clear, her heart lifted. Miss Lane thought that helping the children was a good idea. Sarah's confidence soared. She folded the letter into her apron pocket and hurried about her tasks, making plans for "her school" as she worked.

∽

Cora, too, felt her letter from Sarah was a gift. She set it aside carefully and made plans to use it in her campaign to raise funds for a year-round schoolhouse on Malaga. If one of her students cared this much about education and had received the support of the "King of Malaga," most assuredly the good people of Boston and Malden would find it in their hearts to provide the funds that the city of Phippsburg refused.

She approached her mother for advice on how to proceed, and with Lucy's support they went to speak to Reverend Clark.

Cora managed to restrain her desire to speak up and impatiently participated in the polite small talk that began their visit. She was ready to broach her subject when Reverend Clark said, "I believe that what your father has accomplished among the island people of Maine is most admirable. The church board has encouraged the primary classes to raise the funds needed to provide a motorboat for the Captain's use. Just this week, on Sunday last, Fred Woolley sent the primary children home from Sunday school with a letter reminding the parents of the Captain's mission and requesting contributions."

"Oh, Reverend!" Lucy exclaimed. "How very generous you are. The Captain is out on the water for hours every Sunday and a motorized boat will make his work even more effective. Isn't it wonderful, Cora?"

Cora managed to smile and nod. She knew it really was wonderful. After all, the Captain was in his seventies and often suffered from terrible pain in his legs and feet. *It's just,* she thought, *I really was hoping to start a schoolhouse fund.*

❧

Lucy hooked her arm through Cora's as they walked home together. "I know you are disappointed, daughter, but first things first. The good people of First Church have chosen to gift your father with a boat. We will make the schoolhouse happen. You know that the state of Maine has said that Phippsburg must take responsibility for the children, and they certainly don't want the Malagaites to attend school with the white children. We will be able to raise the money for a schoolhouse and, when that happens, the state will provide a year-round teacher and you will be free from your responsibility."

"But, Mother, I love to teach the children."

"I know you do, dear. It's been a meaningful experience for you, and someday you will be able to use your skills while educating your own children."

"I have no plans to marry."

"But you will. You're much too pretty to remain a spinster." Cora pulled away as Lucy finished, "Let's stop at Miss Allison's and take a peek at the samples. We both need new dresses for the holidays."

❧

TAMARA MERRILL

The holidays arrived with the usual bustle of activities. Jonathan and Cora were considered a courting couple by many and as such were invited out often. Lucy delighted in their growing close- ness and encouraged Cora to wear her most flatter- ing dresses.

"Mother, I'm only meeting Jonathan to help him choose Christmas books for the children. I believe my old cloak will do in this dreadful weather."

"Don't be a silly goose. The new cloak is much warmer." Lucy replaced the old gray cloak Cora was holding with the new deep green cloak and the matching fur-trimmed muff and hood. *There*, she thought, admiring the way the color of the cloak brought out the red highlights in Cora's hair. "Take your fur muff. You wouldn't want to catch cold so close to Christmas. You look lovely. While you are shopping, perhaps you can find a book for your father."

Cora pulled the hood up and slipped her hands into the muff. She loved the warm, soft feel of the rabbit fur. "I wonder if the children on Malaga are warm enough," she mused.

"I'm sure they are fine. Stop worrying about things you cannot change." Lucy kissed her cheek. "Go. Have a good time. If Jonathan asks you to stay for dinner, don't worry about us—I know where you are."

Thoughts of Malaga and Sarah's school were never far from Cora's mind. As she stepped into the car- riage, she decided to spend some of her Christmas money on something for Sarah and the children.

They arrived at the Old Corner Bookstore. Jonathan stepped forward to hand Cora down from the carriage. "You look especially beautiful to-day, Cora," he said.

"Thank you." Cora blushed. "I always love Boston when the snow is fresh."

Jonathan offered his arm, and they crossed the icy sidewalk and entered the store. Cora took a deep breath. "I love the smell of books."

"As does my Elizabeth. She's become quite a little bookworm."

"Well, then, we must choose the perfect book."

Spending time with Jonathan had become very comfortable for Cora. They chatted together as they explored the store, reading bits of books to one another, commenting on the bright covers, and pointing out favorites. Cora searched the Christmas card display, looking for a card to send Sarah. Each image seemed to show more extravagance than the next. She frowned, and Jonathan asked, "Is something the matter?"

"I am looking for a card to send to Sarah, and each of these seems to show a Christmas unlike any the children on Malaga have ever experienced. Sometimes, I find it embarrassing to know how much I have and how little they have. It is only a matter of birth; it is not something I deserve."

"You are truly a good woman, Cora. The children are lucky to have a friend like you. Perhaps this card with the holly and ribbons that simply says 'Best Christmas Wishes' would be appropriate." He handed the card to Cora. "I'd like to add a dollar or two to the card when you send it. Sarah could buy a few treats for the other children."

"Thank you, Jonathan. That would be so generous of you."

"Let's pay for our purchases, and then we can stop at the post office and send the card."

❧

Cora stood in the front parlor admiring the pine boughs tucked behind the picture frames and draped over the piano. The Christmas tree sparkled in the lamplight, waiting for its candles to be lit. She took a deep breath. Everything smelled so good. Jonathan and his children would be arriving any minute for dinner and to attend midnight services with the Lanes. She touched her lips, remembering the kiss they had shared when last she saw him. She'd been kissed before, but never like this. Her stomach flipped a bit as she remembered the excitement. *Maybe,* she thought, *marriage is not always a bad thing.*

The bell chimed. Cora glanced in the mirror and hurried to greet the guests. Jonathan politely kissed her fingertips and her stomach flipped again. She dropped her eyes and welcomed the children. "Come in and see our tree," she offered.

"It's enormous!" Jack exclaimed.

"It is very beautiful," Elizabeth concurred.

"Thank you. All Christmas trees are lovely, aren't they? Tell me about your tree."

Jack clapped his hands together. "It's as big as Father." He looked at Jonathan. "Maybe it's bigger. Did you know that the Christmas tree in the President's house has electric lights?"

"I did not."

"I learned it in my book." He took Cora's hand. "May we play with your house?"

Cora smiled at Jack, delighted by his open joy. "Of course you may. Elizabeth, would you like to play, also?" She walked with Jack to the large Victorian dollhouse. "This was my dollhouse when I was your age, Jack. Every year we put it under our Christmas tree and I decorated it for Christmas."

"Lizzie, come and look at this. It looks just like this house." He gazed in wonder at the tiny family.

Elizabeth couldn't resist his excitement and joined him in moving the family about. She glanced over her shoulder at Cora. "Does the family have a name?"

"I called them the McDonalds, but they won't mind at all if you give them new names."

"Obviously," Jack said, "the boy is Jack and the dog is Rover."

The adults laughed indulgently and turned to other topics.

✍

On Malaga, the islanders gathered together in the schoolroom. A small fir had been cut down and was trimmed in pine cones and a few paper chains that Sarah had helped the schoolchildren make from the newspapers she had gathered on the mainland. They had ripped strips carefully, since Seloma McKenny wouldn't allow them to use her sewing shears on such a frivolous project, and glued them together with paste made of a bit of flour mixed with water. "I think dis is the best Christmas tree ever, Sarah," Joshua said. "It's as good as dat one at da inn."

"It has no candles," Sarah said.

"And, a good thing, too. We don't need da be burning your school down."

"It's not my school, Josh."

"It should be. When I marry you, you can stay on dis island and teach dat school all the time."

"Who says I'm going to marry you?" Sarah stamped her foot.

"Everyone knows you'll be mine someday. Everyone but you." Joshua grinned. "Here comes 'the king' with his fiddle. Happy Christmas, Sarah."

Sarah laughed. "Happy Christmas, Josh. I need to help my mama with the food. Why don't you go dance with Nancy? Maybe *she*'d like to marry you."

༄

Dinner at Captain Lane's home was always an extravagant meal, but tonight Lucy had outdone herself. The white linen cloth was laid with the best china. The silver she had inherited from her grandmother sparkled in the light of the tall candelabras that bracketed an arrangement of white flowers and pine boughs. An elegant Yorkshire pudding accompanied the roast beef, and, much to Jack's delight, the meal culminated in a flaming plum pudding.

The women and children excused themselves and left the men at the table to enjoy port and cigars. Cora showed the children to the washroom. After refreshing themselves, they returned to the parlor. Lucy lit the candles on the tree. Cora picked up the book on the side table. "May I read to you?" she asked the children.

"That would be lovely," Elizabeth said politely.

"Is it a good story?" Jack asked.

"I believe you will like it. There are ghosts and a large roast goose." Cora smiled at the boy as he arranged himself on the hearth. She opened the book and began. "Marley was dead, to begin with. There is no doubt whatever about that."

∽

When the book ended, Jonathan helped his sleepy children into their wraps and boots for the journey home. Jonathan turned to Cora and laid a delaying hand on her. "May I speak to you a moment?"

Cora gazed up at him. The candlelight was reflected in his eyes and she smiled warmly. She hoped he was going to kiss her again.

"You are very beautiful, Cora. I have come to care deeply for you." He paused and cleared his throat. "I spoke to your father tonight and he has given us his blessing." He dropped to one knee. "Will you do me the honor of becoming my wife and a mother to my children?"

Cora's hand flew to her throat. She had not expected this. Was she ready for marriage? She started to shake her head no, but heard herself say, "Jonathan, do you love me?"

"I do, Cora. With all my heart."

"Then I will marry you, Jonathan. When I am twenty-one, but not before."

# CHAPTER EIGHTEEN

## SEATTLE

Treatment began immediately, and once again Henry accompanied her to all the appointments. But Susan knew he wasn't acting the same. One evening, as she sat knitting a sweater for Gabriel, she couldn't stand it any longer. "Henry." He grunted. "Henry, put down that phone and talk to me." He started to speak, but Susan held up her palm in a stop gesture. "We've been married fifty years, Henry. Don't try to fool me. You need to tell me what's wrong."

Henry looked up from his phone and focused on his wife. He removed his glasses and folded them carefully. He rubbed his eyes and sighed. "You know I love you, Susan. I really do. I feel like a fool because I know it shouldn't matter and it doesn't, but ...," he sighed again, "this whole race thing bothers me."

Susan placed her knitting in the basket and took a sip of tea. "Can you tell me why?"

"I think it's because it came out of the blue. I never thought much about race until this. I mean, I was proud to be Irish, but that's not race, that's ethnicity. I just accepted the fact that I was a Caucasian male, and my wife was a Caucasian female, and my children were Caucasian. And now, I find out it's not exactly true. I'm just so confused." Susan waited patiently. Henry continued, "I've read all about it." He gestured at his phone. "There is no law or rule or anything that demands that anyone claim any particular race, but how do you choose what to write on a form, which box to check?"

"I googled it, too," Susan admitted. "The fact that no exact percentage dictates your race actually made it easier for me to understand why no one mentioned African-American heritage in my family. My grandparents were all born in the early 1900s, when there would have been a lot of open discrimination. Perhaps they were afraid and chose to pass as white. My father's parents were gone before I was born and my mother's died before I was ten. I remember them, but only as people who loved me. Mother kept a wedding picture on her dressing table. It showed Mom and Dad with both sets of parents. Everyone just looked happy. I don't remember thinking anything else. I'd like to see that picture now."

They sat in silence for a moment before Susan said, "It does make me wonder about my heritage, and I think, after I beat this cancer, I'd like to find out who my ancestors were. I think the kids will want to know. But for now, nothing is changed; do you understand that?"

Henry nodded. "Okay. Yes. I think I do." He stood and crossed the room to take Susan's hand. "I'm sorry I've been acting so silly. When this is over, we'll trace your roots together."

Susan's initial checkups were promising, but then the tests began to show the cancer progressing at a slow but steady rate. At each appointment they were assured that a donor search was in process. If no donor could be found in the next few weeks, Dr. Ramirez suggested that they could try an infusion from one of the children.

"What exactly does that mean?" Susan asked.

"There is no danger to the donor. They are given the same drug you took to ready the cells and when an adequate number are available, the donor is placed under local anesthesia and the cells are extracted from the donor's bloodstream. The recovery is swift. The donor typically has fully restored marrow and blood cell counts in under two weeks."

Georgia immediately volunteered. "It makes no sense to wait a few weeks. Can't we do it now?" she demanded.

Dr. Ramirez agreed, and Georgia began taking the drugs that would cause her hematopoietic cells to move from her bone marrow into her bloodstream.

Two days later, Marybeth called. "We have a possible donor." She waited for Susan's exclamation of relief. "We need you to come in to the office this afternoon for a physical exam, just to assure that you are healthy enough to tolerate the infusion. The donor is also receiving a physical exam to assure that he is healthy and has no infectious diseases. If everything is a go, we will be able to do your procedure in just a few days."

"When should we be there?" Susan was gripping the phone so tightly that her fingers were white.

"Come at four p.m. Be prepared to check into the hospital. They'll want you to be in isolation and receive chemotherapy to ready your body for the donation."

"Thank you. We'll be there."

Susan clicked off and turned to Henry, her face radiant. "They have a donor." Henry wrapped his arms around her frail body and they rocked back and forth, together. Breaking apart, Susan looked directly into Henry's eyes. "I have a good feeling about this," she said, smiling broadly.

"Me, too." Henry kissed her. "You go pack your bag and I'll call the kids. What time is it in Barcelona?"

"Only about eight p.m."

Jeff answered on the first ring. "Hey, Dad. How's everything?"

"I have good news. They've found a donor."

"On my God! That's great." Jeff's voice faded a bit as he turned and said, "Lola, they found a donor!" Then he was back. "What's next, Dad?"

"Your mother is packing her bag now, and we should be checking into the hospital this afternoon." He explained what they knew and promised to call Jeff again as soon as everything was confirmed.

Henry's call to Georgia was much the same. He promised to let her know when they were at the hospital so she could come.

Georgia called Mitch to cancel their date, and then Linda to pass on the good news. "I'm so glad," Linda said. "I'm so relieved."

"Me, too. I'll call you tonight, after I see Mom."

"Better yet, come by my house. Ken and I are just hanging out at home, and it'll be a relief to talk about something other than wedding plans."

Georgia hugged her mother good night, waved to the nurse at the desk, walked quickly down the long, too familiar hallways, crossed the sky bridge, and found her car in the huge parking structure. As she pulled out, her phone rang. "Hi, Mitch."

"Hi, how's your mom?"

"The doctor says everything is good to go. He's going to do some more chemotherapy and then they'll transplant the bone marrow."

"That's great news. Did they tell you anything about the donor?"

"Only that almost all the important HLA markers match. He'll provide the bone marrow in another hospital and a courier will bring it here."

"I know we canceled our date, but it's early. Would you like to meet for a bite to eat or a drink?"

"I'm actually headed to Linda's. I promised I'd stop by. Why don't you meet me there?"

"Are you sure? If you guys would like to talk alone, I understand."

"It's not a girls' night. I'm pretty sure Ken is there."

"Okay, I'll head over now. Drive careful. I'll see you in bit."

Georgia smiled as she hung up. Mitch was, without a doubt, the least demanding, most easygoing guy she'd ever dated.

# CHAPTER NINETEEN

## MALAGA
## 1907

Sarah McKenny pulled her shawl over her head and ran as fast as she could across the clearing. She burst through the door of her grandfather's house, startling Seloma and causing her to drop the spoon she'd been using to stir porridge.

"Now jus' see what you done. How many times do you have to be told to stay calm?"

"Sorry, Ma'm. Mama's right sick and I can't wake up Daddy."

"Grab that satchel by the bed. Quick now." Seloma pulled the porridge pot from the stove. She snatched the old, brown, tattered shawl from its hook by the door and rushed out, grabbing the satchel from Sarah's hand. "Sounds like this new baby is in a hurry to meet his life. You tell your grandpa where I've gone and then git over to hep me."

Seloma stepped into the small cabin and pulled the door shut. She stood still for a moment, allowing her eyes to adjust in the low light. The faint glow from the night fire reached only to the hearth mat. She could hear her daughter-in-law's low moans. "I be here now, Mattie—we'll get this baby born today, don't you worry none." Seloma moved to the bed. She placed her cool hand on Mattie's forehead and was surprised by her warmth. "Hush now, you done this twice before."

She found Simon sleeping on a mat pulled close to the hearth. She nudged her son with her foot. He groaned but didn't wake, "Damn, boy. You pick a fine time to be needing to sleep off your liquor." Eliza sat quietly on the mat she shared with Sarah, her big eyes intent on her grandmother. Seloma told her, "You be a good girl and get yourself dressed. Then run over to Zorah's house. Her mama will give you breakfast."

Eliza pulled her frayed dress over her nightshirt. Her long stockings were already on her feet. Sarah had taught her to keep them on as a barrier against the cold winter nights. She found her shoes and tugged them over her feet. Most of the shoe buttons were missing, but her daddy had used a piece of fish line to close the gap and she was able to keep them on—most of the time. Eliza approached the bed. Her mother moaned and Eliza drew back.

Mattie managed to open her eyes and focus on her daughter. "It'll be fine, Eliza. Your new brother or sister is coming today. Be a good girl, mind Sarah."

"I will, Mama." Eliza bent forward and kissed her mother's cheek. "I love you, Mama."

"Love you, too, child."

"That's enough now. Run along, Eliza." Seloma shooed her granddaughter toward the door. "If you see Sarah, you tell her to hurry up."

Eliza took one last look at her mother, opened the door, and scurried out. The wind whipped snow into her face. She started to turn back, to pull a shawl from the hook by the door, but a horrible wail curled out of the house, and she turned and ran to Zorah's house.

∽

Sarah found Grandfather Jim down at the shore. "Grandmother said to tell you she's gone to help my mama with the new baby."

Jim nodded. "Where's your pap?"

"He was still sleeping."

"Well, wake him up, girl, and tell him to drag his butt over to my place. He can hep me mend the net."

Sarah nodded and scrambled up the bank. For a minute she felt dizzy. She grabbed a tree limb to steady herself and kept going. She hoped this baby wouldn't take long to be born. Sarah stopped at the wood pile and gathered an armload of logs. It would be good to chase the cold out of the cabin and welcome her new brother or sister into a warm house.

Seloma glanced her way as Sarah entered. "Build up the fire, and try to wake your pap. This baby is in a rush to see the world."

Sarah moved quickly. The fire was soon crackling merrily. She knelt by her father and spoke quietly. "Pap, you need to wake up now. Mama's having the baby and Grandfather wants you to help with the nets."

Simon didn't move. He made no sound at all. Sarah laid her hand on his shoulder. She needed to wake him, but he would be very angry if she shook him. She nudged him a bit. Still nothing. "Grandma," Sarah looked over her shoulder at Seloma, "I think there's something wrong with him. He ain't making any sound."

Seloma rose from her place by Mattie's bed and approached her youngest son. She said loudly, "Simon, wake up now!" He didn't open his eyes. Seloma placed her hand on his chest. She held two fingers in front of his lips and began to cry. Sarah had no idea what to do; she'd never seen her grandmother cry. "Go git your granddad. Hurry."

Sarah spun around, opened the door, and ran as fast as she could. Bursting through the door for the second time this morning, she blurted out her message. "Somethin's wrong with my pap. Grandma says for you to come right quick."

Jim didn't hesitate. If Seloma said to come, he knew it was important. His long legs carried him quickly to Simon and Mattie's home.

Seloma sat on the floor next to Simon, tears running down her face. Mattie's moans filled the air. Jim took it all in with a glance. "He's gone, Seloma. I'll take care of this. You need to help Mattie. It sounds like that baby is about ready." He gently helped his wife from the floor. "What do you reckon happened?"

Seloma shook her head and wiped savagely at the tears. "Don't smell like drink." She crossed the room to Mattie's bed and took her hand. Mattie groaned. Seloma murmured, "It'll be all right. Everything is gonna be all right." She picked up the damp rag and wiped Mattie's hot face. The girl was burning up with fever.

∽

Sarah followed her grandfather. She tried to hurry, but her feet didn't seem to work right. Sarah wiped the sweat from her forehead. Her head pounded with a terrible headache. *I'm so cold,* she thought. *How can I be so cold and still be sweating?* She stumbled across the frozen clearing. Eliza called to her from Zorah's house and Sarah lifted a weary arm to wave.

Inside the cabin, Grandpa was wrapping a blanket around her pap. *He must be cold, too,* she thought. Seloma turned and motioned for her to approach the bed. "This baby will be here in a minute. Git me some hot water and the swaddling cloths. Then come back here and hold your mama's hand."

The water Sarah had placed on the stove earlier had come to a boil. She cooled it with a dipper of cold water and carried the pot to the bed. The swaddling cloths were washed and folded in the bed box. She lifted them out carefully and caught a whiff of the lavender water they'd been rinsed in. It smelled like a summer day. Her stomach whirled, and for a moment Sarah feared she'd be sick. Her head throbbed. She kept her eyes focused on Mattie; she didn't want to know what was happening with her pap.

"You all right, Sarah?" Seloma asked. Sarah managed a nod. "Okay, Mattie, I need you to push. Sarah, hold your mama's shoulders and when she bears down, you hep her."

Seloma pushed Mattie's nightgown out of the way. A bright red rash covered Mattie's bare legs. Seloma sighed and glanced over her shoulder at her husband. "Jim. Check Simon for a rash. It looks like Mattie has the measles."

Mattie groaned and bore down. Her shoulders lifted off the bed. Sarah supported her mother and then with a terrible scream, Mattie was delivered of a baby boy. She sank back, shaking and crying. "You done good, Mattie. It's a fine boy." Seloma cut the cord, quickly wrapped the baby, and placed him in the box that had been prepared for his arrival. "Now, Mattie, I just need another big push and we'll be done." Mattie lay still. "Sarah, show your mama the new baby. Mattie, you can rest in a minute. Open your eyes and look at your fine new baby boy."

Mattie opened her eyes and turned her head to see Sarah. She lifted a finger, as if to touch the child. "Marcus," she whispered. "Take care of my Marcus, Sarah." Mattie's eyes closed again and did not open.

Sarah stood silent beside the bed, the baby cradled carefully in her arms. She stroked his tiny face and bent to place him next to his mother. "No," Seloma spoke sharply. "Your mama and pap are both gone from the measles. Wrap that baby in a warm shawl and take him up to Zorah. Ask her to come here to hep wit the necessary things. You stay over there and take care of Eliza and Zorah's

142

childun, and this here Marcus. I'll be along as fast as I can."

Sarah did as she was told, too numb from the deaths and birth to think clearly. Zorah didn't ask questions, just gave Sarah a hug and hurried out the door. To Sarah's relief, Eliza and the other children were excited by the arrival of the tiny baby boy and only asked his name.

Despite her headache, Sarah managed to keep the children occupied until Zorah returned. She didn't want to think about her parents, or about the fact that Grandma had said they died of measles. Just a few years ago, measles had swept through the island, but only old man Smith and the Wiley baby had died. Her mama and pap were strong; surely there was some mistake.

Zorah lifted Marcus from Sarah's arms. "You all right, girl?" Sarah tried to nod, but her neck was stiff and her head throbbed. She attempted a smile. Zorah touched her forehead. "You burning up, child. Let me see your chest." Sarah was too weak to protest as Zorah unbuttoned her dress. "See this rash here? You got the measles, Sarah. You go lay down on the bed and rest 'til your grandma git here."

❧

The room whirled and dipped. Voices came and went. Someone stripped off her clothes and bathed her skin with tepid water. It was light and it was dark. Sarah drifted. Somewhere she heard Eliza cry. A sip of water was offered. She tried to swallow, but the water leaked from her mouth. A baby cried. Sarah saw her mama by the window and laughed, "I knew you weren't dead, Mama." Sarah stretched out her fingers, grasped her mother's hand, and they flew.

⌒

Seloma grieved for her youngest child. The older children were married and living here and there, sometimes returning to Malaga, sometimes not. They were all gathered around her today, as Seloma managed to hold both Eliza and Marcus in her arms. She rocked back and forth. Tears streamed down her face. Today they'd buried three members of her family, all dead within a day of one another. Now there were two orphans, two little children with no family but each other. "How many more are sick?" she asked her husband. "How many more are going to be sick?"

"It's a hard winter, Seloma. Most every year a bunch of our people get the measles. The good Lord giveth and the good Lord taketh away."

"Ain't no good in a God that would take this baby's mama and daddy. Simon might have liked his liquor, but he never did nothing but put good into this world. Mattie was a kind woman, and Sarah …" She covered her mouth to hold back a sob. "Sarah was goin' to be a teacher, a fine teacher."

"God must have needed them in heaven." Jim patted his wife's shoulder.

"I needed them here," Eliza declared.

Seloma pulled herself together. "Your mama and pap would want you to grow up to be the most helpful, good girl possible. They would want you to take care of Marcus."

Eliza nodded solemnly. She slid off Seloma's lap. "I will, Grandma. Promise."

# CHAPTER TWENTY

## MALAGA
## 1907

Cora flipped her hand back and forth. Sunlight caught in her ring and bounced around the room, creating rainbows on the ornate wallpaper. She opened her portfolio and withdrew a monogrammed sheet of stationery. Over the past months, several of her friends from school had become engaged and two were planning summer weddings. Cora began to write notes declining their invitations, citing the need to be in Maine. Lucy was appalled. "If you don't attend the weddings of your friends, who will attend your wedding?"

"My friends know that I teach on Malaga in the summer. I'm sure that I have offended no one. Both Alexia and Dortha have only included our family on their invitation lists because Father has business with their fathers. A lovely gift will suffice."

Lucy shook her head. "It seems to me that you refuse to see the significance of social niceties. You are marrying an important man, who will expect you to act accordingly."

"I can assure you, Mother, that you have taught me well. I promise I will do nothing to embarrass you and Father or Jonathan. But, I will not interrupt my last summer of teaching by making trips back to Boston for weddings that I do not care to celebrate." Cora twisted her engagement ring. The three-stone diamond ring Jonathan had given her was the envy of all her friends, but sometimes it felt so heavy.

Lucy extended an invitation to Jonathan and his children to visit the Lane cabin on Horse Island. "I should like that very much and the children will be delighted. Perhaps," Jonathan looked at Cora, "I could see Malaga Island and this school of yours."

With everyone in agreement, it was arranged that the visit would take place the last week in July.

The Lane family returned to Maine for the summer of 1907. They were welcomed by the people of Phippsburg and Captain Lane readied himself, once again, to row between the islands every Sunday, spreading the word of God.

Jim McKenny sent Joshua over to talk to the family and arrange the ladies' transportation to Malaga. Cora greeted him eagerly. "It's so nice to see you, Joshua. I have new books and toys for the children. Did Sarah continue the schooling for the little ones all winter?"

146

"No, Ma'm. Sarah be gone."

"Gone? Where did she go? Did she marry?" Cora was aghast, but she knew that some girls married very young, and Sarah might be fifteen by now.

Joshua shook his head, his eyes full of sadness. "Miss Cora, we had the measles somethin' awful this winter. Sarah and her mama and daddy gone to heaven."

"Oh, no." Cora covered her mouth. "How awful! What about the others?"

"Sammy can't hear no more, but nobuddy else dies."

Cora wanted to hug the young man, but she knew enough not to; it would only cause him trouble if someone saw them. Instead she touched his arm lightly. "I'm so sorry, Joshua. I know you cared a great deal for Sarah."

"I was goin' to marry her when she be sixteen. I would have kept her safe." He turned and stumbled to his boat. "I pick you up for teachin' on Monday, Miss Cora."

"Thank you. I'll be ready." Cora's tears flowed freely as she watched the boat pull away. *What a waste,* she thought. *I really think Sarah could have been a teacher.*

On Monday morning, eight children sat in the classroom, anxious to greet Cora and her mother. They stood together as the women entered the room. "Good morning, everyone," Cora said brightly.

"Good mornin', Mrs. Lane, Miss Cora," they chanted together.

Cora surveyed the bright shiny faces. She knew most of the children from last year. Eliza waved shyly from her place on the long bench and Cora gave her an extra smile. *She must miss Sarah something awful,* Cora thought.

"I see an organ has been added to our school," Lucy said.

"The King brung it over in his boat," a small boy explained.

"Who plays the organ?"

"The King do, but mostly he play the fiddle and Miss McKenny, she play the organ."

"Lovely. Cora, will you do the honors today? Bow your heads, children, and we will bless the Lord for the gift of this organ and ask his blessing on our school."

Cora sat at the instrument, waiting for her mother to finish the prayer and suggest a hymn. She knew she should bow her head. Instead she looked carefully at the gathered children. They were all so carefully washed and all so thin. Joshua slumped in the doorway and their eyes locked. Cora knew they were both thinking of Sarah. She quickly bowed her head and closed her eyes.

When the school day ended, Cora slipped away from her mother's conversation with Seloma and walked to the small graveyard. She picked a few wildflowers and found the wooden cross that bore Sarah's name. "I miss you," she murmured. "Rest in peace, Sarah." She laid the flowers beneath the cross and walked back toward the house. Lucy was waiting impatiently for her return, but, noting the look on her daughter's face, and the direction from which Cora appeared came, she held her tongue and stepped into the boat for the return trip.

❦

Summer settled into the now familiar routine of teaching in the morning, tea with friends in the afternoon, and on Sundays Lucy and Cora attended services at the church in Phippsburg, while the captain rowed his boat from island to island. Cora still found teaching to be of great interest and talked often of how much she would miss it after her marriage. "You'll be kept busy with Jonathan and the children," Lucy declared. "And before long, perhaps you'll have a child of your own."

Cora shook her head. "I'm in no hurry to have additional children, Mother. Jonathan has suggested that we travel, and I find that idea intriguing. I should like to see the cities of Europe and perhaps our own Wild West. And, I shall join the National American Woman Suffrage Association."

"Cora! How dare you even suggest such a thing? Your father would be furious."

"He would," Cora agreed. "But I will be married and Jonathan agrees that women should have the right to vote."

"But does he agree that his wife should parade about on the streets of Boston?"

"I'm certain he shall. He knows of my strong feelings on this matter."

Lucy shook her head. *I only hope they marry before Cora ruins her chance for happiness,* she thought. Aloud she said, "Jonathan and the children will be here tomorrow. Why don't you take the pail and pick enough blackberries for a cobbler. I believe the children would enjoy that."

Happy to escape, Cora picked up the bucket and hurried to the door. Lucy's voice stopped her.

"Roll down your sleeves and take a hat. You don't want to be as brown as a Malagaite on your wedding day."

⚬⚬

Jonathan arrived with exciting news. First Church had raised the funds necessary to purchase the motor launch and had commissioned him to help the Captain find such a boat at the Phippsburg Boatyard. Cora congratulated her father and joined in the prayer of thanksgiving that the Captain offered.

The next morning, Jonathan and Captain Lane rowed across the bay together and returned in separate boats. The motor launch, piloted by the Captain, took only a third of the time to cross. The Captain was beaming as he glided toward the dock. He tossed the painter to Cora, who pulled it tight. The children clamored for a ride but the Captain refused, saying, "This boat is for the Lord's work, and only for the Lord's work."

He strode toward the house, calling back over his shoulder, "Come inside, Cora. I have news of the school."

Cora calmed the children with promises of tea served outside and told them to wait on the shore for their father. She hurried after the Captain, anxious to learn his news. She found her parents in the kitchen and forced herself to wait pa-tiently as the Captain told Lucy how marvelous the motorboat was, how easy to maneuver, and how quickly it crossed the water. "Surely, the Lord has blessed our mission."

"Indeed," Lucy agreed.

Noting Cora's arrival, he said, "You are aware that last winter the state of Maine put education on Malaga Island under the authority of the Superintendent of Schools." The women nodded. "Mr. Payton Smith is that superintendent. I have learned this day that he plans a visit to your little school in August."

"Perhaps the state will consider establishing a real school on Malaga," Lucy said.

Cora bit her tongue. She wanted to demand, *If our school isn't real, what is it?* Instead she said carefully, "His visit will be much appreciated. We should plan a special program. Thank you for letting us know, Father. I believe I will return to the dock to wait for Jonathan. I've promised the children that they may have tea in the yard, and I do think that Jonathan and I will join them."

She walked slowly back to the dock. She watched as Jonathan brought the rowboat into the dock and tossed his painter to Jack, who tried valiantly to secure the line. Elizabeth came to his rescue. Jonathan stepped out of the boat. He stooped to hug both the children. Cora smiled. A man who would embrace his children with such joy would certainly make a good husband. Cora lifted her hand and waved. Jonathan scooped Jack up, tucking him under his arm, and reached down to hold Elizabeth's hand. Thus encumbered with both children, he beamed at Cora and called out, "Hello, my darling!"

⁓

Later, when the children were in bed, Cora sat on the end of the dock next to Jonathan. She gazed up at the stars. A sigh escaped her lips. Jonathan lifted her hand and kissed her palm. "Is something troubling you?"

"*Troubling* is perhaps too strong a word. I am concerned that the superintendent will find our little school lacking and will not agree to our proposal to build a schoolhouse on Malaga."

"I believe that he will find your school to have been of great benefit to the children. Certainly, those that are now able to read and write are proof of your good work. He should realize that the state has actually saved money by having you and your mother as unpaid teachers these last three years."

"True, but …"

"But what?" Jonathan prompted.

"But the children are not pure white, and many see no need for education of those less fortunate than themselves."

Jonathan pulled her close. "I know how important the school is to you and how sad you are to be leaving, but, even if it is selfish of me, I'm delighted that you will be my wife." He placed a finger under her chin and tilted her face toward his. "I promise, Cora, that I will do everything in my power to help raise the money to build a schoolhouse on Malaga."

Cora smiled. "And, will you work to assure that women get the vote?"

Jonathan laughed. "I will."

꙳

Cora and Lucy prepared the schoolchildren carefully for Superintendent Smith's visit. On the morning of his visit, Cora and Lucy arrived to find the schoolroom sparkling. The floor and windows had been scrubbed. Jars of mayberry blossoms and wild carrot stood on the organ and on the windowsills. The children filed in, freshly scrubbed and wearing their best clothes. "He's comin', Miss Cora. We see his boat."

"Excellent. Everyone, let's bow our heads and start our day," Lucy said firmly and began the morning prayer.

As they raised their bowed heads, Superintendent Smith entered. The children rose as they had been taught. "Good morning, Mrs. Lane," Smith nodded to Lucy, "and Miss Lane." He nodded to Cora and turned to face the children. Their expectant faces were a variety of black, brown, white, and black with freckles. For a moment he hesitated, not used to seeing children of such a variety in a classroom. Then he said, "Good morning, children."

"Good morning, Sir," the children said together, exactly as they had practiced.

Eliza stepped forward, took a deep breath, and said clearly, "Welcome to Malaga Island School, Superintendent Smith." She dropped a curtsy, grinned at Cora, and took her seat. Cora winked at her.

With such an auspicious start, it was only right that the morning passed quickly and happily. When asked, each child read from his or her primer. The older children demonstrated simple arithmetic skills. Lucy displayed writing samples and Cora kept an eye on Smith's reaction. She was sure it was favorable. As the school visit drew to a close, Cora said, "We have prepared, for your pleasure, a two-part rendition of 'School Days.'

Mrs. McKenny will accompany us on the organ and Mr. McKenny will join us on his fiddle."

The children sang with infectious spirit and soon Superintendent Smith was tapping his foot. They began the final chorus and Smith's deep baritone joined in the happy words: "School days, school days, dear old golden rule days …"

The children were dismissed. Smith spoke to the adults. "There is no doubt in my mind that these children need to be educated. Perhaps it would be most cost effective to send the children to the mainland."

Cora bit her lip, afraid to speak up. Jim McKenny felt no such compunction. "The people of Phippsburg ain't gonna want our children in their schools. The state needs to give us our own teacher. These young'uns are just as bright as them over there, but they don't want to mix."

"Thank you, Mr. McKenny. I'll consider your concerns and make a decision quickly. Do you believe that you can raise the funds to build an adequate schoolhouse on the island?"

"I believe that we can, Mr. Smith," Lucy said firmly. "We will begin our work at once."

# CHAPTER TWENTY-ONE

## SEATTLE

Things should have been perfect but, somehow, they weren't. Georgia jogged around Green Lake, her earbuds blasting Adele's "Rolling in the Deep," but for once she wasn't singing along. She was deep in thought. Susan had received an almost perfect bone marrow donation and, while she was very weak, she was holding her own. Jeff and Lola were planning to be in Seattle for Thanksgiving, They were bringing Gabriel to meet his "other" grandparents. Henry had set up a crib in Georgia's old room, and when she felt well enough, Susan was knitting feverishly to be sure Gabe would have a warm sweater for their visit. The fall semester was going well. Or was it?

"Damn," Georgia said, and stopped abruptly. "Am I letting that idiot, Mark Hedrick, get to me?"

"You okay?" a jogger asked, pausing and running in place next to her.

"Fine, sorry." Georgia moved aside. The jogger waved and ran on. She pulled her earbuds out and dialed Mitch's number. No answer. She left a message. "Hey, just wondered if you'd have time for a cup of coffee. I'm headed to Elliott Bay Books right now."

Bookstores and libraries were always Georgia's first choice for refuge from the world, and Elliott Bay was one of the best.

She pushed open the door and took a deep breath. The sight of thousands of books piled on tables and crowding the shelves gave her spirits a lift. She needed coffee, but first she needed to find a book on interracial dating and marriage. She headed up the stairs to the self-help section. Mark had been so rude at Friday's meeting and she was mad at herself for not calling him on his behavior. *What business is it of his who Linda marries or who I date? He's such a jerk.*

She pulled books out at random, quickly skimming the back cover and then returning the book to its place on the shelf. There seemed to be an abundance of books on every type of relationship. She grinned as she read the cover of a book stating it was for "the man who loves his dog too much." Her search was interrupted by a clerk asking, "May I help you find something specific?"

"Please. I need a book on interracial relationships."

"Personal or in the workplace?"

"Both, I guess. Or something that …" Georgia's voice trailed off. She realized she was actually kind of embarrassed. *Stop it,* she told herself.

The clerk wasn't fazed by her confusion. He pulled several books from a low shelf and handed them to her. "Take a look at these. Perhaps one will be what you want."

Georgia thanked him and accepted the books. She flipped over the first one and read, "Believe it or not, there are still people who have families or friends that disapprove of inter-racial relationships in today's world. Fostering a relationship is tough enough, but with detractors all around you, it can re-ally affect your self-confidence when out in public." She flipped the book over and looked at the cover: a man, a woman, and a crowd of people in the background. This looked like exactly what she needed. She took a quick look at the other books and chose a second one that offered "twelve steps to understand-ing your interracial relationship." She placed the other books on the returns table and carried her choices downstairs to the coffee lounge.

After ordering her latte, she settled into a corner table and began to skim the books. "Hey, beautiful," Mitch said, kissing her swiftly. "I'm going to order my coffee. I'll be right back."

Georgia turned her book choices cover down and placed them on the bench next to her. Mitch returned. "You studying something or just reading a good book?" he asked.

"A little of both." Georgia smiled at him. "Hope I didn't take you away from anything important."

"Nothing is more important than a cup of great coffee in my favorite bookstore. I was thinking about doing my laundry and this," he lifted his cup in a salute, "is much more fun." He took a sip. "So, what's up?"

"I just needed to talk to you."

"Sounds serious."

"Not really, but, well, maybe it *is* serious." Mitch raised an eyebrow and waited for Georgia to continue. "You know Ken and Linda are engaged." Mitch nodded. "So, what do you think about that?"

"I'm happy for them. They seem like a great couple. Why?"

"I guess, I'm just wondering what you think about the race thing?"

Mitch stayed quiet for a long minute. Georgia fidgeted with her spoon; she wanted to take back her question. At last, he spoke. "I'm not exactly sure what you want to know, Georgia. Are you asking me if I approve of a mixed-race relationship? Because that seems kind of strange since I believe you and I are in a relationship."

"I'm very confused about race. Not us, and our relationship or Ken and Linda. But about how other people react to race and how and when to speak up."

"Okay."

"My dad is Irish. It is very important to him. But some things are happening in our family that have everyone very confused."

"You mean your mom's cancer?"

"That, too. But, more. When we were all tested to see if we could donate bone marrow, the test results were pretty surprising." Georgia took a drink of her latte and placed the cup carefully in the exact center of her coaster. "Mom needed bone marrow from a black donor." She looked at Mitch to see his reaction.

He sat perfectly still. Georgia waited. Finally, he said, "Are you trying to ask me if I am bothered by the fact that you have African-American blood?" He didn't wait for an answer but continued. "I'm surprised, and I wonder why you didn't mention anything until now. I'm also wondering how you feel about learning this. Does it upset you to know that you aren't purely Caucasian?"

Georgia dropped her eyes. "I haven't told you because I don't know how I feel. I don't want it to bother me, but maybe it does. And, I feel like such a hypocrite if it bothers me. Jeff doesn't seem fazed at all, but I keep looking in the mirror trying to see a trace of my African ancestors. I never thought I was racist, but if I'm bothered by it, doesn't that make me a racist?"

"I think you need to cut yourself some slack. I don't know how long you've known, but this is a lot to process. I like you because you are warm, funny, smart, and very beautiful. Your race has very little to do with it."

"Very little, or nothing at all?"

"Georgia, that's crazy. You are not Japanese. In my home, anyone not one hundred percent Japanese is different, exotic, sort of forbidden."

"Does that mean if I were Japanese you wouldn't like me?"

"Don't be so literal. If you were Japanese you wouldn't be you. I've dated plenty of Japanese women. Some of them I liked a lot."

"Have you ever dated a black woman?"

"No, but I never ruled it out. Have you dated a black man?"

"No. I wouldn't have dared. I always knew my dad wouldn't approve." Georgia drank the last of her coffee. This conversation had gotten way out of control. "The only thing I was worried about was how to stop Mark Hedrick from making racist/sexist remarks about Linda and myself, and somehow we are talking about dating others."

"Actually, I think we are talking about your fears. However, to make it simple, the most effective way to stop any kind of bully is to call him on his behavior. The next time Mark makes a comment that you feel is inappropriate, tell him so and report him to the department head. In the meantime, stop worrying so much. I like you. You like me. Can you just enjoy that and let the future take care of itself?"

"I can," Georgia said. *But,* she thought, *I still don't know how I feel about anything. Or how you feel about me.*

∽

Late that night, Georgia sat at her desk, staring out into the dark. She pulled a yellow legal pad out of the drawer and began a list:

1. Is it too hard to be in an interracial relationship?
2. Why hasn't Mitch told his family he is dating me?
3. Do I want to get married, ever?
4. Do I love Mitch?
5. If I have children, they might be black.
6. What if I get multiple myeloma? (It is in my genes.)
7. Do I need to claim African American as my race on forms?
8. Why doesn't Jeff care about race?
9. WHAT IS WRONG WITH ME???
10. What is my family history? I want to know. How do I find out?

# CHAPTER TWENTY-TWO

## MALAGA
## 1907

Cora knew that she'd return to vacation on Horse Island, but she'd never again be the Malaga Island School teacher. Leaving Maine in August 1907 was difficult. Saying good-bye to the islanders was harder than usual. She would soon be a married woman. Things would never be the same again. She hugged Eliza, and was reminded of Sarah. The eight-year-old Eliza looked much the same as Sarah had when Cora first began teaching.

"Next year, if the good Lord is willing, you'll have a fine new schoolhouse and a new teacher," she told the children. They sniffled, and Cora tried not to join them. "I will visit your school and I expect to find that you all are advancing through your studies."

❧

Joshua was silent as he rowed Cora and Lucy across the water to their home on Horse Island. He helped Lucy from the boat and then Cora. Lucy said a brief good-bye and hurried up the path to the house. Cora lingered. "I'll miss you, Joshua. You are a marvelous young man."

"I aim to go away, Miss Cora. I jist been staying here to help with the young'uns. I plan to make myself some money and find me a wife, and I don't want to do it 'round here."

"But won't you miss your family?"

"'Course I will. I gonna send money to my mama. You 'member that big boat that was here a couple of years ago? That USONA?"

Cora nodded.

"That be Mr. Child's boat. I been working for him some, and he tell me he named that boat the USONA 'cause this here is part of North America and so is Canada, so we be United States of North America. He say there be another America called South America where lots of people look all different ways. You reckon that be right?"

"It is right, Joshua. The Americas, together, make up a very large continent."

"That what Mr. Childs say. He say I can work for him on that big boat and I can see all the Americas and Europe, too."

"That's wonderful. I envy you the opportunity to see the world."

"Mr. Childs, he give me some books to read. It sure look like there be a lot to see."

"I'm glad you're still interested in learning. When you come back for a visit, you should share your experiences with the Malaga children."

"I do that, Miss Cora, but I ain't never goin' to live here again after I leave."

Cora wished him luck and they parted. She had wanted to ask him why he never wanted to return, but she was sure she knew. Despite the school, the mainlanders still looked down on, and complained about, the Malagaites. Joshua was a bright young man with light skin; he could pass for white if he moved away. She wondered if he would.

⁓

Back home in Massachusetts, plans for Cora's wedding accelerated. Lucy, subscribing to the old nursery rhyme "Monday, for wealth, Tuesday, for health, Wednesday, best day of all, Thursday, for losses, Friday, for crosses, Saturday, no luck at all," insisted that Cora be married at the fashionable hour of high noon on a Wednesday, in the most auspicious month of all, October. When the church was not available on her chosen date, Lucy reminded the Reverend Mr. Clark of the Captain's missionary work and was able to secure the exact time and date she wanted: October 23, 1907.

⁓

Cora sat with her mother writing invitations. She suggested, "Since I'm marrying a widower, with a fully appointed home, perhaps we could add a note asking that donations be sent to the new Malaga School Fund in lieu of wedding presents."

Lucy dropped her pen, creating an ink stain on her white shirtwaist. "Cora!" she exclaimed. "What in the world is wrong with you? Whatever gave you such an insane idea? You can't ask people for money!"

"But, Mother, that's exactly what we have been doing. Just last Sunday you made a lovely plea for support. People will spend much more on a wedding

162

present that I don't need than they will donate to the school. We'd actually be saving them money." Cora grinned. She knew it was wicked to provoke her mother, but she and Jonathan really didn't need a thing. *And*, she thought, *if we do, Jonathan will buy whatever we need.*

"Stop it, Cora. Need I remind you that you will be a married woman soon? A woman with children. Your crazy ideas need to be put aside."

"Mother," Cora's serious tone caused Lucy to pause and look at her daughter, "how did you know that you wanted to marry Father?"

Lucy sighed. "My father wanted me to marry the Captain. I'd seen him at various events and, of course, we'd spoken. He was a Civil War hero, you know?" Cora nodded. "I was twelve when the war ended. By the time I was eighteen, I was courting a bit, but there just didn't seem to be enough eligible young men. The war had killed so many." Lucy sighed, took a deep breath, and continued. "Then mother became ill and I took over her care and that of the household. The years went by so quickly. I was twenty-nine, and a confirmed spinster, when the Captain asked for my hand in marriage. The Captain was forty-seven. I knew my father's choice was a good one. I haven't regretted my decision to marry."

"But did you love him?"

"I grew to love him. He is a very good man. I never expected to have children and I considered your birth, when I was thirty-four, to be a miracle, as did the Captain." Lucy turned back to the envelopes she was addressing. "Jonathan will make you a fine husband, Cora. True love has little to do with what you read in those novels you enjoy so much."

163

"I think I might love Jonathan," Cora confessed. "But I'm not sure I want to be married."

Lucy ignored the comment. "Let's finish these invitations, and we can drop them at the post office and then stop by Miss Allison's for a fitting of your gown."

⁓

Cora watched her reflection in the tall pier glass as Miss Allison fussed with the tiny, satin-covered buttons that marched down the back of her wedding gown. The gown's soft, rich cream-white satin complemented Cora's dark hair and caused her skin to glow. The waist, cut demurely low, was covered in lace. Her arms were encased by long satin sleeves that ended just below her wrists and buttoned with more of the tiny buttons. The sumptuous skirt fell in a graceful waterfall effect and was pulled back into a small bustle.

"It's beautiful, Mother." Cora spun and looked over her shoulder to get a glimpse of the bustle. "Miss Allison, you've created the most beautiful dress. Thank you."

Miss Allison beamed. "Just let me add the veil and train, Miss Lane." Using hook-and-eye closures, she attached the eighty-five-inch train to the skirt and spread it on the carpet. The heavy satin and lace caused Cora to tip slightly.

Lucy smiled. "Remember, the Glover twins will be your pages. They'll carry the train down the aisle, and after the wedding you will use the wrist loop to carry it yourself." Lucy wiped a tear from her eye. "You will be a beautiful bride, Cora. I'm so glad you agreed to the long train."

"It is lovely," Cora agreed, "but it seems like such a waste since I'll never wear it again."

"It is completely appropriate," Lucy spoke firmly, "for you to wear your wedding dress all through the holiday season. An October wedding is perfect, since there are more formal occasions in the fall and winter. Of course, you won't wear the veil, but the train will look lovely at any dance or perhaps at the theater. By Easter, you will need to put it away, but in the meantime, you can enjoy being a beautiful, young bride."

Miss Allison lifted the lace veil over Cora's head and tucked it into place. "Your mother tells me that she has ordered a wreath of orange blossoms, but for now we'll just have to imagine." She stepped away and surveyed her handiwork. "The fit is quite nice. I'll have the dress pressed and delivered to you next week along with the rest of your trousseau."

Wedding gifts arrived on a daily basis. Lucy carefully arranged them, in a lavish display of wealth and ostentatious generosity, on tables covered with gleaming white damask cloths. Three days before the wedding day, Cora and Lucy hosted a tea to thank those who had sent the presents, and to allow everyone to tour the gifts. Cora was overcome with the abundance of the offerings. She found herself to be secretly pleased at the jealousy of her school friends. Her wedding was, without a doubt, the social event of 1907. *Perhaps, I shall enjoy being married, after all,* she thought.

# CHAPTER TWENTY-THREE

## SEATTLE

This time the chemotherapy and radiation took an even greater toll on Susan. Each day she seemed smaller and more frail. Georgia watched her mother suffer and worried that she wouldn't be strong enough to receive the donor cells. Susan, as always, was able to read her mind. "Don't worry so much, darling," she said. "I don't plan on dying anytime soon. I want to meet my grandson."

*From your lips to God's ear,* Georgia thought. Aloud she said, "I love you, Mom."

At last the doctors declared that all the cancer cells were gone and that Susan's immune system had shut down. The donor marrow infusion was scheduled.

Henry stayed by the bed, holding Susan's hand as the allogeneic infusion of the donor cells began to flow into Susan's bloodstream. A movie played on the television set, but neither of them watched it. Susan dozed and Henry sat watch. Nurses came in quietly to check the IV flow. Henry wondered idly how many sets of masks, gowns, and gloves the hospital used each day. Time passed. The IV finished. Susan slept.

∾

"Hi, Mama." Georgia leaned down and pressed a kiss to Susan's temple. The mask kept her lips from touching her mother's skin. She seemed warm. "How do you feel? Are you running a fever?" Without waiting for an answer, she sat down next to the bed and picked up her mother's hand. "Did Jeff call?" Susan nodded and Georgia continued, "Did they schedule a flight yet?"

Susan smiled slightly and shook her head. "One question at a time. Yes, I have a very low-grade fever. And, no they haven't scheduled a flight. Dr. Ramirez says I'll be in isolation until they find donor cells in my blood. And Gabriel won't be allowed to visit during that time, so I told Jeff to wait until we get the approval."

"That makes sense," Georgia agreed. She opened her phone, pulled up the gallery, and handed the phone to her mother.

"Oh," Susan sighed. "Isn't he beautiful? Ten months old today and I still haven't met him. He looks just like Jeff did at that age." She returned the phone and closed her eyes.

Georgia adjusted the blanket and watched Susan drift off to sleep. Tears filled her eyes. She blinked them away. The thought of losing her mother was unbearable.

Some days Susan seemed stronger, some days weaker. One week post-infusion turned to two and then three. The doctors monitored her progress carefully, watching for signs that the transfusion graft was beginning to create new, healthy cells. When she spiked a fever, they added antiviral medication and assured the family that such setbacks were common.

Susan never complained. When she was awake, she asked about Henry's day, Georgia's classes, and, always, asked to see the most recent picture of Gabriel.

Five weeks post-infusion, the blood tests began to show an increase in both red and white cells. Dr. Ramirez seemed optimistic that Susan was showing improvement. At six weeks he lifted the isolation order. Georgia called Jeff with the good news.

"Come as soon as you can. Mom and Dad really want to meet their grandson."

"I've already arranged time off work, so we'll get on a flight as soon as possible. Tell Mom we'll be there in just a day or two."

Georgia began to cry silently. She took a deep breath and tried to keep the tears from her voice as she said, "Hurry."

"We will. Just hang in there, Georgie."

His words were as good as a hug. Georgia managed to pull herself together and returned to her mother's bedside to report that Jeff was on his way.

The news that her first grandson would soon be in her arms made Susan very happy. She brushed away a tear as she said, "Please check to be sure your father has Gabriel's room ready. He put up the crib and brought my old rocker down from the attic, but make sure it looks pretty."

"I will, Mama. The bedding you chose has been delivered. I'll make sure it is washed and ready."

Susan smiled. "And buy flowers for Lola and Jeff's room. I'll make a list of groceries for your father to buy. Do you know if Gabe is eating solid food?"

Georgia grinned. It felt great to have Susan sounding like herself, making plans and worrying about the family.

⟡

Gabriel was delightful. He had no fear of anyone and was soon enamored with Susan, holding his arms out whenever she entered a room. Susan's happiness in her grandson inspired everyone. Things returned almost to normal.

Susan bravely brought up the topic of her donor and of his race. "We need to talk about this, kids," she said one night. "I've been doing a lot of reading and remembering. Henry brought down some old papers and things that we had stored in the attic after my mother died. Going through them, I found a lot of old pictures."

"I'd love to see them," Jeff said.

"Me, too," Georgia chimed in.

"There are some surprises. Or maybe, I'm just looking at things differently. Henry, please get that stack of photos on my desk." Henry rose to follow his wife's bidding, as Susan continued. "I was astounded to discover that we are not one hundred percent Irish, or a mix Irish and Northern European. I know these revelations must be hard for all of us."

"Well, Mom, we were both surprised by the results of our tests but relieved to know that you and Dad are our birth parents. Not being told we'd been adopted would have been a bigger shock. I'm curious, though, and I'd like to know the whole story. How about you, Georgia?"

Georgia nodded.

Henry returned with the stack of pictures and handed them to Susan. She looked down at the first picture and smiled as she said, "This is my parents' wedding picture. You've seen this before. I have a copy on my dressing table." She passed the photo to Georgia. "Look at it carefully."

"Grandma was very pretty, and Jeff kind of looks like your dad." Georgia passed the photo to Jeff.

Lifting the next photo, Susan said, "I think this is a picture of my mother. On the back it says '1934, Geraldine and Anna.'" She handed the picture to Georgia. Jeff moved to see over her shoulder.

"So, who is Anna?"

"She looks like Grandma, but ..."

"Don't be afraid to say it, Jeff. She looks like your grandmother but she is definitely an African-American child."

Henry sat, quiet, twirling his glass around and around on its coaster.

"This picture," Susan picked up another, "is much older. The ink on the back is quite faded, but I think it says 'Eliza and Marcus, 1911.'"

Jeff took the picture. "She's white and he's black. I think we have a genuine mystery here. Didn't your parents ever talk about their lives?"

"Not much. They were busy. My grandmother lived with us for a short while—maybe a year or two—and I remember her white hair. It was curly and so was mine. I liked that. I don't think she was black. Mother never knew her father. He'd died in an accident when she was just a baby."

"What about cousins? Did she ever mention Anna?"

"No, and I never saw this photo. When we cleaned out Mother's house, I only kept this box of papers because it didn't seem right to throw them away. I had your father put it in the attic and I forgot about it."

She bent forward and spread the rest of the pictures across the coffee table. "Most of these have nothing at all written on the back. I have no idea where that old schoolhouse is—or was—located, and I don't know any of these people. Except, as you can see, my grandmother seems to be in many of them."

"And," Henry said, "the races are mixed."

# CHAPTER TWENTY-FOUR

## MALAGA
## 1908–1909

With Superintendent Smith's promise that a teacher would be provided if the people of Malaga Island could build an appropriate school, and with her daughter safely married and on her honeymoon in Europe, Lucy increased her fund-raising efforts. Six hundred dollars was a large amount of money, but Lucy's determination was formidable.

School Superintendent Payson Smith's letter of January 17, 1908, stated that "the schoolhouse for this Island should have two rooms. One to be used as a schoolroom and the other equipped for teaching simple manual training and domestic science," and with that direction in mind, Lucy reached out to the community. Mr. Woolley established the Malaga School Fund and the good people of Malden, Portland, and Boston began to contribute; some gave pennies and a few gave as much as twenty-five dollars.

Cora and Jonathan returned from their honeymoon and joined the fund-raising efforts. As spring approached, Mr. Woolley felt assured that a building could be constructed and informed Mr. Payson of their success. He responded by sending the current regulations for the management of schools in unorganized townships and assured them that a teacher would be found as soon as the construction was complete.

"But, that's unfair," Cora protested when she heard the news. "The children look forward to school each summer. Last October he agreed to place the Malaga school under the state's supervision. Why can't a teacher be provided while the school is under construction?"

"The regulations are quite clear. A teacher cannot be hired until there is an approved schoolhouse and residence," Jonathan said. "The fundraising is going very well. Perhaps construction can begin soon."

"The weather in Maine precludes breaking ground before late June or early July," Captain Lane explained. "The children can wait. Patience is a virtue that they best learn."

Cora fisted her hands in her lap and swallowed her angry retort. It did no good to argue with the Captain.

∽

Later, as she brushed her long hair and plaited it for the night, Cora mused over the plight of the Malaga School. Just this week, a wealthy woman in Boston had donated a dozen chairs and desks. It seemed impossible that the school could not reopen in June. Cora noticed Jonathan watching her in the mirror and smiled at him. He stepped closer, placed his hands on her shoulders, and kissed the top of her head. Cora tilted her face up and accepted his lips.

Jonathan whispered, "I know what you are thinking."

Cora laughed, "I doubt that."

"You want to teach one more summer."

Cora dropped her hairbrush and it clattered to the floor. "How do you know that?" She frowned at her husband. "Can you read my mind?"

Jonathan laughed. "Oh, my darling, there is no need to be a mind reader. You have made it known how much you enjoy teaching the children on Malaga. And, your face gave away your complete dismay when your father suggested there would be no school until after the schoolhouse is built."

"Would you mind terribly? I know it's wrong for a married woman to work, but… this is God's work."

"I am proud of the work you and your mother have done on Malaga. If you want to spend the summer months continuing your mission, I fear it would be wrong to stand in your way." Cora stood and faced him, watching his face carefully as he continued. "Jack and Elizabeth would enjoy a summer in the wilds of Maine. If you do not think it would be too much for your parents to have the three of you living with them, I see no reason why you shouldn't teach."

Cora wrapped her arms around her husband and hugged him close. She drew his face down and kissed his lips. "Thank you, Jonathan."

"I will miss you all terribly, but I will come up to the island as often as possible."

"Perhaps the children would like to attend classes on Malaga?" Cora chattered on, making

173

plans to tell her parents and to make the necessary arrangements. Jonathan kissed her again and drew her toward their bed.

※

The Malaga School Fund rose to 580 dollars and the Lanes returned to Horse Island. Cora traveled with her parents while Jonathan headed south with the children for a visit with their grandparents. Arriving in Maine on June 1, 1908, the Lanes found the Malagaites more destitute than ever. The clam-digging season had been shorter than usual and several new families had taken up residence. The new chairs and desks were welcomed and soon the school was open again, this time under the control of the state. Twelve students of varying ages filled the seats and waited eagerly to learn. Cora greeted the students she knew and introduced herself and her mother to the newcomers.

Eliza's familiar face was wreathed in smiles as she dropped a curtsy. "Morning, Ma'm. You be Missus something now, not Miss Lane."

"Yes, Eliza. I was married last November. I am Mrs. Smithson."

Eliza bobbed her head. "My granny say Marcus need to stay with me if I want to come to school. Be that right? I'll make him be good."

"Marcus is very young."

Tears welled in Eliza's eyes and she brushed them away with the back of her hand. "He almost two. I gotta take care of him. I make him be quiet, I swear."

"It will be fine, Eliza. I want you to come to school. Why don't you and Marcus take a desk by the door and you can slip out if you need to do so."

"Thank you, Ma'm." Eliza tugged Marcus toward the desk. "I been practicing all winter, Miss Cora; I can read real good."

"That is excellent, Eliza. Now take your seat," Lucy interrupted, speaking firmly. "And remember to say 'Mrs. Smithson.'"

"Yes, Ma'm." Eliza blushed and then grinned when she caught Cora's wink.

Mr. Woolley helped Lucy reach out to the people of Maine, inviting them to tour Malaga and to contribute. The Malaga School Fund continued to grow. A site was chosen on a rocky bluff at the easterly side of the island. The school would nestle among spruce and firs. Visitors flocked to the island. They came to see the classroom and then to enjoy a tour of the schoolhouse site. The students, understanding the importance of the fund-raising, greeted the gawkers politely, answered questions, read aloud, and did sums. Cora found the exhibition to be distasteful, and she complained to Jonathan about the need for the children to be viewed "like animals in a zoo."

"I know, love," Jonathan said, "but the children don't mind and it's all for a good cause. The sooner the school is built, the sooner you will be able to return to Boston."

Cora nodded. "I miss Jack and Elizabeth. It will be fun to introduce them to Eliza and Marcus. When will they return from Atlanta?"

"Their grandparents are enjoying having the children this summer. They have asked if Jack and Elizabeth can stay until school resumes. SaraBeth is teaching Elizabeth to knit and Jack is delighted with a litter of new pups." Cora frowned, and Jonathan hurried to complete his thought. "Without the children underfoot, you will have more time for fund-raising and teaching."

Cora turned away and nodded. "I'm sure your right, Jonathan." *He doesn't want them to attend my school,* she thought. *Not even for a few hours a week. Is he afraid that exposure to Eliza and Marcus will hurt them somehow?* She straightened her face and kept her eyes on the trees. "We are planning a flag-raising for the schoolhouse site on July sixth. Will you be able to stay for the event?"

Monday dawned bright and clear. The bay was calm as people began arriving. Soon seventy-five mainlanders crowded the schoolhouse clearing. They spread picnics on the grass and chatted among themselves about their contribution to the "self-improvement and moral reform" of the Malagaites. Cora smiled politely and bit her cheek to avoid pointing out that the children could overhear and understand every degrading remark.

The Reverend Mr. Wilkins rose to begin the ceremony. "Let us pray." The crowd quieted. "Dear Lord, we are gathered today in appreciation of the good people of Maine and Massachusetts. You have led them to open their hearts and pocketbooks in a kindly, helpful spirit and the children of this ignorant, backward island now have a chance to learn simple skills that will encourage them to walk upright in your grace. We ask your blessing on this schoolhouse and on the work that will proceed here. We thank your humble servant, Captain Lane, for without his ministry, this island would not have been brought to God. Amen."

The crowd echoed his amen, but Cora and most of the islanders remained silent. The schoolhouse was a good thing and a year-round teacher would be wonderful, but the Malagaites were no different than anyone else. They worked hard, against great odds. It was wrong to speak poorly of them. *Next week,* she thought, *I'll teach a lesson in humanity, believing in yourself and ignoring the naysayers.*

The children sang a hymn and Captain Lane gave a speech. "School Superintendent Mr. Payson Smith could not be with us today, but he has assured me that as soon as the building is complete and adequate lodging is arranged, he will provide a teacher. In this clearing we will build a shingled, hip-roof, frame building twenty-two by twenty-six feet. The school will consist of three rooms: the schoolroom, a reception or social room, and a kitchen. It is hoped that by providing such a modern building, a little of what is termed domestic science can be taught to the mothers, and that the opportunities for a gathering place will be appreciated.

"Your generosity has brought us here today to begin this project. The funds contributed have reached six hundred dollars." Whistles and clapping interrupted and he raised his hand to quiet the crowd. "However, owing to the difficulties that have been encountered by the situation making transportation of material expensive, and on account of the high cost of labor and material, we will need to continue our efforts. It is hoped that the amount raised may speedily reach the eight-hundred-dollar mark. I have asked two children to pass through this charitable and benevolent crowd with baskets. Reach deep into your hearts and pockets today and the Lord will bless you. As the flag is raised for the first time in the Malaga School yard, Mrs. Lane will lead the children in a rendition of 'America.' Please rise."

The week after the flag-raising, supplies and workmen arrived. Jim McKenny and the other men and boys worked with the building crew, and by August first the lot had been cleared and the frame laid. As August drew to a close, Cora again said good-bye to her students. She assured them that as soon as the work was finished, a "real" school would open.

Back in Boston, Cora resumed her duties as a wife and mother. Jack and Elizabeth were lovely children, but they were in school all day and she found herself with time on her hands. She avidly read the news of the suffrage movement and, without asking Jonathan's approval, joined the newly formed Equality League of Self-Supporting Women. She might not be self-supporting, but she reasoned that she could be.

Lucy was furious. "What is wrong with you?" she demanded.

"Mama, I think that women are at least as capable as men and I want my daughters to enjoy the same opportunities as my sons."

"Women will never be the equal of men, Cora. As long as we are mothers and caregivers, we will need to rely on men for support and guidance."

Jonathan laughed and squeezed Cora's hand. "Lucy, I'm afraid you've raised a modern woman. I'm in agreement with Cora that women should be allowed to vote. After all, they are the gentler sex. Perhaps they can have a civilizing effect on mankind."

"'Allowed' is not the issue. We are equal—just as intelligent, just as strong, and it is our right to vote."

Captain Lane growled, "Women are too emotional to vote. Play your little game, Cora. Soon you will have children of your own and you'll see that it is best to leave things as they are. Now, enough of this silliness. Jonathan, do you care for a smoke?" He pushed back his chair and Jonathan followed him from the room.

Despite Cora's desire to break the habit, Sunday, October 6, 1909, found Cora and her new family dining with her parents. It was expected, and Jonathan insisted that it would do no harm. "After all," he maintained, "your father is getting older, and your mother is always happy to see you and the children." Cora reluctantly agreed.

179

"A teacher has been hired," Captain Lane said, unfolding his napkin and reaching for the roast. "I believe the family should be represented at the opening of the school; therefore I will travel to Phippsburg and stay at the home of Reverend Wilkins. No one else need make the journey." Cora started to speak. Jonathan laid his hand on hers and shook his head slightly. The Captain continued, "I am aware of your desire to see the school, Cora, but you would be a disruption. The children need to get to know, and learn to respect, their new teacher."

"A good point, Captain," Lucy said, spooning additional gravy over her husband's meat. "What do you know about the teacher?"

"When will the school open?" Cora spoke at the same time.

"One at a time." Captain Lane cut a large piece of his meat and chewed slowly.

Cora tapped her foot under the table and bit her lip.

"The teacher will arrive on October twenty-third to begin classes. The following Sunday there will be a special service in the reception room. I have, of course, been invited to speak and I will do so."

Cora drank from her goblet to avoid interrupting. She knew from experience that her father could not be hurried.

"The required forty-cents-per-inhabitant assessment has been collected and sent to the state treasurer. I am afraid that some required assistance and it was extended to them through the Malaga Island Settlement Association, who as you all know is handling the building funds and will act as the state's agent. This cannot be allowed in following years, and everyone has been informed that they must be prepared to pay next year's school assessment in April. I sincerely hope that they will comply, but a mixed-race individual has an inferior brain and…" He glanced at the children and choose not to continue.

"As for the teacher, Payson has found a fine young woman of strong Christian ideals. Her name is Evelyn Woodman. She will teach reading, arithmetic, Bible subjects, and social graces. Without a doubt she will set an example for the women and children to follow."

"Where will she live, Captain? Will she need to row across from Phippsburg each morning?" Lucy asked.

"She has been hired to teach year-round. Rowing across the bay would be arduous. However, since she cannot live in a home where the races are impure, we have added a small room to the side of the schoolhouse that will serve her well. The residents will provide her with food, although she has been informed that she may want to insist that the food be brought to her, rather than that she eat with them."

"Seloma McKenny's house is as clean as mine, Papa. And, I'm sure she's a better cook." Cora almost choked on her indignation. "The Malagaites will give Miss Woodman nothing but their best."

"Perhaps, but their best is not up to scratch."

"Cora," Jonathan said calmly, "you and your mother have provided a wonderful beginning. You should be very proud of your efforts. Now it is time for the state to take up the challenge and, if possible, raise the standards of respectability for the people of Malaga."

∽

Cora, who had always loved learning, became more and more interested in not only suffrage, but in the field of eugenics. She attended as many meetings and rallies as she could fit in the social schedule she was expected to keep as Jonathan's wife. She learned the names of the women who were leaders in both movements: Victoria Woodhull, Elizabeth Cady Stanton, Susan B. Anthony, and others. She read everything she could find on their lives and ideas. It seemed true that, as Margaret Sanger espoused, it should be the choice of the individual woman whether or not to have children, and it also made sense that it would be best if all children could be born to physically fit, moral, well-situated parents. The arguments confused her. Surely, not all children could be classed so easily. Her students had been a fine example; others had said they could not learn, yet the children had proved them wrong.

Jonathan was always willing to discuss her ideas and they often talked late into the night. Jonathan spoke of how eugenics had deep roots in the world's history. "Even Plato," he reminded Cora, "specifically endorsed murdering 'weak' children in favor of the 'strong' and the belief that only men and women with superior characteristics be allowed to bear children."

Neither felt that it was right to deny rights to anyone on moral grounds, but Cora admitted, "All of the best minds seem to disagree with us."

"True, we may be in the minority, but not all of the best minds disagree, just the most vocal."

"I fear for the island people of Maine. The newspapers continue to cast them in a poor light."

# CHAPTER TWENTY-FIVE

## MALAGA
## 1909–1911

Life in Boston kept Cora from visiting Maine the summers of 1909 and 1910. She worried about the children, particularly Eliza, and asked her father for updates on the islanders.

The Captain was willing to talk of his ministry, but he had no news of the individual children. He fretted that the islanders did not seem to realize the importance of work. "I have spent these past years counseling the Malagaites on the value of economy and thrift, and yet I fear it is impossible to change the base nature of these beasts. Just last summer I encouraged one family, who was especially impoverished, to fish, dig clams, and to sell bait to the trawlers. They seemed to understand. By the end of August, they had saved about seventy-five dollars among them. The family could have reached 'March Hill' in comfort. But, no, they used the shingles we provided to repair their miserable hut as kindling. And with the cash they bought six dogs in order that each member of the family could have its own pet, and spent the rest of the money for sweets, pickles, jellies, and fancy groceries. The Malagaites are as inattentive as little children. I fear there is no hope for the mixed race; they are simply inferior and will always be so."

"Surely, you can not mean that," Cora reproached her father. "Miss Woodman is teaching moral responsibility."

"You can't teach what cannot be learned, Cora. Mr. Darwin's theories are correct."

"But, Captain," Lucy, too, was distressed by his words, "surely the fact that the islanders are able to read and write disputes that."

"No, my dear. I fear you ladies are much too kindhearted to understand that they are trainable, as any animal is, but they are not the equal of white men."

"Father can't be right, Jonathan," Cora complained after they left. "I see no difference between you and I and the majority of the Malagaites. Certainly the islanders suffer from a lack of worldly goods, which we do not. However, that should not be the deciding factor of a person's value."

"I'm afraid that is exactly the argument the scientists use to prove their hypothesis. Just last week I read an article that quoted Mr. Darwin as having stated in his book, *The Descent of Man,* that white, upper-class Northern European persons should be giving birth in greater numbers than the impoverished persons. His studies have provided ample proof that there is a direct correlation between wealth and intelligence."

"Certainly, even Mr. Darwin doesn't believe that wealth is all that is necessary for intelligence."

"Not the only indicator. But an important one. I believe he presents a very strong case that race is even more important. And that the undiluted white race is the most evolved."

"Jonathan, I have read Mr. Darwin's book. He is without a doubt a brilliant man, but I fear he is wrong in this regard. I will not change my opinion on this, but I do not care to argue with you."

"Nor I with you, my dear."

"I should like to read the opinions of other scientists. I believe in making up my own mind and I have, as you may recall, seen firsthand the ability of the poor to learn."

"I'm not unhappy," Cora tried to explain to her friend Olivia. "I just want to make a difference."

"Most would say that you *have* made a difference. You taught those children to read and you raised the money to build that school. When you have a child of your own, you'll be too busy to brood."

Cora blushed. "That's exactly what Mother says." She sighed. "I'm not sure I want to have a baby."

"Of course you do. You and Jonathan are exactly the type of people who should have many children."

"Why do you say that?"

"It's obvious. You are smart and pretty. He is tall and rich. Your babies will be smart, good-looking, and rich. The perfect combination."

"My baby will be no different than any other baby." Cora could feel her anger growing and changed the subject. "I have joined the Woman Suffrage Party."

"What does your husband think of that?"

"He approves, of course. Jonathan agrees with me that women should be able to vote."

"I can't imagine why you would care about such a thing. It really doesn't matter." Olivia finished her tea and rose to leave. "If women should be expected to vote, I, like most gentlewomen, will ask my husband for whom to vote. I don't see that it will make any difference at all."

Olivia kissed Cora's cheek at the door. "I must get home to my babies. Stop thinking so much, Cora. It isn't good for your complexion."

Lucy understood Cora's frustration. She, too, had seen the children of Malaga brighten and become excited at learning. Lucy took it upon herself to discover what was happening on the island. She was able to report to Cora that the school seemed to be doing well. Miss Woodman attended the Phippsburg Church and the congregation thought highly of her demeanor. "She is a godly young woman," Lucy assured Cora. "I have visited the school this summer and there are about fifteen students most days. I believe Eliza and Marcus are among those who regularly attend."

While this was reassuring to Cora, the newspaper articles about Malaga Island and its residents continued to speak of them as an embarrassing eyesore to both local and year-round residents. Jonathan explained, "The coast of Maine is becoming a resort area, and the citizens of Phippsburg and the surrounding area wish to take advantage of this modern trend. Your father told me that there has been talk of building a fine hotel on Malaga Island."

"But the island is owned by the people who live there, isn't it?" Cora protested.

"I believe there is some question about the title. As I recall, a few years ago, perhaps in 1904, the state of Maine ruled that the Perry family are the legal owners of the island. I believe that no Malagaite pays rent or taxes and, therefore, legally they are squatters, with no rights."

"That can't be true. The Darling family settled that island a long time ago and the McKenny family has been there almost as long."

Jonathan shook his head. "There is more that you should know, Cora. There has been some talk of using the new Binet intelligence test to determine if the children are feeble-minded."

"And, why would they need to do that? Those children are as bright as any other." Cora rose and began to pace the floor.

"The Maine School for the Feeble-Minded, in Pownal, may be a better place for the children to live."

"Jonathan!" Cora's voice rose. "How can you say such a thing? The children are happy where they are, surrounded by their families and friends."

"They are. But they know nothing else. At the Maine School they would live on a farm and learn skills that would be of value to the community when they were released as adults."

"The Malagaites are not defective or deficient. They are as normal as you and I."

"Perhaps, Cora, but others believe differently."

"This must stop, Jonathan. It is almost the end of 1910; men must learn to respect one another. I shall go to Malaga in June and see for myself."

⌒♋⌒

Miss Woodman was a fine teacher, perhaps not as pretty or nice as Miss Lane, but still, school was the best part of Eliza's life. Each school day she rose with a song in her heart, hurried through her chores, and made sure Marcus ate something for breakfast. She was glad her grandparents were too busy with everyday life to pay much attention to what she and Marcus did all day.

She glanced quickly around the cabin, making sure that everything was tidy. Grandma Seloma demanded a clean house. She brushed a few crumbs from the table and hurried Marcus out the door. They scurried past the graveyard. Eliza allowed herself a glance at the headstones marking the graves of her mama, papa, and sister, Sarah. She didn't pause. Miss Woodman didn't cotton to late-comers. Marcus stumbled. She caught him up onto her hip. At almost five, he thought he was too old to be carried. She hushed him and made it to the school just as Miss Woodman began to ring the bell. Eliza straightened Marcus's clothes and ran a hand over her hair. She hadn't had time to re-braid her hair. Miss Woodman would notice.

Eliza was the best reader in the school. Most days Miss Woodman asked her to read the daily devotional from the special book she kept on her desk. Eliza slid into her desk seat and folded her hands, the way she'd been taught. Today, however, Miss Woodman didn't pick up the blue book. Instead she said, "Children, we have a new student with us today." Eliza looked around. She knew everyone on Malaga and there weren't any new families. Her eyes widened. A white girl was sitting behind her. Eliza looked back at Miss Woodman. "Mary Elizabeth Cranston of Phippsburg will be attending our school."

One of Marks boys demanded, "What she doing here?"

"Mary is here to learn. The same as everyone else. Her parents have chosen Malaga School. Eliza," she turned to look directly at Eliza, "please help Mary learn our ways."

Eliza nodded, too stunned to speak. She glanced over her shoulder and smiled at the new girl. Mary stared back. Eliza wondered what Grandpa Jim would say.

∽

"Yup," Grandpa agreed over supper. "She's from Phippsburg alright. Her father paid her school tax to that superintendent, so I reckon she's allowed. I 'spect she's too smart for them young'uns over in Phippsburg."

Eliza nodded.

Marcus said, "Nobody reads good as Eliza. Bet she's smarter din that white girl."

"You be nice to her, hear?" Grandma Seloma frowned at the children. "Ain't her fault she comin' here to learn."

"Miss Woodman told Eliza to take care of her," Marcus piped up.

Seloma turned to Eliza; concern showed on her face. "Somethin' wrong with that girl?"

"No, Grandma. Miss Woodman just wants me to show her how we do things. She hardly talked at all, but I think she's just scared."

"Right then, like I said, you be nice. She white and we don't need no trouble. Maybe they think our school is good enough for their young'uns, they stop writin' 'bout us so much," Seloma said.

"Who writes 'bout us?" Marcus demanded.

"Ain't none of your business," Grandpa said. "Jus' you pay attention to your chores and your schoolin'."

Eliza tapped Marcus on his leg, her code to him to leave well enough alone. Marcus dropped his eyes to his plate and stopped talking. He'd never known any mother but Eliza and he trusted her. Eliza vowed to ask Miss Woodman what people were writing about Malaga and where they were writing it. She'd never read anything about it in her schoolbooks.

The next morning when Eliza asked her, Miss Woodman blushed slightly and brushed the questions aside. "I believe your grandfather was referring to some newspaper reports that the island is not well maintained." Eliza frowned. "Nothing for you to worry about." She began to ring the bell, summoning the children into the classroom. "Hurry now, Eliza. I have some exciting news to share today."

The fifteen students rose for the prayer and the hymn and then settled into their desks with the usual clatter. Miss Woodson called them to attention with a rap on her desk. "I have important

191

news." She waited as the final rustle settled. "Governor Plaisted is planning a visit to our school in just under two weeks."

"Who dat?" Marcus asked. The others snickered. They weren't sure either, but he sounded important.

"Who is that?" Miss Woodson corrected, but she didn't wait for Marcus to repeat his question. "Governor Plaisted is the most important man in the state of Maine. It is a great honor that he has chosen to visit your homes and our school. It is important that you make a good impression. We will prepare a special program of singing and recitations, and we must do it quickly."

Mary Cranston raised her hand. "I know several long poems, Miss Woodson. I recite Lord Tennyson's 'Crossing the Bar' very nicely. It brings my father to tears each time."

"Thank you, my dear. I think it would be quite nice if our new student would lead our presentation."

*New, heck,* Eliza thought, *Miss Woodson just wants to show off the white girl.* She turned her head and smiled at Mary, remembering her grandmother's admonition.

The island buzzed with preparations for the governor's visit. The schoolhouse windows were washed. All the desks were scrubbed, and loose papers and books disappeared. The children were reminded to wear their best clothing and to scrub behind their ears.

At home Eliza overheard Grandpa Jim telling Jerry Murphy, and the other men, that the real reason "that damn politician is comin' here is 'cause they want all us undesirables to disappear."

"I ain't leaving this island, Jim. I built that house with my own hands. They ain't got no right to take our land."

"They have any right they claim to have. We ain't going to have anything to say in the matter. The school look good, but they ain't goin' to care about that. They jus' want the governor to side with the ones that want us gone."

Eliza kept her eyes on the bread she was kneading. Grandpa Jim didn't like eavesdroppers. She wanted to know more, but the men moved outside and she didn't dare follow. She glanced around the house. It was all she had ever known. Grandma kept everything clean as possible. They had real glass in all the windows. *I wonder who they are that want us gone?* she thought. She covered the bread to let it rise and went outside to be sure Marcus was doing his chores.

On June 11, 1911, Governor Frederick Plaisted, and his entourage of politicians and reporters and clergymen, arrived on Malaga. He stepped ashore, smiling broadly at the Malagaites who had gathered to meet him. The children, scrubbed to within an inch of their lives, and checked that morning by Miss Woodson, sang a welcoming hymn. Jerry Murphy led the group on a tour of the island. They inspected the homes and asked how many persons, of what ages, were housed in each. The reporters scribbled frantically, making notes of each comment from the governor, and of everything they saw.

The school was saved for last. The visitors seemed surprised to find everything in order. The governor listened to the performance that they had prepared. He announced, "I am pleasantly surprised to find that our little school is so well thought of that a white family would send their child here to be educated."

Eliza's temper rose. She felt Mary Cranston preening beside her, and bit her cheek to keep from making a sound.

Governor Plaisted continued his speech. "Superintendent Payson has done these poor, ignorant people a mighty service by providing this building and a fine teacher." He beamed at Miss Woodson. "It is not an easy task for a young woman to leave her family and come to reside in hardship, among such as these."

*What hardship?* Eliza thought. *She has her own room and outhouse.* The governor's next words drew her attention back to his speech. "The conditions on this island are deplorable. The best plan would be to burn down the shacks with all their filth. Certainly, the conditions are not creditable to our state, and we ought not to have such things near our front door. I do not think that a like condition can be found in Maine, although there are some pretty bad localities elsewhere. But, the people cannot be forced to leave their poor homes."

That night Grandpa Jim seemed to be in a better mood. "Seloma," he said, "perhaps livelihood and home are safe after all."

194

Seloma shook her head. "Those rich white folks still don't like us. If they be wantin' this island, they'll find a way."

❦

Cora read the report of the governor's visit in *The Brunswick Record*. "Did you read this, Jonathan?" she asked.

"I did. I think you can rest easy this summer. The governor has stated that islanders will not be forced off the land."

"Mama says Miss Woodson is engaged to marry and a new teacher has been found. Perhaps I will not go to Maine this summer."

Jonathan smiled. "I would be relieved. I did not want to dissuade you, but in your condition, travel is not advised."

Cora patted her still flat stomach and resumed her needlework. *I'm sure everything will be fine,* she thought.

# CHAPTER TWENTY-SIX

## SEATTLE

Discharged from the hospital and back in her own home, Susan was content. The family worried that her strength didn't seem to be returning, but her spirits were high. When Gabriel napped, Susan napped. When Gabriel ate, she ate. When Gabriel was awake, she stayed near him, talking to him, singing softly and playing games. Lola watched, taking care to lift Gabe off and onto Susan's lap, making sure that he did not exhaust his grandmother.

One afternoon, Gabe fell asleep in Susan's arms. Lola moved to lift his solid little body. "You know I'm not getting better, don't you, Lola?" Susan said sadly, reluctant to give up the child.

"I do," Lola admitted. She placed her hand on Susan's shoulder. "But I will keep your secret until you want to tell your family."

"Thank you." Susan kissed Gabe's forehead. "I'm so glad you brought Gabe to meet me." Lola nodded. "You'd better take him now—my arms are very weak."

Lola scooped up her son. "We'll stay, Susan. We will not leave you alone. I'll just put Gabe down and be right back."

Susan carefully stretched, and shook out her fingers. *I don't want to die,* she thought.

Lola returned and gently helped her stand and move to the sofa for a nap. As Lola pulled the cover over her, she caught her hand. "I'm not ready to die," she said.

"Then you won't, not yet. Get some sleep. Gabe will be up in an hour."

Susan dreamed of a meadow. She flew above the grass, the breeze blowing her hair. She gazed down and saw Henry. He sat alone and she knew he was crying. Then Jeff and Georgia appeared. They hurried to their father, lifted him to his feet, and surrounded him with love. Suddenly Gabe was there, laughing and pulling at his grandfather's hand. Susan awoke. Her face was wet with tears. She turned her head and saw Lola sitting in the big wing chair watching her.

Lola smiled. "You were dreaming."

"I was," Susan said.

"Do you want to talk about your dream?"

"I don't think so. It was very sad, but happy, too. I think it meant that when I die Henry will be okay, that life will go on."

"Mostly, a good dream then," Lola said.

"I have something to tell you all," Susan said. "I love all of you, so very much. Henry," she smiled across the room at her husband, "you are a wonderful husband. I'm so glad I married you, even though my mother told me not to."

"What? Why not?" Henry straightened in his chair and set his after-dinner coffee down with a thump. "I thought your mother liked me."

Everyone laughed.

"She liked you, she just wasn't sure you were the right choice for me. She never explained why and I was too much in love to ask. By the time the children were born, she seemed to think you were perfect." She patted the sofa on either side of her frail body. "Georgia and Jeff, come sit by me." They did, and

Susan reached out to hold hands with them. "You two are the best children a mother could hope for. I've loved every minute of time that I've spent with you." Georgia started to talk, but Susan squeezed her hand and continued. "It doesn't look like I'm going to beat this cancer."

A stunned silence filled the room for a long second and then everyone, except Lola, began to protest in earnest. "I don't believe that." Henry's statement rang out above the others.

"Henry," Susan spoke softly, "please believe. I'll need your help." Henry moved to the sofa and knelt on the floor in front of his wife. He wrapped his family in his arms as they cried together.

It was as if acknowledging the severity of her illness allowed Susan to let go. While the rest of the family moved through the next days in stunned silence, she brightened. On a sunny afternoon, Susan called Georgia to her side. "Honey," she said, "you are here all the time. When was the last time you spoke to Linda? Or went out on a date with that nice Mitch?"

"Mom," Georgia choked back the tears that seemed to be close to the surface at all times, "I just want to spend my time with you."

"It isn't healthy, Georgie. I want you to have a full life, now and forever."

"But, Mama, my life will never be full with you gone."

"It will, if you allow it. I want you to call Linda right now and make a plan to see her tonight." Georgia shook her head. "Yes, take out your phone and call right now. I promise I won't die tonight." Georgia's eyes overflowed, but she pulled her phone out of her pocket. "And, don't spend all night feeling sorry about this." She waved her hand up and down, indicating her body. "You two have Linda's wedding to plan and I intend to be there."

Georgia hugged her mom and did as she was told.

Ken opened the door and swept her into a big hug. "I'm sorry about your mom."

"I know." Georgia took in his bare feet, the computer desk in the corner covered with books and papers and a huge monitor, and grinned. "Are you guys living together?"

"We are." Linda hurried in from the kitchen and hugged her tight. "And, as you can see, he's a big slob. His stuff is every-where. Let me grab you some wine and we can talk."

Georgia curled into her favorite chair and said, "Tell me everything. When did all this happen?"

"Just ten days ago."

"Why didn't I know about it? I see you at work almost every day."

"I wasn't keeping it a secret. I just didn't want to tell you when Mark would overhear. Haven't you noticed he's always watching you?"

"I have. He told me that if I needed additional time off, he could arrange it, but that I should understand that taking time off might affect my standing at the college."

"What a jerk!" Ken exploded. "That guy is an idiot. He asked me yesterday if English was my second language. I said, 'Dude, I was born here.' It didn't even faze him."

Linda cringed. "Let's not talk about all that stuff tonight." She took a big drink of her wine. "Let's talk about our wedding plans."

"Good idea," Georgia said. "My mother is expecting a full report. Better yet, you should stop by and tell her yourself."

"Is she up for visitors?"

"First, she considers you one of the family, and second, she actually seems better, more relaxed. They've stopped all treat-ment." For a long minute the room was completely silent. "It's what she wants," Georgia whispered. She shook herself. "So, wedding plans. Tell me everything."

⁓

The next day when Mitch called, Georgia accepted his invitation to dinner. "I'll meet you there, at seven thirty. I just want to stop by and see my mom first."

Susan expressed her happiness that Georgia had a date. Jeff teased her in a brotherly manner, and for a moment everything felt normal.

⁓

She greeted Mitch with a quick kiss and a brief hug. The conversation flowed quickly from Susan's health to Ken and Linda's wedding plans. "Have Ken's parents decided to accept Linda?" Mitch asked.

"Accept? That seems like a strong word."

"Well, last time I talked to Ken, they were refusing to attend the wedding."

"When was that?"

"I don't know exactly, a few days ago."

Georgia's head was spinning. Linda had seemed fine last night. *Maybe,* she thought, *Ken hasn't told her.* "What is Ken going to do?" she asked.

"He wants his parents' approval, but he says it doesn't matter. He'll marry the woman he loves, no matter what."

"How sad. The wedding is only weeks away. Why would they refuse to attend? Linda practically grew up in their home."

"Like my parents, they think they know what is best for their son. They love Linda, but they want a Japanese mother for their grandchildren."

"That seems so messed up. How can it matter so much?"

Mitch looked thoughtful. "It wasn't that long ago that you were struggling with your feelings over the discovery of your own ancestral background."

"But they love each other."

"A good marriage is based on much more than love. Couples with similar backgrounds have a greater chance of success."

"My parents have a great marriage despite their racial backgrounds," she protested.

"True, but when they married, they believed their backgrounds were very similar."

Georgia couldn't argue with that; it was true. She remembered how quiet her father had been when Susan had showed them the pictures. She wondered how he really felt. Did he love his wife and children less?

"How about you? If you fall in love with someone your parents don't approve of, will you marry her?"

Mitch took a moment and then sighed. "Probably not. I really like you, Georgia, but to be honest, they would never accept someone with mixed blood. My family is important to me. I don't think I could ever choose to cut myself off from them."

"Good thing we aren't in love then," Georgia managed to say as her mind reeled from his words.

♏

Georgia raised her hand to tap on Linda's office door just as the door swung open. She jumped back. "Hey, I was just coming to talk to you."

Linda grinned and stepped back. "Come on in."

"I have something I need to tell you," Georgia started.

"Me first. Ken and I are going to get married at city hall next Thursday."

"Huh, what about the wedding plans?"

"His parents are refusing to attend, so we don't need them. We just want you and Mitch, and a few other friends, to be there. Will your parents come?"

"Wow!" Georgia hugged Linda. "Are you okay with this? I thought you wanted a big wedding."

"I'm delighted. I want a big party. Not a big wedding. We'll still have that, and if his parents don't come, who cares. We love each other and we are going to make beautiful babies."

"Not right away, I hope."

"Well, no, but soon. I want to have a family like yours."

"Mixed race?" Georgia laughed

"Yep. Look how good you and Jeff turned out."

Georgia kept her thoughts to herself. *I wonder if it would be easier if I'd always known, or would it be harder? It's all so confusing.*

"So, girl, what did you have to tell me?"

"Nothing important." She hugged Linda again. "I'm so happy for you. Tell me all the details and I'll be there."

∽

Susan leaned back against the pillows piled high on her bed. "Linda was a beautiful bride. She and Ken looked so happy."

Georgia agreed. It had been a nice ceremony, followed by a lovely brunch. Now Susan looked very tired. Georgia pulled the covers up and tucked them around her mother's shoulders. "Sleep a bit."

Susan pulled her hand out from the blanket and caught Georgia's hand. "I want you to find happiness, darling. Mitch isn't the one for you, but someone special is out there. I will miss seeing you marry and meeting your children. But, I'll know."

Georgia bent and kissed her mother's cheek. She didn't argue; it was obvious her mother's health was failing. "I love you, Mama. I promise to fall in love and marry a wonderful man, and I will name my daughter after you."

Susan smiled and closed her eyes.

# CHAPTER TWENTY-SEVEN

## MALAGA
## 1911-1912

Captain Lane and Lucy spent the summer of 1911 on Horse Island. Cora's pregnancy was much on Lucy's mind. She was looking forward to meeting her grandchild in December. Lucy did not discuss such womanly matters with the Captain, but the women of the Phippsburg Church rejoiced with her. The new teacher was installed on Malaga, but Lucy did not visit the island. The Captain brought back news, and that was enough.

Early in July the state of Maine, again, ruled that Malaga Island was owned by the heirs of Eli Perry. The city of Phippsburg buzzed with the news. It was common knowledge that the Perry family was determined to build a resort on Malaga, and the city looked forward to the surge in revenue that tourists would bring.

The Perry family filed papers to have the islanders evicted. On August 7, Attorney General Pattangall served the forty families living on the island with orders to vacate their homes and the island by June 1, 1912. When Captain Lane told

Lucy the news, she responded by saying, "It is best that we don't mention this action to Cora. It would trouble her mind, and I'm certain nothing will come of it."

"Perhaps you are right. However, the Governor's Council will meet soon and will undoubtedly discuss the continuing drain on the state budget that is Malaga Island. I fear the school is not making a difference in their shiftless attitudes."

∽

Jim McKenny was aging and the press, taking notice of that fact, were now calling Jerry Murphy the King of Malaga. "I'm tired," Jim admitted to Seloma. "Let someone else talk to them damn reporters and govemint men."

The adults on Malaga met together in the community room of the school. Tempers ran hot. Rants and threats against the Perry family were made. "If we are forced to leave our homes, where will you go?" the Malagaites asked one another.

"It will not come to that," Jerry Murphy declared. "This is the United States of America. They cannot take our land."

Jim McKenny wasn't so sure. "We have no clear title to our land. The courts have given it to those damn Perrys. We may need to make a plan to leave."

Much shouting ensued as consternation broke out. Eliza could hear the loud voices from her perch on the front porch. Grandpa Jim had told her to stay away from the meeting and when she'd ask why, Grandma had warned her to 'mind her own business.' "I'm almost thirteen," she muttered, scraping her bare toes through the dirt. *Something is going on and I think it's bad,* she thought. She decided to pay closer attention to the adults.

That weekend, the oldest McKenny son, Jim Jr., returned to the island with the news that the Governor's Council had met and the published minutes stated that the government was paying too much to aid the poor in towns that were, in their words, "a blot upon the state." Three towns were specifically mentioned, including Malaga. They had determined that they would not abide continuing a "drain on the treasury" that was encouraging the paupers to attract "around them a thriftless, lazy gang, to help them in consuming supplies furnished by the commonwealth."

"It says here," Jim read aloud to the gathered Malagaites, "that it was decided that 'the good of the State and the cause of humanity demands that the Malaga colony be broken up and the people segregated.'" Jim shook his head. "This ain't good, is it?" He picked up the dispatch and continued reading. They recommend that 'to rid the Island of its population, and to prevent further squatting, the State should hold title to the property.'"

"Sounds like some politician hopin' to get rich made a crooked deal, don't it? I bet them Perrys had a plan all along to sell this island to the state," Jerry Murphy said.

∽

"This is the last Sunday we will be in Maine, Lucy. Perhaps you would like to join me for the preaching on Malaga. Cora will question you and it would be good to have firsthand knowledge," Captain Lane declared.

Lucy agreed, and on Sunday she went along to Malaga. The new teacher greeted her warmly and showed her the students' most recent work. "The children are, for the most part, cheerful and willing, if a bit lazy. I fear most can never achieve a standard of education that will prepare them for real work."

"It appears that some have quite nice handwriting," Lucy commented.

"They are like little animals, learning little tricks and stories, but not really comprehending. They are no different from the parents, who have little understanding that when the state tells them to evacuate the island, they must do so."

"Surely, the parents are making plans. I found them to be quite pleasant when my daughter and I taught here."

"Pleasant, surely, but the state has requested that the Malagaites be tested using the new Binet intelligence test. I doubt that anyone can pass, with perhaps the exception of one girl, Eliza McKenny. But her level of intelligence may be due to the fact that she is more white than most."

"Her older sister, Sarah, was quite bright, also, and she, too, was very light-skinned."

"I know nothing of her. They are an aberration, no doubt."

"She died young, from measles I believe. It is time for services. Shall we?" Lucy led the way into the community room. She sat through the preaching, paying no attention to her husband's words. Silently she fumed that these children were deemed unteachable simply because of their skin color.

∽

As their boat cut through the water, Lucy asked the Captain, "What do you know of this intelligence test?"

"I believe that it was developed in France and is a very scientific method of distinguishing between mentally retarded children and those children who are of normal intelligence, but are lazy. Children are asked a variety of questions, using a variety of formats. Scoring is very precise, and the results are considered very accurate. Why do you ask?"

"I was told today that the state intends to test the children of Malaga. Why would they do this?"

"The state is now responsible for the island, and it is a costly responsibility. The testing will be used to determine if the islanders are capable of supporting themselves. It may well be that the children are best served by being removed from their current circumstance."

"Surely, the families will move together."

"They are not welcome on the mainland."

∽

The Malagaites were unsure where to turn. A few families talked of leaving but weren't sure where to go, or how they would survive. The intelligence testing commenced, using a test based on knowing information that the Malagaites had never been exposed to: they were asked to explain how a light bulb works, to identify a picture of a phonograph, etc. Despite their best efforts, the intelligence of each person tested was found lacking.

Their skulls were measured and the bumps on their heads analyzed to determine their mental abilities. Soon a doctor was called upon to sign commitment papers for those unable to pass these tests.

On December 12, 1911, three men came to the Marks family home: a doctor, a sheriff, and a judge. They held court in the tiny home and declared the entire family, seven persons between the ages of two and fifty-six years, unfit for society.

Immediately upon judgment, the family was removed and taken by boat to Bath, by train to Portland, and by stagecoach to The Maine State School for the Feeble-Minded in Pownal.

Jim McKenny raged against the state. He kept his children and grandchildren close at hand and refused to allow the doctors to test them. A few families moved away during the fall of 1911, settling in the fishing villages of Sabasco and Harpswell, but the residents were not happy with the new settlers and complained to the legislature that allowing the Malagaites to settle on the mainland was "much like spreading smallpox throughout the state."

As the bitter winter dragged on, the Malagaites, once again, turned to the state for additional resources. The remaining forty residents began to make plans for a move they did not want to make.

❧

Without saying good-bye, a few more families left the island. The government men sometimes came and took away a child, sending them off to the school in Pownal. Eliza kept her head down and listened to every conversation she could. The adults were worried. She was sure of it, but when she asked, she was told to hush and given extra chores to do. She quit asking, but she didn't stop watching.

As soon as the ice was out of the bay, the men went fishing every day. They kept only a small amount of the catch and sold the rest. Grandpa Jim gave the money he earned to Seloma and she hid it in a lard can under a floorboard. Eliza saw her do it and knew something was happening. Usually a good catch meant a good dinner, but now it seemed that they were only concerned with saving cash. She screwed up her courage and asked, "Grandma, what are you going to buy with all that money?"

"It ain't much, girl. Only a few dollars, and don't you tell anybody 'bout it. We gonna buy a new start."

"What's that?"

"Ain't none of your business. You git now and do your chores."

Slowly the days grew warmer. Then one day in June, the teacher up and left. "How come we ain't havin' school no more?" Marcus whined.

"I thought you didn't like reading and writing," Eliza teased.

"I likes it better than chores."

Eliza laughed at her little brother. He was five now and almost too heavy for her to lift. But she grabbed his arms and swung him around and around until the both grew too dizzy to stand. They lay together on the ground, arms spread wide, waiting for the sky to stop spinning.

"I love you, Eliza." Marcus patted her arm. "You ain't never gonna leave me, right?"

"I love you more." Eliza turned to her side so she could tickle him. "Everybody has to leave sometime, Marcus. But I'll always love you and watch over you, even if I have to go far away."

"If you marry some boy, I'm gonna live with you."

Eliza laughed. "I'm not in any hurry to get married, Marcus. I want to be a teacher."

"Like Miss Woodson?" Marcus wrinkled his nose.

"No. Like Miss Cora. I want to like the children I teach. Come on," she pulled him to his feet, "let's see if those mean old chickens laid any eggs today."

The Tripp family moved onto their scow and left the island. Marcus thought it would be fun to live on a boat, but Eliza didn't think it would be warm. She liked having a house with a fire. Marcus had often played with the Tripp boys and he missed them.

Grandma Seloma kept both Eliza and Marcus busy. They helped her pack up the few family belongings into feed sacks. Eliza was instructed to keep her clothes and her few books separate. One afternoon, Seloma handed her a silver-backed hairbrush. "I want you to have this, Eliza. Put it with your things. It was my mother's, all I have left of her. You're a good girl. It'll help you remember."

"It's beautiful, Grandma." Seloma hugged her, something that almost never happened. Eliza hugged back. For a moment she thought Grandma was going to cry.

"Go along now. You get to bed. It's going to be a long night and you'll need your rest."

Eliza started to ask why the night would be long, but Grandma looked so sad that she simply lay down next to Marcus and watched the flames until her eyes grew heavy and she fell asleep.

Moments later, Grandpa Jim was shaking her shoulder. "Wake up, girl. I need you to take Marcus to the boat. Wrap him up warm and come back right fast to help us carry."

"What's happening?"

"We leaving, girl. No eviction man goin' tell me where I gotta go. Hurry now."

Eliza did as she was told. The people still on the island moved quickly, not speaking. The fishing boats were cast off on the rising tide. Marcus leaned against her, confused by the nighttime journey. "Where we goin', Eliza?"

"I don't know, Marcus. I ain't never been off this island before. I think it is an adventure like in that story 'bout Robinson Crusoe."

The boats didn't stay together during the night. Each family seemed to head in a different direction. The movement of the boat rocked Eliza and Marcus back to sleep. When the sky began to lighten, Eliza awoke. Without waking anyone, she eased her way to her cousin Nelson. "Where you taking us?" she asked.

"Bath, Eliza. It's a nice big town. We'll be okay there while we wait for Pa."

Eliza nodded as if she knew what he meant.

Agent Pease arrived on Malaga early on the morning of July 1, 1912. He came with a sheriff, a doctor, and a few willing citizens. They expected trouble. Instead, as they approached the island, they saw no boats and no movement. There was no wood smoke rising over the pine trees. Even the seabirds were quiet.

They climbed the path to the settlement, hands on their guns. No one and nothing greeted them. The island was bare. Every house had been dismantled and was gone. The only thing left standing on Malaga was the Malaga School and seventeen tombstones in the old graveyard.

Pease looked around in astonishment, then said, "I call this a job well done. My report to the governor will state that Malaga Island is no longer a reproach to the good name of our fine state."

Cora finished nursing her son and opened the *Boston Globe*. She gasped when she read the headline, "Malaga Island Cleared of Degenerates." Quickly, she placed the baby in his cradle and read the article. "Jonathan," she called, "how is this possible?"

Jonathan hurried into the room, afraid that something dire had happened to the baby. When he saw her trembling with anger, shaking the paper, he knew at once what she had read. "Your parents told us of the eviction notice. It seems that the islanders were not ready to give up their freedom."

"But where have they gone? How will they live? Malaga was their home." She sank into a chair. "They have moved the school to another island and taken the caskets from the cemetery. Where will they bury those poor people?"

"I understand that the caskets have been moved to the cemetery at the School for the Feeble-Minded."

"But that is wrong. The dead were not feeble-minded." She spread the paper across her lap and pointed. "It says here that Mrs. Tripp died of exposure while her children watched." She covered her eyes and wept. "I should have done something."

"There was nothing to be done. The state evicted the Malagaites, not you. The feeble-minded and insane will be taken care of and the others will go on to live their lives."

"I want to find Eliza and her brother Marcus. I need to know that they are safe. I will not rest until I know where they are."

"Calm yourself, Cora. I'll help you. It may not be easy. I understand that some of the people have disappeared or are, perhaps, in hiding. But we will do our best."

# CHAPTER TWENTY-EIGHT

## SEATTLE

Susan's death had changed everything. Jeff and Lola were still at the house with Henry, but everyone knew they would need to go back to Spain soon. Jeff couldn't expect that they would hold his job open forever. Georgia felt lost. She'd always been close to her mom, and losing her felt like she was missing a part of herself. She worried about Henry. He was devastated by the death of his wife of almost fifty years. She did know that the only thing that made him smile was Gabriel crawling into his lap or demanding his attention.

One afternoon, when she arrived at the house, Henry handed her a letter. "I thought you and Jeff might want to look at this."

Georgia flipped the envelope over. The return address was the National Donor Marrow Program in Minneapolis. "What is it?"

"It's the donor number of your mom's donor and how you can contact him. If you want to. He doesn't have to respond, but they suggest that many donors welcome contact from the family." Georgia gazed down at the letter, unsure what to do. "Jeff read it this afternoon. I think he wants to know why this black guy matched your mom. And, probably, matches you two, also."

"How do you feel about it, Dad? Do you want to meet him?"

"I don't think so." He sighed. "Not because he's black. Because your mom died. But don't let me stop you. Jeff already has a son and you'll have children someday; health information is good to know."

"Thanks, Dad. I'll talk to Jeff." She hugged him and blinked away her tears.

∽

Jeff wanted to write.

Georgia was hesitant. "What are we going to say? 'Hello, Sir, please explain why your HLA markers—which are inherited, by the way—match our mother's markers—and incidentally, some of ours—when we have always been under the assumption that we are a lily-white Irish family'?"

Jeff laughed. "I guess that's the gist of it, but I'm sure we can be more tactful than that. Maybe we start with 'thank you for donating.'"

"Yeah, 'Thanks—but too bad it didn't work.'"

"Georgia, lighten up." He saw the tears welling in her eyes and hugged her. "I want to know, but we don't need to contact him until you're ready."

"I'm just being stupid. Yes, of course, we should send a letter and say thank you and ask if he would like to meet us."

"Exactly. The agency letter says not everyone wants to meet the family. So we leave it up to him." Jeff grinned. "But, if we meet him, we're bringing all those pictures and all our questions. Agreed?" Georgia nodded. "Okay, I'll write the letter tonight. Now I've got some other news. Where's Dad? I want to tell you at the same time."

Henry was in the kitchen helping Gabe eat his Cheerios while Lola cooked dinner. Henry pretended to eat a Cheerio and Gabe chuckled. "Hey, Dad," Jeff said, interrupting the fun. "Lola and I talked it over and we'd like to stay another six months. My company wants me to write a manual and I can do it remotely. We'll get our own apartment so we won't be underfoot all the time. What do you say?"

Henry sat stunned for a moment and then he grinned at Gabe, who grinned back and spit out a Cheerio. "I say that's an excellent idea. But this house is way too big for just me. I want you to stay here." He looked at Lola. "If that's all right with you, dear."

"Gabe would love it, and so would I." She turned from the stove and hurried to hug Henry. "My parents will want to come for a visit."

"Susan always says ... said ... the more the merrier."

"Okay, that's settled. Now we just need to find a husband for my sister and all the loose ends will be tied up." Georgia hit Jeff. Gabe yelled and Henry wiped away a tear.

Georgia removed the box of papers and photos to her apartment, and she spent most evenings gazing at them, trying to find a hidden message. Linda, who was a whiz at fashion, had helped her place the pictures in chronological order by using the clothing to determine the year they were taken. *If these were her ancestors, who were they, and why didn't Mom know who they were? Or*, Georgia pondered, *perhaps she did know and kept it a secret. But why?* Susan had never been a secret keeper. It made no sense. Much more likely, her mother had told the truth when she said that the box had come into her life when her mother died and she, busy with her life and children, had put it away and never opened it. She gazed again at the wedding picture of her grandparents. Jeff did look kind of like his grandfather, but he looked more like Henry. She took the photo into the bathroom and compared her features to her grandmother's. She saw no resemblance at all, but Susan had always said that Georgia looked like her mother. *Maybe it was all in what you wanted to see*, Georgia thought. She stared at the picture again. They both had dark hair. She could see nothing that would make her think they were of African American descent.

She called Jeff. "Hey, what do we actually know about mom's family?"

"I've been searching my brain, too. Not much. I asked Dad and he says Mom's parents were from Canada, maybe. So, really not much."

"We know Mom was born in the US. So, if they were Canadian, it was before Mom was born. Did you write that letter?"

"I did. And, I sent it. Now go read a book or something and quit thinking so much. Love you to the moon and back."

"To infinity and beyond."

"Forever and always." Georgia was smiling as they hung up.

"Hey." Linda stuck her head into Georgia's office. "You and Mitch want to come over for dinner this weekend? Ken's cooking, so you don't have to be afraid."

Georgia grinned. "If he doesn't cook at your house, he doesn't eat."

"I know. But he does cook and I eat. So, want to have dinner?"

Georgia frowned and shook her head. "I don't think that's a good idea."

Linda stepped into the office and plopped into a chair. "That look tells me there is trouble in paradise. Things not working out so well with Mitch?"

"I don't know. He's nice enough, but the race thing is a big deal. He says it doesn't bother him that I'm mixed race but that his parents would never accept it. And ... I know he'd never go against their wishes. So, no to dinner or any other setup. I think we'll just be friends."

"Okay. Then I'll start looking for someone else. Married women want their best friends to be married, also."

"You and Jeff. He wants me to be married, too. I'm not sure I'll ever be. Right now I'm obsessed with finding out who I am. I want to know my family's history, and I don't think I can move on until I do."

༻

When the letter from the donor arrived, Jeff took it straight to Georgia's office so they could open it together. A snapshot was enclosed. They examined it closely. A tall, very dark African-American man with gray hair had his arm around a lighter-skinned woman in a turban and a dashiki. They were flanked on either side by two young women who appeared to be identical. They flipped it over. On the back was written, "Me with my wife and daughters."

Georgia took another look at the picture. "Am I crazy, or do the daughters look like Mom?"

"Not crazy, Georgie. It was the first thing I noticed. They definitely look like our mom and a lot like you. At least in the picture."

"Read the letter. Does he want to meet us? What's his name?"

*Dear Jeff,*

*Thank you for your letter. I was saddened to hear of your mother's passing. When I was informed that our HLA match was so close, I entertained great hopes that the transplant would help. I am sorry that it did not.*

*I am Lawrence (Larry) McKenny. I am married and the father of lovely twin daughters. We reside in San Diego, CA, where I was a high school teacher before my retirement.*

*You mentioned in your letter that until this time you had no idea that your family was racially mixed. I am sure you have many questions. If we are related, as we appear to be, our family's story is convoluted and strange. I would be pleased to meet with you, and your sister, at your convenience. I will place my phone number and email address at the end of this letter. Please use them as you see fit.*

*I will tell you that my grandfather was born in 1907, on Malaga Island, in the state of Maine. The story of Malaga is not a pretty one, but you may want to read about it before we meet.*
  *Sincerely,*
  *Larry*

Georgia was already typing "Malaga Island, ME" into her search engine. The results filled her screen.

1. Malaga Island: A Century of Shame
2. Malaga Island: A Story Best Left Untold
3. Malaga Island – Wikipedia
4. The Dark Secrets of this Now-Empty Island in Maine

Jeff pointed at "A Century of Shame" and said, "Start there."
For next two hours, as evening fell and the building grew quiet, they read the sites and watched the videos. The awful story of how eugenics, racial prejudice, religious zeal, and greed combined to force the Malagaites from their homes was overwhelming. Finally, they pushed back from the computer and sat quietly. "We need to understand this," Jeff said.

The papers and the photos in her grandmother's box seemed more important now. She read each one carefully. The love letters addressed to Geraldine Tyler from a young soldier, Lloyd McKinney, who was to become her husband, were especially sweet. He was proud that a teacher had agreed to be his wife and told her often how much he missed her. She found memorabilia of events that meant nothing to her. In the bottom of the box was a brown-paper, accordion-style Filofax. The elastic band was brittle with age. Georgia opened it carefully.
The pockets were labeled neatly: *Geraldine, Steven, Confidential, Malaga.* Georgia took a deep breath. She called Jeff,

announcing, "I think I found something. Grandma's box has a really old file with a section labeled *Malaga*. It says *Property of Eliza Tyler* on the outside."

"Wait for me. I'll be there in thirty minutes."

Georgia carried the folder to the kitchen, made herself a sandwich, and ate it while staring at the file. As much as she wanted to see what was in it, she was glad that Jeff would be there when she actually looked at the contents. When he arrived, she asked, "I was thinking we were related to Larry through Grandpa McKinney. Even though the names are spelled differently, it makes more sense. Doesn't it?"

"I thought that, too. But, let's see what you found in Great-Grandma's file. Let's start with Geraldine—we know she was our grandmother."

They found a record of birth for Geraldine Louise Tyler born on September 21, 1926, in Rumford, Maine. She was listed Female, White, Legitimate, and the first child. Her father was Steven Tyler, White, no age listed, born in the US, currently residing in Rumford, Maine, no street address, Occupation: Mill Worker. Her mother, as expected, was Eliza Tyler. Maiden name: Lane, White, no age listed, born in the US, residing in Rumford, Maine, Occupation: Housewife. It was signed by a Harriet Millford, and was received by the Town Clerk and registered on December 30, 1927.

"I wonder what took so long to register the birth," Jeff said.

Georgia considered for a second and then guessed, "Probably a home birth; it's not signed by a doctor. I think that was kind of normal procedure."

"Okay, let's see what we have on Steven." He pulled out a letter and a death certificate. "This says he died January 15, 1927. He was only thirty-nine years old."

Georgia quickly did the math. "And the baby was only four months old when he died. How sad. What's the cause of death?"

"Just says 'accidental.' What does that mean?"

Georgia had opened the letter. "He was injured on the job. This is a letter stating that the mill is paying his widow, Eliza, eleven hundred dollars, and is held harmless in his death."

Silently Jeff, reached for the letter, read it, and slid it back into its envelope. "Confidential or Malaga next?"

"Confidential."

Jeff extracted the papers and laid them on the table. First was a normal school teaching certificate, certifying that a widowed white woman, age thirty-six years, had completed the requirements to teach in a Maine State School. "It looks like we come from a long line of teachers."

Georgia picked up the next paper. "This is a letter of recommendation from a Mr. Foxton, saying that Eliza Lane has provided education to students in the rural areas of Quebec for the past five school terms, August 1919 through July of 1924." Georgia raised her eyebrows at Jeff. "There's the Canada connection Dad knows about."

"Maybe," Jeff said. "Anything else?"

"Just that she comported herself in a manner befitting an unmarried woman and that he is recommending her abilities." Georgia laid the letter aside and picked up the next item, a newspaper clipping. "This is an obituary for a Cora Smithson, née Lane, of Boston, Massachusetts. She was some kind of society lady who was active in the suffragette movement. She died in 1918. Maybe her maiden name, Lane, is a clue."

"Curiouser and curiouser." Jeff picked up the next envelope and slipped out the card inside.

"This is it, I think," he said.

Georgia sat perfectly still, waiting.

"This is an invitation to a college graduation in 1967, for a Lawrence McKenny. Someone wrote on it, 'Don't expect to see you but thought you should know.' It's signed with a capital A." They were silent for a long moment. Then Jeff said, "Pull out the stuff from Malaga. We might as well see it all."

The Malaga section was stuffed with newspaper clippings, mostly from the early 1900s but some as new as the 1950s. Each article they read maligned the people of Malaga Island. Some had names underlined, and Georgia wondered if they were people her great-grandmother had known. A few of the clippings had no date, but always they repeated the adage that the people of Malaga were tainted with mixed blood and moral depravity.

"I think we need to go to San Diego now. Let's call Mr. McKenny and set a date."

❧

"Are you nervous?" Jeff asked as he maneuvered the rental car out of the airport garage.

"A little. Do you think we made a mistake agreeing to meet at his home?"

"Actually, I've decided it's a good idea. He has things to show us and, if that stuff we read is any indication, this might be a pretty emotional meeting."

The GPS took them to a ranch-style home on a street in Clairemont Mesa. Except for the sunshine and palm trees, it could have been a street in any suburb in America. They parked next to the curb and each drew in a deep breath. A voice boomed, "Welcome, welcome."

The man approaching them thrust out his hand to grasp first Georgia's and then Jeff's hand. "Come on in and let's get to know each other." His warmth put them at ease. "This is my lovely wife, Chloe. The kids wanted to be here, but I told them it would be too much to meet us all at the same time. Make yourselves comfortable. I'm betting you have a million questions."

"We do, but first, thank you again for trying to help our mom. She was very grateful that the transplant gave her time to meet her grandson," Jeff said.

"My pleasure, son. I'm sorry I couldn't do more. Now, let's figure out how we're connected."

After they were all seated, Georgia pulled the Filofax from her bag. "We've found some paperwork and old photos that may help. We've read everything we could find on the Internet about Malaga Island. It is appalling that such a thing could happen and almost no one knows about it."

Larry nodded his head. "There is a lot of history that folks don't want to talk about. The eviction on Malaga Island was bad enough, but what is worse is the other things that happened to our families." Georgia wasn't sure she believed she'd had family on Malaga, but she kept silent and listened. "No one who was evicted from the island was unaffected. Most of the people who were sent to that School for the Feeble-Minded never left there. Some died shortly after being locked up, but some lived long lives. I think Lottie Marks was the only one who was released, but she wasn't the only one who should never have been sent. Many of the forty or so exiled in 1912 survived, and they made new lives for themselves wherever they could. They hid their heritage. Some moved away and passed for white. Some stayed in the area and suffered the continuing slurs that have never stopped. Do you know that to this day in that part of Maine, people insult one another by saying, 'Stop acting like a Malagee,' or, 'You want people to think you're from Malaga'?"

Chloe commented, "The saddest thing is how it tore families apart. Here you are, looking to be the same age as my twins and none of us even knowing the other part of the family exists. My family is from the South and we have plenty of bad history, but we all know each other and we all love each other."

Georgia pulled out the pictures and sorted through them. She found the one of the two young girls. "I'm not sure how we are related. This is my maternal grandmother, Geraldine, with someone named Anna." She passed the picture to Larry.

Larry smiled. "Anna was my mother. She's Geraldine's first cousin."

"But Grandma was white. It said so on our mother's birth certificate."

"She looks white, but I'd say she was passing. Probably never told anyone about it. My mother used to fume about those who passed for white; she was angry all the time. But my grandpa Marcus used to tell her to calm down, that people only ever did what they had to do. I think I know most of this story; if you want me to tell it, I will."

# CHAPTER TWENTY-NINE

## SAN DIEGO

"When I was a kid, I spent a lot of time with my grandpa Marcus McKenny. My mom and dad both worked and I guess he was taking care of me, but I just thought he was my friend and the smartest person I knew. We lived in Bangor, Maine. You ever been back there?" Jeff and Georgia shook their heads. "It's pretty enough, I guess, but the weather is vicious. My dad grew up out here in San Diego. He'd joined the Navy as soon as World War II started and got stationed in Maine. He met my mom when she was seventeen, and I was born in 1942. Before you ask, they never got married, but he was around most of the time. I think he always hated the cold because when Grandpa died in 1960, we moved out here right quick. It was pretty rough being a black boy, not like today and not like in the South. We went to our own schools and churches and kept out of the way.

"When I'd complain, Marcus would tell me the story of his own childhood. He was born in 1907 on Malaga Island. His mama and daddy both died of the measles on the night he was born. His oldest sister, Sarah, died a few days later, and he and his surviving sister moved into their grandparents' home; King Jim McKenny's house. The first five years of his life were good—his sister took care of him, carted him to school with her, played with him, all that—and then the eviction happened. He was only five that night, so mostly he remembered the boat ride and having to stay quiet. He always said, 'I was with my sister, so I wasn't scared.' But then, Eliza disappeared."

Georgia leaned forward. "My great-grandmother Eliza? But she was white and her last name was Lane."

"Maybe. As a child, Marcus only knew that Eliza took care of him and that she disappeared. But when he was older, he learned that Eliza had been very fair-skinned. Their grandfather, Jim McKenny, was Scotch-Irish and his wife, Seloma, was a mix of Black and Indian. Simon, Eliza and Marcus's father, was mixed. Their mother, Mattie, had dark skin, blue eyes, and red hair, so mixed race, also. I've been told that Sarah, the sister that died, was fair-skinned. Marcus was dark, as dark as I am."

"But how did Eliza disappear?"

"Jim and Seloma, her grandparents, decided it would be best if she passed as white. Jim took her to a house that was advertising for help, said she was his daughter and that her mother was dead. She was hired as a maid. In those days, I guess they thought that was best. Whatever their reasoning was, Marcus didn't see his sister again until 1934.

"Marcus was working in a boatyard, married by then, and had a daughter, Anna. He sometimes wondered what had happened to Eliza, but she'd been gone a long time. Back then when you knew someone who was passing for white, you didn't talk about it. Same way you didn't tell outsiders that you had any connection to Malaga Island. So, one day when he walked in from work and found a white lady with her little white girl in his house, his first thought was to wonder if he was in some kind of trouble. The lady started crying and saying, 'Marcus, Marcus,' over and over. She hugged him and he stood real still, afraid to be touching a white lady.

"He stepped back and she said, 'I'm Eliza, Marcus. Don't you remember me?' and in that second he did. He always chuckled when he said this next part. He looked at her and he said, 'I remember you, but you white now.' And then she said, 'I've always been this color; you just didn't notice.'

"So, you'd think this was a happy ending, right? But it wasn't. Eliza's husband had been killed in an accident and she'd used the compensation money—"

"Eleven hundred dollars," Georgia interrupted.

Larry nodded. "Eleven hundred dollars, to get a teaching certificate and a new job, and she was moving out West. She was passing for white, her husband had been passing, her daughter had a birth certificate that said she was white, and she intended to continue passing for white. She'd just wanted to see Marcus one more time to be sure he was okay. So, they had that one afternoon and evening. Eliza must have had a camera and taken that picture of her daughter, Geraldine, with Marcus's daughter Anna. Like I said, my mama and your grandma were first cousins."

Jeff and Georgia sat in stunned silence. Until Jeff said, "But..."

"I know," Larry agreed, "there is more to the story. I've pieced together most of my birth family and I can make some guesses about yours. However, if your great-grandmother Eliza never shared the truth with her daughter, Geraldine, or if Geraldine knew and never shared it with your mother, the truth is lost."

Georgia was stunned. "We know that Eliza taught in Quebec before she married. How do you think that happened?"

"I actually know that; I just skipped over some of the stuff that Eliza told Marcus that day. She'd wanted to be a teacher from the time she'd learned to read. When her grandfather left her to work as a maid, it was in the home of a professor. She spent the next four years studying everything in their library. When she was seventeen, she read an obituary for Cora Lane Smithson, her first teacher. She quit her job, rode a train up to Quebec, and applied for a job as a teacher in a tiny rural school using the name Eliza Lane. Quebec is close enough to Maine that she was afraid someone would recognize the name McKenny and connect her to Malaga."

"Wasn't Marcus angry that his sister was passing for white?" Georgia asked.

"Maybe, but if he was, he never let on. He talked about her some to me. Said how proud he was to have a sister who had achieved her dream. Told me I shouldn't ever settle for less than what I truly wanted. When I told him I wanted to be a teacher, he was thrilled. Told me I had the brains for it. He was proud that I was the first person in our family to graduate from college. And, when Vietnam happened, he prayed I'd get a deferment. He told me to be proud of who I am, but to never tell anyone—not even anyone in California—that I had a connection to Malaga Island.

"So, I didn't. In fact, it really didn't matter to me. As far as I knew, no one had ever heard of Malaga and I quit thinking about it, too. After we'd moved to San Diego, being black was more important than ever, but in a good way. I was proud to be black. We said 'black' then, not African American. I protested for racial equality and against the war. I loved college, I met my lovely Chloe here, and I loved teaching. I've had a very good life. Malaga didn't matter to me until 2010."

"Why 2010?" Jeff asked.

"I woke up in 2010. Did you read that stuff about the governor's apology?"

# CHAPTER THIRTY

## SAN DIEGO

Larry accepted a glass of tea and settled in to continue the history lesson. He began, "Evicted from their homes, the Malagaites dispersed and went into hiding. Some hid in full view, some by moving away from the shore, some left the state of Maine—going to Canada and to the West. As you know, a few changed their names and chose to pass as white. No matter what path they took, all the Malagaites had one thing in common: they did not talk about their past. The media continued to report on the island of 'degenerates and imbeciles' that had been 'exterminated by the state of Maine.'

"Individually, the Malagaites decided to turn away from their heritage. As generations were born, they were not told the story of their roots. Malaga Island faded away. After the caskets and the schoolhouse were moved, no one ever lived on the island again. The state sold the island, but it remained empty. Fishermen from Phippsburg began to store their lobster pots on the shore. Occasionally, a story was told that someone had seen a ghost on the island. By 2000, even those stories had faded away.

"Gradually history was rediscovered. Over one hundred years of concealed persecution and shameful actions were brought to public attention in books, national publications, television productions, university studies, and a prominent Maine Public Radio production, 'Malaga Island: A Story Best Left Untold.'

"In 2012, the Maine State Museum announced a special exhibition, telling the story of Malaga Island, for the one-hundredth anniversary of the eviction. Descendants of John Darling, James McKenny, Jerry Murphy, and others began to question the stories they had heard from parents and grandparents.

"With all this attention focused on the past, on April seventh, 2010, the State Legislature issued a proclamation that acknowledged the expulsion of the Malagaites from their homes. Hold on a minute. I've got it right here." Larry unfolded a paper and read:

"'RESOLVED: That We, the Members of the One Hundred and Twenty-fourth Legislature now assembled in the Second Regular Session, on behalf of the people we represent, do recognize with profound regret the tragic displacement of the Malaga islanders in 1912, in the name of the disgraced Eugenics Movement, with its overtones of prejudice against poverty, racism and stereotyping; and, while rebuking this past, rededicate the future to the ideals of tolerance, independence and equality of all peoples in our ever-changing world, which are the birthright and heritage of all proud Mainers; and rededicate ourselves as lawmakers to the social and economic justice that is the right of all peoples; and be it further

RESOLVED: That suitable copies of this resolution, duly authenticated by the Secretary of State, be transmitted to the Maine Coast Heritage Trust, the Maine Historic Preservation Commission, the Maine Historical Society and the NAACP.'

"Now, you are probably thinking that the resolution was a good thing. The state had apologized and that should be that. And maybe it would have been, but they didn't announce that resolution in advance, so no one heard, not the descendants or any stakeholders, just the legislators who happened to be in attendance when it was read into the record. Of course, word got out. It was reported by a journalist, Colin Woodard, that while this statement, provided by Governor John Baldacci, seemed to be a gubernatorial statement of regret, in fact, only hours before, the governor had queried his office as to why the issue had been left to the legislature in the first place. Since the 1912 evictions were orchestrated by one of his predecessors, he seemed to feel no need to accept responsibility. The extremely low-profile apology was just another insult in a long line of insults.

"The descendants started to talk and spread the word on social media. This is when I woke up. Finding others on the Internet stirred me to join with them and seek a true apology. The Malagaites deserved no less. In fact, we deserved a great deal more. We began a campaign to receive a public apology, some type of restitution, and to have the graveyard restored to its proper place."

Larry paused to take a breath and drink his tea.

Georgia and Jeff sat dumbfounded by what they were hearing.

Larry picked up his story. "It took a while. On Tuesday, September fourteenth, 2010, the governor came to Malaga Island as part of a celebration marking the dedication of Malaga as part of the Maine Freedom Trail. There were nearly thirty descendants in attendance and he made a proper apology to them. He said, and I quote, 'Let me just say that I'm sorry. I'm sorry for what was done. It wasn't right and we were raised better than that. We're better people than that. It's reprehensible what happened to your families and, you know, the spirit which you bring to today is a spirit that others can learn from.'

"I wasn't there; however, I've heard from those that were that it was a healing experience. The families of the Malagaites no longer felt the shame of the past and began to heal."

Georgia wiped the tears from her eyes. "I wonder if my mother knew this."

"I think not. By 2010, your grandmother had taken her secret to her grave and the story of an island in Maine would have meant nothing to your mom, just another racial incident."

Jeff was pacing the room, deep in thought. Trying to absorb everything he'd heard today. He picked up his grandparents' wedding picture and stared at it. "Remember," he turned to Georgia, "when we were all together and Dad said something about Grandma not wanting Mom to marry him, and Mom said she liked him fine after you and I were born?"

"Vaguely, why?"

"Take a good look at this. I think both she and our grandfather were passing."

Larry and Georgia studied the picture. Larry nodded. "Could be."

"I think Grandma didn't want Mom to marry a pale-skinned, redheaded Irishman for fear that her children would have dark skin. Then after you were born, and Mom knew she couldn't have more children, Grandma relaxed."

"She felt she needed to keep the secret," Larry confirmed.

"My head is spinning." Georgia stood and looked at Larry. "If my grandma and your mother were first cousins, then you and my mother are second cousins. So, what are we to you, third cousins?"

"You are precious new relatives that I am delighted to know," Chloe interrupted. "Larry, the girls are on their way over. They want to meet Georgia and Jeff."

"Quick then, before the noise starts, I have just a bit more to tell you." Georgia and Jeff sat, not sure they could handle any more. "In 2012, the Maine State Museum staged a wonderful exhibit titled 'Malaga Island, Fragmented Lives.' Chloe and I went back for the opening, and Governor Paul LePage apologized again and promised to open a scholarship fund for descendants. The Malaga 1912 Scholarship Fund was funded in 2014. The first awards were made in 2015. That scholarship opportunity is over. The final awards were distributed in September 2018.

"The remains of the original Malagaites are still buried at Pinelands, the former Maine School for the Feeble-Minded. In 2017, the state erected a six-foot-tall, granite monument engraved with the names of the seventeen exhumed islanders and the names of the exiled islanders who died at the school." He took a deep breath and concluded, "Not a story with a completely happy ending, but real life is seldom tidy. Some say it is a story best forgotten, but I think it is a story everyone should know and remember."

# CHAPTER THIRTY-ONE

## SEATTLE/MALAGA

Georgia was very quiet as she and Jeff waited for their flight home from San Diego. Jeff watched her but left her alone; he knew she would talk when she was ready. *It's been quite a day,* he thought. *I'm not sure what I feel either.* He pulled out the journal he always carried and started to make notes. Georgia saw what he was doing and pulled out her own journal.

She began to doodle her thoughts. She drew an island covered with pine trees, then a boat filled with people. She added a dark cloud over the island, scrawled MALAGA in big bubble letters, and then wrote Black? White? And crossed them both out. She sighed. "I'm so confused," Georgia confessed to Jeff.

He closed his journal and waited.

"It was interesting to learn all this stuff, and Larry and Chloe are lovely. But I really didn't feel any connection until Sarah and Seloma showed up with their kids. Those two really do look like Mom."

"Yeah, that was weird. You didn't say anything, so I didn't know if you were okay with the resemblance to Mom."

"It was hard to miss." She glanced at her doodling. "It was like seeing double. They could have posed for those pictures we have of Mom with a dark tan, playing with us on the beach in Hawaii."

"Mom was in her thirties then and our cousins are thirty-six."

"Cousins? Is that what we are?"

"Well, maybe fourth cousins or something, but definitely related."

"Do you feel related to them?"

Jeff took his time answering, as he considered the day. "Yes, I think I do. In fact, I know I do."

Georgia dropped her eyes to her journal and began to draw a family tree. "I want to go to Maine. See that island. Maybe meet some more of the descendants, something."

"Okay, let's do it. You have a spring break coming up, right?"

❧

Approaching the east coast of Maine, the plane made a slow, wide turn so they would land in Portland from the east. Georgia peered out the window. It was a perfectly clear day. The coastline was beautiful; she could see what looked like hundreds of small islands, some dotted with houses, some looking to have nothing but rocks and trees. She wondered if she was looking down on Malaga Island.

They'd made no specific plans. Larry had provided directions to Phippsburg and warned them that the descendants who lived in the area preferred to be left alone. They checked into a hotel, ate dinner, and agreed to drive to Phippsburg the following day.

❧

On the advice of the desk clerk, in the morning they drove to Portland's East End and had breakfast at the Portland Pottery Cafe. The food was delicious. The waitress refilled their coffee cups and asked, "Where are you visiting from?"

"Seattle," Jeff responded. "This neighborhood looks like it would be fun to explore."

235

"Yep, it is. Just passing through, huh? Where you headed?"

"Over to Phippsburg. We just learned that our ancestors came from Malaga Island."

"Oh, yeah." She pulled the check from her pad and laid it on the table. "Pay the cashier when you're ready."

"Whoa, what did you do to offend her?" Georgia teased.

"No idea." They both looked to the kitchen area and saw the waitress whispering to a cook. She pointed, and they turned to look at Jeff and Georgia. "Let's get on the road," Jeff said, shrugging off the incident. "It'll take about an hour to drive. We just go north on 295 until we hit Route 1, and then in Bath we go south on 209."

"Got it. You drive and I'll look out the window."

It was a pretty drive. The houses seemed to be mostly historic and well kept. They passed through towns with names that were familiar from history books. Neither one had visited Maine before and they found everything interesting. They commented often on what they saw. Bath looked especially inviting. As they turned south on State Route 209, they grew quiet. The Phippsburg Town Hall, a small white building by the side of the highway—no town in sight—was right where Larry had told them. They parked and went in.

A middle-aged woman greeted them from behind the desk, asking how she could help. Georgia picked up a guide titled "Walking Phippsburg." "We are interested in Malaga Island."

"Lots of other places around here that are prettier and easy to get to. Sure you want to go out to that island?" She eyed them suspiciously. "Nothing out there but lobster pots and a trail. No facilities."

"Yes, we understand, but we'd like to see it. How do we get there?"

The clerk pulled a brochure and photocopied map from under the desk. She tapped on the map. "This is Town Hall; that's where you are. You follow the road this way." Her fingers traced the route. "The most likely place to get a boat this early in the season is at the Rock Gardens Inn. Somebody there might be willing to take you across."

"Thank you for your help." Jeff smiled politely.

The clerk passed him the brochure. "This is from the Heritage Trust people. It's a guide to that place." She turned back to her desk without saying good-bye.

Back in the car, Jeff said, "I'd heard that the people of Maine are reserved, but that's two today who seemed downright hostile."

"I think it's when we mention Malaga Island. Up until then, the natives seem friendly."

"Larry did warn us that they don't like to talk about Malaga or the events that happened there."

At the Rock Gardens Inn, they had no problem finding a young man who was willing to take them across the brief stretch of water and wait for them. "It'll only take you an hour or so. There isn't much out there to see. I got a book in my backpack, so you don't need to hurry." They agreed to his terms and were soon stepping out on the undeveloped shore of Malaga Island. He pointed them to the trailhead, warning them to stay on the trail and to watch out for poison ivy and ticks.

"Well, at least he didn't seem to disapprove of our visit," Georgia said, heading up the trail. "I have no idea what poison ivy looks like."

"Three shiny leaves, remember."

"I think I'll just stay away from everything." Following the paper guide, they found the location of the McKenny House and sobered. The names on the guide were familiar from their reading, and here in the quiet of the pine forest it all became real. "Those poor people," Georgia murmured. "They were only living the best life they could, just like everyone else."

They completed the circuit and returned to the beach. Georgia asked, "Do you think this is the beach they used when they had to flee in the middle of the night?"

"Hard to tell; things change over a hundred years." Jeff turned and looked back into the trees. "Pretty place, isn't it?"

On the quick trip back, the boatman was more talkative. "Spooky out there. My dad stores his traps over there." He gestured to a pile of lobster traps on the beach. "My school took us to that exhibit the museum did. It was pretty interesting. None of us had ever known where the word *Malagee* came from; we used to call each other that all the time, but the teachers put a stop to it." He pulled in alongside the dock and held his boat tight so they could climb out.

Jeff thanked him and started to walk away. He turned back. "You know any of the descendants?"

"Suppose I might, but we don't ask and they don't tell. Except for that group that got the Trust to take over the island and built that big monument at Pownal. That bunch talks about it some. Rest don't."

"Why is that?"

"Don't expect they believe it's anyone else's business." He waved them off.

"I don't think there is anything else to see here. Let's drive back to Bath for lunch, and then we can find that monument at Pinelands," Georgia suggested.

࿇

Over lunch, Georgia looked up Pinelands on Google. "It's a park now. I guess I was picturing a locked mental health facility."

Jeff chuckled. I hadn't thought about it much. I never looked it up either. What else does it say?"

"Started as School for the Feeble-Minded, where the patients lived, received treatment, and worked the farms. There is a brief mention of the Malaga Island residents and the relocation of the cemetery to the grounds of the school. Wow, it says here that the sterilization law allowed sterilization to be used 'for eugenic purposes or for the therapeutic treatment on feeble-minded and others suffering from certain forms of mental disease.' They sterilized one hundred and eighty-nine patients. In the 1930s, they cared for fifteen hundred patients. That's a lot. Must be a big place. Then, due to changing times, it was a well-known training hospital for mental illness, and then a residential facility, and it closed in 1996. In 2000, a foundation purchased the property and it became a park. Looks pretty nice." She tipped her phone so Jeff could see the website. "There's nothing on here about the monument. I bet we can find it."

⌀

The granite monument was beautiful. Jeff and Georgia stood quietly in front of it as they read the list of names, and the inscription:

**From the 1860's, until 1912, a community of laborers and fisherman lived on Malaga Island off the coast of Phippsburg. A controversial community for its time. White and black residents, married and lived together on the small island, until the State of Maine, evicted them in 1912. Included in the eviction was the state's removal of the island cemetery to the grounds of the Maine School for the Feeble Minded, where some island residents were committed. Remembered here are the community members exhumed from the Malaga Island cemetery by the state, and those who died here as patients.**

Jeff took Georgia's hand and they silently returned to the car and to the hotel.

"I'm ready to go home," Georgia said. She twirled her wine-glass and watched the legs of wine float down and subside. "This knowledge has changed my life." Jeff waited. "I'm no longer afraid of being African American and Irish. I proud of my ancestors on both sides. We come from a powerful line, Jeff."

"We do," Jeff agreed. "I will tell this story to my son and make sure he never forgets."

"If I have children, I will tell them, too. I will never be ashamed of my heritage. And, I believe that if Mom had been told about her mixed parentage, she would never have been ashamed. She would have told the world."

# CHAPTER THIRTY-TWO

## SEATTLE

Georgia pulled her *keikogi* over her head and folded it into her duffel bag. "That felt great," she told Linda. "I really needed to hit something tonight."

"I don't think that is quite the calmness of mind our sensei tells us we are supposed to be striving to achieve." Linda grinned. "The way you were hacking that bag with your *bokuto*, I thought you wanted to kill it."

"No murder intended. I'm just so frustrated by everything I've learned about my heritage. I tried to draw a family tree last night." She pulled a folded piece of paper from her bag and handed it to Linda.

"Did it help?"

"I don't know." Georgia shook her head.

"Come on, girl. Let's go get some dinner and I'll help you trace your roots." Linda tucked the paper into the side pocket of her purse and swung open the locker room door.

✍

"All right." Linda pushed their empty plates aside and spread open the drawing. "This seem pretty straightforward. What's the problem?"

"I worked off the government reports form 1911. I discovered that my great-great-grandfather, Jim McKenny, and his wife had four children. There might have been others, but three were alive in 1911 and I know that Simon died from the measles—so four children."

Linda nodded, tracing her fingers across the drawing. "Simon and Mattie had three children."

"I think that's right," Georgia agreed. "Sarah, the oldest, died with her parents in 1907. So that left Eliza, my great-grandmother, and Marcus, Larry's grandfather."

"And ..." Linda encouraged her to continue.

"Larry told us that Eliza changed her name to Lane because it was the name of a schoolteacher." Linda nodded. "Who is this person? It must be someone fairly important."

Linda picked up her phone. "Let's see what we can find on Google."

"You don't think I've already tried that?" Georgia protested.

"It's all in how you search," Linda declared. "I am a master. Starting with...." She thought a minute. "*Teacher Lane Maine.* No," she backspaced, "*Teacher Malaga Maine.*"

Google suggested three sites about the shameful history of Malaga Island. None of the three contained anything about a teacher. Searching for *School Malaga Maine* brought up a few more sites. Linda added *Lane* to her search: *School Malaga Maine Lane.*

"Look at this." She showed Georgia the results:

**The Lane School on Malaga Island - Vita Brevis**
Jun 5, 2014 – "A history of parts of Capt. and Mrs. **Lane's** and their daughter's work among a neglected people on **Malaga** Island, **Maine**" (Mss A 1900), ...

"I told you I was a master searcher."

The two women quickly read their screens and found that Cora Lane had been the first teacher on Malaga Island. "Well, that explains the name choice. She was probably Eliza's first teacher. I wonder what ever happened to this woman."

"That's an easy one. I'll just search in Ancestry.com and find the marriage records for a Cora Lane of Malden, Massachusetts."

"You don't know when she married or even if she was ever married."

"But, I can search and ... here it is." Linda gloated. "Miss Cora Lane wed Master Jonathan Smithson on October twenty-third, 1907." She waved her phone in Georgia's direction. "Let's see what happened to her. The death records on this site are excellent."

A few more minutes of searching brought up an obituary for Cora Lane Smithson, survived by her husband, Jonathan Smithson, an unnamed infant son, and three surviving children, William, Jack, and Elizabeth. "Read this." Linda handed her phone to Georgia.

Georgia quickly skimmed the contents, pausing to read some parts more slowly than others. "This is so sad. Cora was only twenty-eight when she died, and she had already taught school for three years, been a leader in the suffragette movement to win the vote, and given birth. I wonder why she died."

"Probably in childbirth, or shortly after. It was pretty common, and the infant son isn't named."

Georgia nodded in agreement. "If Great-Grandmother Eliza chose to use Lane because of Cora, I'd say she made a good choice."

Georgia found herself sitting once again in a faculty meeting. Mark Hedrick droned on as Dean Kellerman dozed, Martha nodded at his every word, Linda smirked, and Georgia doodled. *How can everything have changed and yet still be the same?* She forced herself to concentrate on Mark's words.

"The final item today is quite simple. HR is reviewing everyone's biographical data. If anyone has additions or changes to their biography, marital status, etc., you need to submit them by Monday. I will, of course, be adding the book I published in January of this year."

"Hear, hear," Martha said.

"I have a change also," Georgia said. "I will be changing my race to Mixed."

"You can't do that," Mark sputtered.

"Yes, Mark, I can. I have discovered that I am of mixed blood, African American and Caucasian. I am proud and excited by this discovery and I would like it reflected in the records."

"Your mother would be shocked." Mark was outraged.

"Mark, just shut up," Dean Kellerman interrupted. "Congratulations, Georgia. Discovering your lineage is an important part of the human experience. I look forward to hearing your story if, and when, you decide to share it. Meeting adjourned."

Chairs scraped back and the faculty scattered. Linda punched Georgia's arm gently. "Way to break the news. "

"I'm sure he and Martha are having a fit right now."

"What about Mitch?"

"Linda, I'm good with this. I really am proud of both sides of me. The Malagaites struggled against terrible odds at a time when they had no rights. They were forced to hide and deny any connection to the island. But now, we are beginning to discover our family history and each other. I already have six new members to add to my family." She grinned. "If Mitch is not willing to accept me exactly as I am, he is not the man for me."

❧

# ARTICLES AND QUOTES

The articles and quotes references in the
book are contained in this section.
They are listed in chronological order.

I choose to keep the original spellings and
statements wherever it seemed possible.

Boston Journal
August 11, 1903


## Monarch Rules Maine's Most Lawless Colony

**Portland, Me., Aug. 11** - That there should be within a short distance of the watering places and charming summer resorts of Casco bay an island on which a colony of people is living in the utmost ignorance, ungoverned by any law, either civil or moral, and under the predominating will of an erstwhile "king" so called by the members of the colony, was the astonishing, but veritable fact ascertained by a party of philanthropic people who last Tuesday visited Malaga island, some distance off the coast of Cape Small Point and in the near vicinity of Cundy's harbor.

The party consisted of Mrs. L. M. N. Stevens, Miss Anna Gordon, the Misses Mary and Helen Daggett of the Cambridge, daughters of Gen. A. S. Daggett of the United States army; Rev. E. H. Cotton of the Baptist Church, Harpswell; Mrs. Cotton, his mother; Rev. W. S. Randall and others who went simply to enjoy the sail, and they were conducted to the island in the magnificent yacht, Usona, owned by A. W. Childs of New York, who with his wife is summering at Harpswell this season.


**Philanthropist at Work**

In speaking about the purpose and results of the trip Mrs. Stevens told an interesting story concerning conditions as they now exist on the island.

"I happened to take the trip," said Mrs. Stevens, "as the result of a letter which I received about ten days ago from Miss Daggett, who is philanthropically inclined and who had heard enough of the rumors concerning Malaga Island to desire an investigation. Accordingly, I in turn invited Miss Gordon to accompany us, and we joined the other members of the party on board Mr. Child's handsome launch.

"We left at 12 o'clock last Tuesday, taking along a licensed pilot, since the waters about Malaga Island are treacherous for navigation, and arrived at the island about an hour and a half later. Two trips of the tender carried those who desired to land ashore, and then we looked about us to see where we were situated. We first saw walking toward us a white man of fisherman like appearance, whom we saluted.

## Approach of the King

"I am the King," said he as he looked out over his several acres of domain, but instead of treating the visitors with majestic haughti- ness, he conducted them about with some degree of politeness and an evident feeling of curiosity, answering their questions with a 'yes,' 'no' or 'I suppose so,' with perfect nonchalance, although volunteering no information which was not asked for.

"I could not tell much about conditions as they have been previously by inquiry from the members of the colony and people who had heard rumors and the most that I found out was of a general nature through personal observation. I should say as a rough estimate that the island contained between thirty and forty acres of land, and as near as I could find out, there were about forty people in the colony, a good many of whom were children. Some were colored, others were white, while still others appeared to have mixed blood.

# TAMARA MERRILL

## Children Live on Rocks

"They were mostly sitting about on the rocks aimlessly, and there were no signs of work or industry on the whole island. There were between seven and ten hovels erected, and although we did not see the insides of many of these, we saw enough to realize that their filth was as repelling as that of the lowest slums of New York or London. But the redeeming feature which gives most of the children good health is the outdoor life on the rocks, which is of course denied the children of the slums in large cities.

"We first talked with the 'king,' as the people call him. He is an ordinary appearing fisherman, and said that the people depended mostly on sea food for their living. When asked if they did any gardening he replied that they did not. I asked him why they did not keep a cow. 'Well,' he said leisurely, 'we thought some of getting one, and perhaps we will this fall.'

"The next one we talked with was a very bright appearing white girl whom her mother said was 13 years old. I asked her if she could spell her name, but she was unable to. Her mother said that most likely she could if she were not embarrassed, and when I asked the mother to help out, she appeared herself embarrassed, and failed to assist in the spelling.

## Poverty and Degeneracy

"And so we continued about the island seeing everywhere signs of poverty and degeneracy, until we were ushered into a room which contained the one bright gleam of civilization in the entire colony. The floor had been washed clean and the contents had been arranged neatly. We found that an attempt had been made by Mrs. Lane, wife of

248

a doctor, summering at Horse Island, to provide some education for the children. Some kindergarten articles were distributed around, showing that a definite step had been taken to bring enlightenment into the barbarous settlement.

"On returning to the launch we were served a bounteous supper by Mr. Childs, and finding that much was left over we left several baskets of the food on the island more especially for the children, whom we last saw on the shore, waving their hands, since they had no handkerchiefs, and eating fruit and pastry with great relish."

## Epidemic Swept Island

Last winter Malaga Island was afflicted with an epidemic of the measles and this first brought the inhabitants to public notice. The State was obliged to send food and other articles to them, or they would practically all have perished. The island belongs really to the town of Phippsburg, but it is a most unwelcome possession, and receives no attention from the authorities.

"There should surely be some steps taken to improve conditions on the island," said Mrs. Stevens, when asked what she would suggest, "and I should say that with first attention to the children, the young members of the colony should be taken from the island by the State and placed in some of the institutions for the poor or delinquent. The adults should then be taken from the place and given work on the mainland, for there is plenty of it to enable them to live respectably. The only other method of reforming them that I can think of would be to get a man and his wife to do settlement work on the island, but I do not think this would be profitable because the colony is not large enough to employ this method. The colony has been in existence for a number of years and the 'king' told us he had lived there thirty-five years, so it seems as though something should be done before the colony increases."

It is safe to say that it is the most lawless colony in Maine, although there is not much opportunity for drinking and stealing on account of its very isolation, and some steps to bring about a reformation will, in all probability, soon be taken.

The Boston Daily Globe
December 31, 1905


**ISLAND COLONY IN NEED**


**People of Malaga Island at Mouth of New Meadows River in Maine Feel Pinch of Winter.**


**BATH, Me. Dec 30** - The people of Malaga island, at the mouth of the New Meadows river, are again suffering this winter for clothing and food. This half island is inhabited by a colony of half whites and blacks. They work only when it is absolutely necessary, and gain a living by fishing and make but little preparation for the winter.

About 10 days ago a large bundle of clothing and some food was sent them by people who knew of their destitute condition.

TAMARA MERRILL

**The Bath Independent and Enterprise**
**February 17, 1906**

"Their homes are of the most part the most miserable huts, in which there is no pretense to cleanliness. Families of six or more eat, live and sleep in one room. A bed is the exception rather than the rule; a mattress a luxury few can afford. They sleep on the floors in heaps of dirty rags, and seldom remove their clothing. Their faces and hands show accumulations of grime; their clothes are little more than rags, the cast-offs of people from the mainland, worn until they will hardly hold together."

# SHADOWS IN OUR BONES

Boston Transcript
August 1906

**Dear Churchman Afield:** I noticed your column last Saturday **A Malden Layman's Summer Work a** request for information about summer religious work and I send you this account of a modest but noble enterprise: On one of the islands of Casco Bay, almost entirely covered with trees and with but two houses, lives during the summer season an old veteran of the sea, Captain Lane, now over seventy years of age. He goes early in the season from his home in Malden, Mass., to this island, where his wife, daughters and a few friends later join him, and he stays alone late into the autumn. This has been his custom many years, and his coming to his island home each year is looked forward to in many scattered settlements of this section of the Maine coast. These people, eking out a poor living by lobstering, digging of calms or fishing, living along the coves or small harbors, heartily welcome the captain as he comes across in his rowboat, some three or four miles. For they love him. On him they depend for any religious service. He preaches in a little schoolhouse on Sundays, gives of his substance for their needs, gives consolation and cheer in cases of bereavement, and whatever of the Christ spirit he can carry to these neglected people. He gladly sacrifices himself for them; for his age and an infirmity resulting from Civil War service often handicaps him. His wife and daughters give regular instruction to the children, which they find growing up under conditions morally and physically adverse. How much he might be helped in this if he could have a good motor boat.

F. H. W.

TAMARA MERRILL

Lane School Scrapbook
No source or date
Late 1906

## Captain Lane's Maine Parish
By F. H. C. Woolley

Following the sea from boyhood; serving the
navy during the Civil War as commander of a gun-
boat under Admiral Farragut; sailing along the
coast of the Carolinas in a small boat, stopping
at out-of-the-way settlements preaching Christ;
doing this same work later along the Maine coast
and establishing Sunday schools; then having to
give up much of the coast work on account of
infirmities, constitute an experience which would
seem to entitle a man at seventy-three years of
age to "lay to"; rather, to anchor finally in
some harbor of rest; bur Captain Lane may still
be found at his summer home on Horse Island, in
Eastern Casco Bay, actively interested in doing
a great deal yet for the Lord.

Resting he is, indeed, but every fair Sunday
finds him starting off early, with his family and
friends, for the Sunday trip in the motor boat,
first to Bethel Point, where some years ago a
chapel was built through his efforts. It is about
a forty-five minutes' sail, and the services begin
as soon as the Captain arrives. A simple text is
taken from the gospels and after a service of song
he preaches vigorously. His large experience in
life, especially among sea-faring and naval men,
makes his illustrations telling and impressive.
After the sermon there is freedom in the meeting;
many in a simple way speak of their Christian
experience. It is both novel and picturesque to
watch the departure from church in boats, for most
of the people live on neighboring islands.

254

Captain George W. Lane

The afternoon service is held at Card's Cove, some two miles distant, at three o'clock, which gives about three hours for lunch, rest and the further journey in the motor boat. The little schoolhouse is filled, and an ideal summer afternoon's quiet pervades the place. At this service are many families from nearby farms on the hills along the shore, as well as the island people, who have come over again in boats. No bell calls to the service; no ushers are here; the people choose their places among the old-fashioned seats and desks of a real country schoolhouse. No Jarring sound of the electric car is heard nor any whistle of steam train; only a song-sparrow's sweet notes, a distant thrush, the call of some crows float into the window. The meeting is carried on by the Captain with the same earnest spirit and vigorous preaching as if it was the only service of the day. The singing is good and the words of testimony are helpful. It is about five o'clock before the motor boat is pointed homeward, and it's a pleasant trip as the sun lowers in the west and Horse Island is reached about six o'clock.

Last summer the school on Malaga Island was well established. Malaga Island is about a half mile north of Horse Island and lies at the mouth of New Meadows River. The forty people living here by lobstering and fishing are a mixed race. Their condition appealed so to Captain Lane and his family that a few years ago a work of uplift, education and help was begun there. Mrs. Lane and her daughters secured the use of a room in a fisherman's home and there started teaching these children, growing up in ignorance and vice. The school was held each summer season during July and August for three years; and last year was placed under authority of the state, to whose attention the matter was brought by the state superintendent of schools

Many of the chapels along the Maine coast in small harbors have sprung from the Captain's works, as he used to go in and out in his sailboat, stopping to preach or organize a Sunday school. Increasing age and infirmities have caused him to curtail his work, but his little parish in the vicinity of Horse Island will still love him and welcome his cheery presence so long as he is spared.

*Malden, Mass.*

Boston Transcript
August 7, 1907


**Excerpt: Description of James E.
And Salome McKinney's home**
By F.H.C. Wooley

"The floor was washed clean, the windows up;
wild carrot and mayberry blossoms in vases stood
on the little organ. The children filed in, cleanly dressed. They had bright faces. Some were
black, some white and some; black and freckled."
Two long boards across the room at one end supported on uprights served as seats and desks. The
children sang with heartiness. The organ had the
accompaniment of a fiddle played by the father of
this home."

Boston Transcript
August 19, 1907


## DIVERS GOOD CAUSES
## An Island School

**To the Editor of the Transcript:** I wish you could have looked into a little home of a humble native of Malaga Island in Casco Bay, Me. It was a bright sunny forenoon when Mrs Lane and her daughter rowed over to the island, about a mile off. The welcome from the children and the mother showed how much these poor neglected people appreciated the love and the service that Captain Lane and his family are doing. This island has recently been described in a Boston paper as a lawless colony, ruled by a king; as a people who do nothing and live in indescribable filth. I was there several times and did not see the "king"; found that the men were away early in their boats after bait or a clam digging, lobstering or doing small jobs for mainland people. The houses are small; few have over two rooms, and the term "filthy" is certainly applicable to several. There are eight children from these homes that attend the school. They range from 10 to 18 years. The best room of the two she had on the first floor of the little house was given up by a mother for the school. The floor was washed clean, the windows up; wild carrot and mayberry blossoms in vases stood on the little organ. The children filed in, cleanly dressed. They had bright faces. Some were black, some white and some "black and freckled". With long boards across the room at one end supported on uprights served as seats and desks. The children sang with heartiness. The organ had the accompaniment of a fiddle played by the father of this home. A year ago these children could not read or write or tell days of the week; in fact, nothing had been done for them. Today the majority can read short sentences, can count, spell and do some excellent written exercises; they readily appreciate this summer-time effort for them and this patient loving service put forth by Captain Lane and his wife and daughters for these people and for others scattered along these island shores is beginning to tell for good. Some whole settlements have been changed for the better. But there is a need of help. Probably no one better understands these people and no one has done more to help them spiritually and materially than Captain Lane and his family, who are not blessed with riches but with a consecrated purpose to do as much good as they can. The captain, who has had a trouble with his feet for many years, is often laid by many times when he would go on his mission, but his courage is good for a man over seventy, and he is soon "up and on". The motor-boat, which the people of the First Church of Malden, Mass., and others interested in contributing for is a reality and the miles has rowed across the past year will be lessened as the new boat speeds him on.

F.H.C. Woolley
Horse Island, Me.

TAMARA MERRILL

No Publication Information


## MAINE'S SOUTH SEA ISLAND AT SCHOOL
## Phippsburg Faces Possibility of
## Having to Educate the Malagoites

PHIPPSBURG, Me., Sept. 13, 1907. As a result
of his recent tour of inspection among the little
communities along the Maine coast, Payson Smith
of Auburn, state superintendent of schools, will
probably call upon this town to furnish the il-
literate children of Malaga island at the mouth
of the New Meadows river with an education.

This quaint island, which was recently described in The Sunday Herald magazine as the
kingdom of Jim McKinney, its shrewdest and stron-
gest inhabitant, is still educationally about
as remote from civilization as if it lay among
the South Sea archipelagos. The origin of its
inhabitants is not a part of its history, and few
trustworthy traditions of any sort exist among
the Malagoites themselves.

Phippsburg once claimed sovereignty as a town
over the inhabitants of the island, but several
hard-headed citizens at once raised the point
that if the town recognized such ownership its
treasury would certainly be called on frequently
to make disbursements for the alleviation of the
islanders' miseries, and the matter was dropped.

As Harpswell, on the opposite side of the
river, also declined to take charge of the
Malagoites, the state stepped in and adopted
Malago as its own. Now it looks, however, as if
the state intended to turn over the burden of the
education of the young Malagoites to Phippsburg.

The curious type of children who are born of
this peculiar and ignorant race have never yet
come ashore for the purpose of attending the
public schools, and the result of Supt. Smith's

260

investigations will be watched with considerable interest.

People generally in this town do not believe that parents will want their children to attend the same schools with the Malago children, while on the other hand, the Malagoites are so little given to obeying the mandates of others, that it does not seem probable that they would be steady attendants at school.

The establishment of a special school, either on the main land or the little island, to be attended only by the children of Malago island, has been suggested as a way out of the difficulty.

TAMARA MERRILL

Clipping from the Lane school Scrapbook
No Source or Date


## REPORT ON THE MOTOR BOAT FOR CAPTAIN LANE

The movement for a motorboat, which began among the primary children last October, has been successful; for, with the help of friends in the church and outside, the boat was secured in August, and has been in service since then. There is a balance of $46.00 to be raised to settle the bill, which in all amounted to $259.17. Mr. Woolley visited Captain Lane this summer, and went with him to the various places where he is helping the people scattered in little settlements along the coast of Maine near Horse Island. The little school on Malagos Island, established a year ago and maintained by Mrs. Lane and her daughters, is prospering, and this year the Maine State Superintendent of Schools. Mr. Smith has visited the school and has promised that the State will maintain the work, providing a little schoolhouse can be built. Nothing has been done for these children, growing up in ignorance and vice, until Mrs. Lane kindly started this work. This little mission appeals to the children and friends of our Primary Department, and we believe the necessary money to pay for the boat will be forthcoming. Photographs of the children of the islands, Captain Lane's residence on Horse Island, and the school at Malagos, and sketches will be gladly shown in the Primary Room.

# SHADOWS IN OUR BONES

**Casco Bay Breeze**
**October 1907**


"The next step is clearing the really beautiful island of its unsightly huts and squalid
beaches and beginning its regeneration as a summer home for some wealthy citizens of New York
or Brooklyn. Las spring Bear Island, Malaga's big
neighbor was sold to Mr. James Williamson of New
York, and he has greatly improved it. The was
a practically uninhabited virgin forest covered
island. But in Malaga the proposition becomes
more complicated. Here are a score of negro families, who have been for the most part recipients
of bounty and charity from individuals, if not
from towns for many winters."

TAMARA MERRILL

**From the Lane School Scrapbook
No source or date**

**For Malaga Island (Me.) Schoolhouse**

**To the Editor of the Transcript:** The following amounts have been contributed toward building the schoolhouse on Malaga Island:

| | |
|---|---|
| A Maine Woman - | $1.00 |
| Robert C. Ogden - | $25.00 |
| G. ? G. - | $10.00 |
| Mrs. M. L. Quincy - | $3.00 |
| C. P. Whitcomb - | $2.00 |
| C. M. Vaughn - | $1.00 |
| A Friend - | $2.50 |
| A. W. Hartwell - | $2.00 |
| A Friend - | $3.00 |
| Mr. Gray - | $0.50 |
| A Friend - | $1.00 |
| | $55.00 |

Further contributions will be gladly received and acknowledged by

F.H.C. Woolley
147 Franklin Street

From the Lane School Scrapbook
No date


**Sunday School Messenger**
**1st Church of Malden**

**REPORT ON THE MOTOR BOAT FOR CAPTAIN LANE**

The movement for a motor boat for Captain Lane, which began among the primary children last October, has been successful; for, with the help of friends in the church and outside, the boat was secured I August, and has been in service since then. There is a balance of $46.00 to be raised to settle the bill, which in all amounted to $259.17. Mr. Woolley visited Captain Lane this summer, and went with him to the various places where he is helping the people scattered in little settlements along the coast of Maine near Horse Island. The little school on Malaga Island, established a year ago and, and maintained by Mrs, Lane and her daughters, is prospering, and this year the Maine State Superintendent of Schools, Mr. Smith, has visited the school and has promised that the State will maintain the work, provided a little schoolhouse can be built. Nothing has been done for these children, growing up in ignorance and vice, until Mrs. Lane kindly started this work. This little mission appeals to the children and friends of our Primary Department and we believe the necessary money to pay for the boat will be forthcoming. Photographs of the children of the islands, Captain Lane's residence on Horse Island, and the school at Malagos, and sketches will be gladly shown in the Primary Room.

# TAMARA MERRILL

Letter from: STATE OF MAINE
OFFICE OF STATE SUPERINTENDENT OF PUBLIC SCHOOLS
AUGUSTA, Maine
January 17, 1908


Mrs. Geo. H. Lane
Malden, Mass.

Dear Madam:

I am hoping that we may open the school at Malaga Island as early as possible in the summer. I am sincerely interested in your efforts to secure for this Island a new schoolhouse. A school may be opened under the circumstances of last year, but I should be very much gratified to know that the school was likely to go into a new building during the summer. I believe the schoolhouse for this Island should have two rooms. One to be used as a school room and the other equipped for teaching simple manual training and domestic science. Your efforts in the direction of providing a schoolhouse for this Island have my warmest approval and I trust will meet with full success. A building to serve the ends of the community would cost six or seven hundred dollars exclusive of the land.

Very truly yours,
Payson Smith

STATE OF MAINE
EDUCATIONAL DEPARTMENT

Augusta April 1, 1908

## REGULATIONS
### Governing the Management of Schools in Unorganized Townships

Agents appointed to manage the schooling of children in Unorganized Townships will carefully observe the following conditions and regulations.

*Under no circumstances must bills be contracted* until the following conditions have been fully complied with:

1. That an enumeration of the persons of all ages resident in the township on the first day of April, and an enrollment of all children between 5 and 21 years of age, shall have been made and returned to the office of the State Superintendent.

2. That the sum of forty cents for each inhabitant of the township shall have been assessed, collected and transmitted to the State Treasurer, by the Agent thereof. Agents have the same authority for the collection of this per capita tax, as collectors in towns have for the collection of personal and poll taxes, and may proceed to collect it in the same way.

3. That no school shall be established in any township till there has been provided, *without expense to the state*, a suitable place for holding such school.

The state will defray expenses incurred for the following purposes *and no other*:

1. Wages and board of teachers for twenty weeks per year;

2. Fuel and janitor's services;
3. Necessary appliances for teaching;
4. Tuition and transportation or board of children sent to the schools of an adjoining town, plantation, or township. It will also furnish necessary school books to be loaned to pupils in the schools established townships, for use during term time.

The duties of agents are:
1. To make the enumeration, enrollment and returns required by law and by the blanks furnished by the State Superintendent.
2. To assess, collect and transmit to the State Treasurer the per capita sum required by law.
3. To employ teachers and purchase fuel and necessary school appliances, and to make contracts for the instruction and transportation or board of children sent to schools of an adjoining town, plantation, or township.
4. To approve and transmit to the State Superintendent for payment all bills contracted by them. Bills for wages of teachers must be accompanied in every case by the school register of the term. All bills must be receipted before being transmitted for payment. They must show, by No. And Range when so designated, the township on account of which they have been contracted, and the name and P.O. address of the party to whom checks in payment are to be sent.
5. To have custody and charge of the books furnished by the state for use in the schools under their charge, to see that they are safely cared for during vacations, and to report the condition of the same at the end of the school year by transmitting to the State Superintendent the school book

registers kept each term by the teacher thereof.

6. To act as truant officers and as such "may in their discretion compel the regular daily attendance at school of every child in their townships between the ages of seven and fifteen years by arresting and taking to school any such child when absent therefrom; and any parent or guardian of any such child or children, willfully refusing to allow said children under his control to attend school, or opposing said agent in arresting and taking said children to school, may be prosecuted by said agent in the name of the state, before the nearest trial justice, and if found guilty, shall forfeit a sum not exceeding twenty dollars for the of the schools in the township wherein said children are resident, or shall be imprisoned for not exceeding thirty days."

Agents will be paid not more than two dollars per day for services actually performed, and also for all actual expenses incurred in the performance of their duties

In employing teachers, they will look to efficiency first, but will not pay unduly large wages. They will see that all teachers employed hold either state certificates or certificates from the school board of the towns of their residence.

Inquiries from agents desiring information or suggestions relating to matters under their charge, not contained in this circular, will receive prompt attention.

PAYSON SMITH,
State Supt. Of Public Schools

From State Archives
No Publication or date

## Flag-Raising at Malaga Island, Me.

Monday, July 6 was an eventful day for Malaga Island, Me., for on this date occurred the flag-raising on the site of the new schoolhouse.

The exercises consisted of singing by the children of the island who are now being taught by Miss Lane in one of the houses there. Remarks were made by Captain George W. Lane of Malden, Mass., through whose efforts these people are enabled to build; and Rev. Mr. Wilkins who is sojourning at Sebasco, Me., made an address. James McKinney raised the flag while the audience of about seventy-five cheered lustily. This was followed by the children saluting and the singing of America by all.

The fact of the flag-raising and the landing of the lumber for the building mark an epoch in the history of this neglected island which is noteworthy.

This schoolhouse is being built by public and private subscription. Part of the amount necessary has been subscribed, and efforts are being made to secure the remaining amount this summer. Contributions may be sent to Captain George W. Lane, Sebasco, Me., or to F. H. C. Woolley, 147 Franklin, Boston.

The Bath Independent and Enterprise
Wednesday, October 21, 1908


## New Building in Prince Jerry's
## Domain Opens for Fall Term

**Bath, Maine** – Monday the schoolhouse at Malaga Island was opened for the fall term of school. This house has been built and paid for from subscriptions of Maine club women, and others and Massachusetts philanthropists. The teachers are to be paid for by the State.

Forty persons live on the island. 11 of them children, and within the past few years they have had no educational privileges at all. The past few summers, however, Miss Lucy M. Lane of Boston has been conducting a school for the greater part of the summer. Through their love for music, Miss. Lane has won the children and her labor at the island is a labor of love. The little hall in the new building is the only public place for a meeting place on the island.

Mrs. F. L. Odlin, chairman of the educational committee of the Maine Federation of Women's Clubs, has received the following letter from Miss Lane:

Sebasco, Me. Oct. 17, 1908

My Dear Mrs. Odlin - Was very glad to receive your letter and hope that the clubs will interest themselves in the educational of the children of Malaga Island.

We have succeeded in raising money nearly sufficient to finish the schoolhouse. If it will be ready for the fall term commencing on Oct. 19th. There is still much to be done there. We need furnishing for the kitchen, furniture for a small reception room that we want furnished neatly and attractively as an object lesson. We also want the surroundings improved. The people will do the work, but the material is needed and whatever can be done to improve their condition will be greatly appreciated.

Hoping to hear favorably from you, I am,

Most sincerely.
LUCY H. LANE

# SHADOWS IN OUR BONES

Boston Transcript
Tues Eve, Nov. 24, 1908

## MALAGA ISLAND SCHOOL

### The True Story of a Praiseworthy Effort to Help the People of a Lonely Island in Casco Bay

When Captain Lane and his wife of Malden, Mass., went on to Malaga Island in eastern Casco Bay, Maine, to see what they could do to help the people, some three years ago, they found there a mixed race making a poor living by clam-diffing and fishing, existing in unsanitary conditions and regarded by some of the mainlander's and others as a worthless community to spend any efforts upon. Captain Lane had been known in these waters for many years as he sailed along the Maine Coast, anchoring now and then in some little bay to preach to the people in a small settlement or to establish a Sunday school, and wherever he went his genial manner won him friends. This same warm-heartedness he carried when he went ashore at Malaga and soon a work of uplift was planned. It did not take Mrs. Lane long to see the importance and hopeful side of a work of educating the ten children then growing up in ignorance and vice. Starting that summer, a little school in one of the homes there, with the help of her daughter, she became convinced at the end of the season, that the next summer ought to see a movement on foot that should result in a good substantial schoolhouse suited to the needs of that island. Mr. Payson Smith, State superintendent of the schools of Maine, was communicated with, the whole situation explained, everything looked into, for Mr. Smith personally visited the island and sanctioned the movement, promising the State's support to a teacher if a schoolhouse could be built. The laws of Maine prohibit the use of funds for buildings of this character, so private means had to be employed. In the spring of this year in Malden a move was made by Mrs, Lane among interested people and friends to raise a fund to build the Malaga School. Mrs. Margaret Deland of Boston gave one of her noted readings and the proceeds she donated to the fund, which increased at a jump. From time to time the amount grew until in the early summer it seemed justifiable to go ahead and contract for building.

Arriving at their summer home on Horse Island, just south of Malaga, Captain Land and family, June 1, found the people of Malaga more destitute than ever on account of the short clam-digging season; also, that several new families had taken up residence there. The little school was opened again, this time as a school under the auspices of the State, in the house of Mrs. McKinney, with twelve pupils. A gift of enough desks and chairs from a Boston lady helped. Miss Cora Lane taught the school throughout June, July and August, rowing over and back each day to the Island, except when the weather was too stormy to get across. Many summer people visited the school and saw what had been accomplished. The contrast in these children form the conditions and ignorance of two years was marked. Indeed. On July 6th, a flag-raising took place on the site of the proposed schoolhouse on a rocky bluff at the easterly side among the spruces and firs. About seventy-five people came together. On Aug. 1st the frame was laid and on Oct, 23rd the building was completed and school began that week there for the fall term. It is a shingled, hip-roof, frame building, 22x26 feet, finished in good shape with three room - the schoolroom, a reception or social room, and a kitchen. These are to be adapted to the needs of the island and it is hoped that in some way a little of what is termed domestic science can be taught the mothers; and that the opportunities for a gathering place will be appreciated is not to be doubted, for at the services held there on Sunday, Oct. 25, the place was crowded and great was the rejoicing.

Now the interesting part of this is that so many have entered into this little project in so kindly and helpful a spirit. It was intended to raise $600. Of that amount $580 has been contributed mainly by people in Malden, Portland and Boston. The list includes some of the most representative men and women, and one of the largest churches, the Federation of Women's Clubs of Maine, and other organizations, and it is hoped the amount may speedily reach the $800 mark, which amount will be necessary owing to the difficulties that have been encountered by the situation making transportation and material expensive, and on account of high cost of labor and material. And further help will be gladly received by Mr. F. H. C. Woolley, treasurer of the Malaga Schoolhouse Fund, 149 Franklin Street, and any information regarding this work will be freely given.

TAMARA MERRILL

Harper's Magazine
1909


## Queer Folk of the Maine Coast
By Holman Day

Between Kittery Point and Quoddy head "re-sorters" have acquired hundreds of headlands and thousands of islands. A phalanx of cottages fronts the sea. More than half the States of the union are represented in these summer colonies. Cove and cape, the coast is pretty well monopo-lized by non-residents; "no-trespass" signs are so thickly set that they form a blazed trail. The man from the city resents intrusion. For that matter, the queer squatter people who have been dispossessed find little relish in being stared at as human curiosities."

"To counsel on economy and to preachment on thrift they are as inattentive as little children would be. A coast missionary (George Lane) took in hand one especially improvident family of six… Spurred by him, they fished, dig clams, sold bait to trawlers, and at the end of the summer saved about seventy-five dollars among them. Then the missionary went away, confident that at least one Malaga family would reach "March Hill" in comparative comfort. When his back was turned, they used for kindling the shingles that he had given them for the repair of their miserable hut, bought six dogs in order that each member of the family could have its own pet, and spent the rest of the money for sweets, pickles, jellies, and fancy groceries."

The Boston Globe
October 28, 1910


## SAYS MAINE HAS MOST DIVORCES

**Leads All East, Prof Sprague Finds.
Suggests More Dignified Civil Wedding
as One Remedy.
Charities Conference on Portland Tour.**

**PORTLAND, Me, Oct 28** Prof B. J. Sprague of the
university of Maine suggested to the state conference of charities and corrections yesterday
the following measures to mitigate the divorce
evil:

That a civil marriage be given more of the ele-
ment of dignity and impressiveness; marriages to
be confined to churches, homes and public rooms;
publication of the intentions of marriage; the
requirement of a separation for one year before
the granting of a divorce and the cooperation of
the people and churches to work for a sounder
public sentiment.

Maine stands at the head of all states east
of the Alleghany mountains in the number of divorces, said Prof Sprague, and 14 percent of all
families are broken up by the divorce courts. He
said that in the five years following 1877 there
were 2511 divorces in Maine, and in the five years
following 1902 the number was 4389. He continued:
"Divorce it not the evil in itself - if properly
guarded. The real evil to be combated is the
diseased and unhealthy family and not primarily
the divorce system. Divorce granted for sufficient
causes and under proper regulation is a benefit
to society and not an evil and adds to the sum
of human happiness.

"It Is the surgical operation on the social body, regrettable, but made necessary by a diseased condition of the family organism."

He found among the causes leading to the obtaining of divorces a greater degree of individual liberty, crabbedness, the fact that with changed modern conditions women no longer fear to face the problem of getting an independent living, unrest and a desire for a change of location and lax marriage laws.

Mrs A. R. Scott of Bangor also discussed the family in the home.

The large attendance in Kotzsohmar hall showed increased interest in the subjects discussed.

In the morning the delegates in automobiles visited the state school for boys, the Maine school for the deaf, the children's hospital and the fraternity house on Center St, where many children are helped to lay the foundation of an education.

Pres Hyde presided at the afternoon session. The conference discussed the treatment of defective children. Dr George S. Bliss of the Maine school for the feeble-minded at Pownal said it is necessary that the feeble-minded shall be taught by bright and interesting people who can set them a good example.

Mrs Clark H. Barker of Portland of the board of overseers of the poor spoke of the Maine institution for the blind, where brooms have been made, chairs reseated and mattresses manufactured or made over. From the receipts of this work the superintendent has turned over to the treasurer over $4700.

At the evening session a state board of charities was advocated by Robert Treat Whitehouse of Portland and Alexander Johnson, secretary of the national conference of charities and corrections.

**Boston Journal**
**August 1911**


"The island really belongs to the town of Phippsburg, but it is a most unwelcome possession, and receives no attention from the authorities."

TAMARA MERRILL

## Phenology Chart and Intelligence Test Sample Page

The first modern intelligence test in IQ history was developed in 1904, by Alfred Binet
(1857-1911) and Theodore Simon (1873-1961). The
French Ministry of Education asked these re-
searchers to develop a test that would allow
for distinguishing mentally retarded children
from normally intelligent, but lazy children.
The result was the Simon-Binet IQ test. This IQ
test consists of several components such as logi-
cal reasoning, finding rhyming words and naming
objects. The score for the IQ test in combination
with a child's age, provides information on the
intellectual development of the child: is the
child ahead of or lagging other children? The IQ
was calculated as (mental age/chronological age)
X 100. The test came to be a huge success, both
in Europe and America.

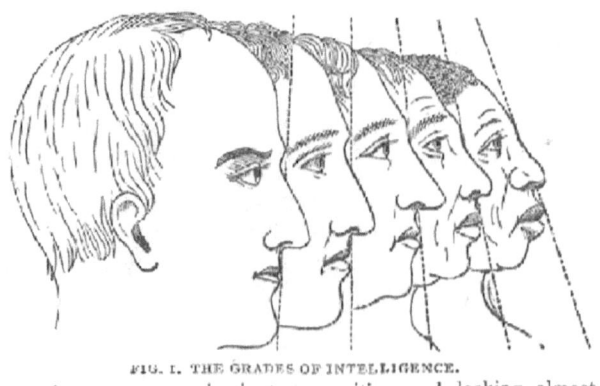

FIG. I. THE GRADES OF INTELLIGENCE.

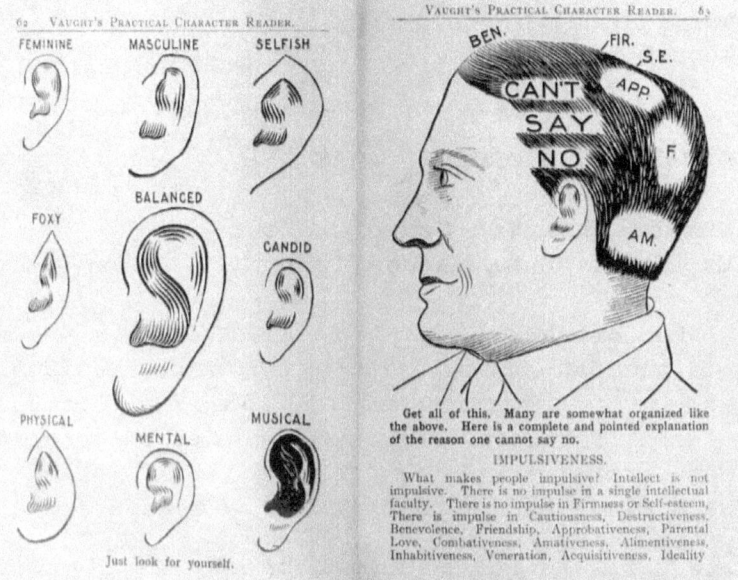

*Note:* The test pictured below is an example of a Beta test. Each picture has a part missing. Identify the missing part in as many pictures as possible within three minutes. (The answers appear on page 180.)

Example of a Beta test taken by army draftees in 1917.

TAMARA MERRILL

Wilmington Morning Star
August 9, 1911


**DEGENERATES ORDERED AWAY.**

**Summer Visitors Cause Order of
Expulsion from Malaga Island.**

**Bangor, Me., Aug. 7.** - Aroused by the com-
plaints of Summer visitors and nearby residents
in the beautiful town of Phippsburg, Attorney
General Pattangall has given notice to about 40
degenerates now Inhabiting the little Island of
Malaga, at the mouth of the New Meadows river,
to vacate the island.

Descended from a Portuguese sailor and a white
woman, these benighted people, only a mile from
the seat of one of Maine's leading colleges at
Brunswick, live like savages, only recently ob-
serving the laws of God and man. They are com-
posed of negroes, Portuguese and whites, and,
neglected by mankind, have lived a life under
almost unimaginable conditions. The old tribal
customs still prevail among these people. They
have a king in John F, Murphy, who is boss of the
island, and the most intelligent and only self-
supporting citizen of Malaga. He owns a motorboat
and makes a good living lobster fishing and taking
Summer visitors sailing and fishing.

These people pay no taxes, observe no laws and
five or six years ago were so low in the human
scale that a local justice of the peace went over
to the island, shot a half dozen dogs and married
all the couples he could round up. The death of
the dogs caused the more comment.

The days of the week, calendar dates, people's
ages, definite paternities - these things are
unknown quantities among the Malagaites. They
live in hovels that, for lack of sanitation, are

282

almost inconceivable. With one or two exceptions the shacks have dirt floors and a single room. Here men, women, children, blacks and whites, cats and dogs, to say nothing of other crawling things, live and have their being.

There are more dogs and goats in Malaga to the square foot than anywhere else in the world, possibly excepting Constantinople.

TAMARA MERRILL

**Copy of the Commitment Form for Lottie Marks
December 12, 1911**

Form 1.

# State of Maine.

*To the Trustees of the Maine School for Feeble Minded.*

GREETING:

Whereas, upon application and after due notice and a proper hearing, it has been made

to appear to me, *James S Lowell* Judge

of the Probate Court for the County of *Sagadahoc*, that

*Lottie Marks* of *Malaga Island* in the county of

*Sagadahoc* in said state is a fit subject for the Maine School

for Feeble Minded.

Now, Therefore, you, the trustees of said School, are hereby ordered and required to

receive the said *Lottie Marks* of the *State*

of *Maine* and to detain *her* in your care until

*she* be discharged by law, or by the trustees, as provided by law.

Witness *Hon. James S. Lowell* at *Bath*

this *12* day of *December*

in the Year of our Lord one thousand nine hundred and *eleven*.

Attest: *Arnold Wrongler*

Register of Probate for the County of *Sa...*

284

The Boston Globe
December 14, 1911


COLONY BROKEN UP.

Seven to Be Taken From Malaga
Island. Are Committed to Maine
School for Feeble-Minded.

**BATH, Me, Dec 14** Today probably will see the
first step of the proposed disintegration of the
colony which for years has occupied the island
of Malaga.

At Tuesday's, session of the Sagadahoc County
Probate Court Judge James S. Lowell, on petition
of George C. Pease of Phippsburg, agent for the
State of Maine, ordered the following persons of
feeble mind on Malaga Island committed to the
Maine School for the Feeble Minded: Jake Marks,
Etta Marks. Lizzie Marks, Lottie Marks, James
Marks, Abbie marks and Anna A. Parker.

The disposition of these people will not rid
the Island entirely of Its population, but will
leave 30 or more persons remaining, most of whom
are able-bodied and can earn their own living,
which it is said the State now proposes they
shall do. Any action on the part of the State
to throw the remaining inhabitants upon the town
of Phippsburg will be strenuously opposed by
the officers of that town, who declare they can
demonstrate that Atty Gen Pattengall Is wrong in
his contention that the island lies within the
boundaries of this county.

285

# TAMARA MERRILL

## Executive Council Report 1911
## Conditions at Malaga Island.

Jake Marks family.

He and his wife are octoroons. He is 55 years old; his wife 45. One boy, James, 30 years old, feeble minded, sore on face hag eaten away the moat of one cheek and into his eye. Nearly blind. Remains indoors most of the time. Lizzie Marks, 28 years old, has a child 2 1/2 years old; father of child supposed to be William Griffin. Lottie Marks, 18 years old, courted by William Griffin, who assists in supporting her. Cost of this family to State for first nine months of 1911 $185.07.

Robert Tripp and family,

Robert Tripp is 40 years old 1/4 negro. Nearly blind. Wife 45 years old, 1/2 negro. Well and strong. 4 children, ranging from 3 to 12 years of age. Three of the children have a white father, one Edward Barnes. Cost of this family to the State for first nine months of 1911 $113.41.

James McKenney and family

James, 64 years old, troubled with asthma, not able to do much work. Wife 60 years old. James is white and his wife an octoroon. Wife is well and strong. No children at home or dependent. Boards Mrs. Annie Parker, for which state pay $3.00 per week in Summer and $3.50 in Winter. Cost to State first nine the of 1911, $12.15, in addition to amount paid for board of Mrs. Parker. Expense of Mrs. Parker to State for first nine months of 1911 was $126.50, which includes an occasional doctor bill.

Frank Gomez and family.

Frank is 68 years old, a Portuguese, well and strong. Wife is younger and feeble minded. Has left him and is living in Harpswell. Have two children in the feeble-minded school at Pownal. Son, Charles Gomez, married, lives on the island, has two children. This family have lived on the island about four years, and have a settlement in Phippsburg. Have never received help.

Nelson McKenney and family.

Nelson is 48 years old, white, lost one leg. Complains all the time of being sick. Wife 35 years old, daughter of James McKenney. Well and strong. 5 children, ranging from 6 to 16 years old. One child blind, others bright and smart. Family has a settlement in Harpswell, and are helped by Harpswell.

Henry Griffin and family.

Henry is 70 years old, well and strong, brightest man on the island. Wife is dead. Lives with George Marks. Is said to have been intimate with Sadie Johnson, a girl 14 years old, the daughter of William Johnson who is an inmate of the Soldier's Home at Togus. This girl now lives with Emery Griffin. Emery Griffin is a woman. George Marks and Robert Tripp are the sons of John Eason's wife. Henry Griffin cost the State $18.63 during the first nine months of 1911.

(3)

Jerry Murphy and family.

Jerry is 48 years old, white, well and strong, drinks considerably. Wife 48, daughter of James McKenney, half—breed, well and strong. 4 children, ranging from 6 to 16. Cost state for first nine months of 1911, $4.00. This is for a doctor's bill.

James McKenny Jr. and family.

James is 35 years old, white, strong, good to work. Wife 28, white, well and strong, good to work. 3 children, oldest about 5 years. Nearly self—sustaining. Have cost State nothing, but probably would sooner or later.

John Easton and wife

John is 65 year old, full—blooded negro, well as average man of that age, rather intelligent. Can do good mason work, but lazy and won't work. Wife 65, negress, complains of being sick all the time and unable to work (?). As already stated, Mrs. Easton is the mother of George Marks and Robert Tripp. Cost state for first nine months of 1911, $63.76.

Eliza Griffin

47 years old, half-breed, well and strong. Will fish, dig clams or potatoes, do a man's work. Lives in a small hut. Provides for Sadie Johnson, who lives with her, and has for four years. Cost to State $55.25 first nine months of 1911. Very little help this Summer, but must have more this winter.

(4)

Emery Griffin

Emery Griffin is a woman, sister to Eliza, 50 years old, negress, well and strong, good to work, will take in washing or do anything for a living, lives alone, has supported herself this Summer, but will need help this Winter. Has cost the State $15.89 the first nine months of 1911.

| Families | No. of People | Cost 9 months |
|---|---|---|
| Jake Marks | 6 | $185.07 |
| Robert Tripp | 6 | 113.41 |
| James McKenney | 2 | 12.15 |
| Mrs. Annie Parker | 1 | 126.50 |
| Frank Gomez | 5 | 0 |
| Nelson McKenney | 7 | 0 |
| Henry Griffin | 2 | 18.63 |
| Jerry Murphy | 6 | 4.00 |
| James McKenney, Jr. | 5 | 0 |
| John Eason | 2 | 63.76 |
| Eliza Griffin | 1 | 55.25 |
| Sadie Johnson | 1 | 4.00 |
| Emery Griffin | 1 | 15.89 |
| | 45 | 598.66 |
| Agents, salary and expenses, | | 72.42 |
| Total expense, nine months | | 671.08 |

Suggestions made by Agent Pease.

State should own island. It could then prevent people from settling there, and turn off the undesirable ones.

What could be done under this condition.

| | |
|---|---:|
| Order Gomez family to Phippsburg, | 5 |
| Order Nelson McKenney and family to Harpswell, | 7 |
| Buy out James McKenney, Jr. who would probably sell his place for $100.00 and leave the island, | 4 |
| Order Jerry Murphy and family to leave. He has stated that he would go when ordered, but it might be necessary to pay him a little, probably $100.00 | 6 |
| Order William Griffin and Geo. Marks to leave the island. William Griffin has a house that probably cost $25.00, which might have to be paid for. | 2 |
| Place Mrs. Annie Parker in the home for feeble minded. She is a fit subject, | 1 |
| Commit Sadie Johnson to Bath Military and Naval Orphan Asylum, | 1 |
| Order Eliza and Emery Griffin from the island. They can get a living anywhere, | 2 |
| Commit Lottie, Lizzie and James Marks to the home for feeble minded, fit subjects, | 3 |
| Send Lizzie Marks child, 2 ½ years old, to Mrs. Hunt, at Portland. She wants the child, | 1 |

32

By this disposition, 32 people would be removed from the island.

Under this arrangement, there would be left on the island the following:

| | |
|---|---:|
| Jake Marks and wife, | 2 |
| James McKenney and wife, | 2 |
| Robert Tripp, wife and children, | 6 |

John Eason and wife,                                    2

Henry Griffin,                                          1
                                                    _____
                                                       13

    The four Tripp children could be accommodated with school privileges at small expense on the main land.

    If this plan were carried out, Jake Marks' wife would probably leave. Jake is in poor health, and probably won't live long. James McKenney is an old man, not well, and probably will not live long. John Eason and wife are in poor physical condition for people of their age.

    If conditions remain as they are now, in five years there would be a large increase over the present population for the State to care for.

    Agent Pease says that the State could purchase the island from the Perry heirs and receive a good title for the sum of $400.00. He further says that if the State is not in a position to buy at present, it could obtain an option on the property at a nominal gum for a reasonable time to purchase at that figure.

**Brunswick Times Record**
**July 21, 1911**


Governor Frederick Plaisted visited Malaga Island in 1911, along with his Executive Council, to see the island for himself. The governor reported he was encouraged by the progress of the children in school, but was not convinced the community would ever accept a middle-class style of living. During his visit, Plaisted remarked, "the best plan would be to burn down the shacks with all their filth. Certainly, the conditions are not creditable to our state, and we ought not to have such things near our front door, and I do not think that a like condition can be found in Maine, although there are some pretty bad localities elsewhere."

# SHADOWS IN OUR BONES

Mower County Transcript
Lansing, Minnesota
February 14, 1912


What a lesson in sociology is contained in the following brief item: Seven inmates arrived last week at the Maine school for feeble minded. They represented four generations of one family, their ages ranging from three to seventy years.

Bath Independent
March 9, 1912

## Report submitted by Nelson Leighton McKenney

"Another dried up native says how he will be the last nigger that leaves his old home after seventy years, the most of it on Malaga… "The others of us are having hard times to find homes anywhere; all on account of folks saying we've got the catch-cramp in fingers and take too many things what are lying 'round loose'. But it's all a lie; we don't steal if we are poor."

NEWSPAPER UNIDENTIFIED
1913

## Cleaning Up Malaga Island—No Longer a Reproach to the Good Name of the State

In little more than one year, Malaga Island had been cleared of its inhabitants and their ancestral remains. Structures left behind were dismantled, including the school house, which had operated as a public school for barely three years.

# TAMARA MERRILL

**Reports on Lottie Marks**
**1917 and 1919**


John Gould, a founder of the Malaga Island Settlement Association, wrote to the school (Maine's School for the Feeble Minded) in 1917..."to check on 'my old friends' from Malaga", but also commented, "The day will come sometime, I hope, when such people as those Marks, etc., etc., will not be allowed to reproduce their kind."

"She is a colored girl, now twenty-five yrs. Of age, of the moron type, or the type which is generally conceded to be the most dangerous to be at large, because of the marked tendency to become a source of social menace."

1919 report on Lottie Marks by schools superintendent (Maine School for the Feeble Minded)

The History of Pineland Center
Published: 1974


## By Judith Kleinberg

From an administrator at the Maine School
for the Feeble Minded: "...preventative measures
had to be taken, which would not permit 'tribal
aggregation and perpetuation'...There are a number
of scattered hamlets throughout the state peopled
by subnormals in ancestral shacks."

HP1327, 124th Maine State Legislature
JOINT RESOLUTION RECOGNIZING THE TRAGIC
EXPULSION OF THE RESIDENTS
OF MALAGA ISLAND, MAINE IN 1912 AND
REDEDICATING OURSELVES TO THE MAINE
IDEALS OF TOLERANCE, INDEPENDENCE
AND EQUALITY FOR ALL PEOPLES

PLEASE NOTE: Legislative Information *cannot* perform research, provide legal advice, or interpret Maine law. For legal assistance, please contact a qualified attorney.

## JOINT RESOLUTION RECOGNIZING THE TRAGIC EXPULSION OF THE RESIDENTS OF MALAGA ISLAND, MAINE IN 1912 AND REDEDICATING OURSELVES TO THE MAINE IDEALS OF TOLERANCE, INDEPENDENCE AND EQUALITY FOR ALL PEOPLES

**WHEREAS**, Malaga is a small rugged island of less than one square mile situated in Casco Bay off the shores of the Town of Phippsburg in Sagadahoc County and the Town of Harpswell in Cumberland County; and

**WHEREAS**, from about 1870 to 1912, Malaga was home to a mixed-race Maine community of people of Scots, Irish, Anglo, Native American and African-American ancestry, among others, struggling to survive as boatmen, fishermen, carpenters and laundresses, as did many rural islanders of that era; and

**WHEREAS**, in that era, for fear of being taxed to support alleged "chronic pauperism," nearby towns denied that Malaga existed within their town waters, and amid lawsuits actual ownership of Malaga lay in dispute for decades; and

**WHEREAS**, in that era, the now-disgraced Eugenics Movement claimed poverty and intemper-

298

ance were genetic traits due to "impure blood," using pseudoscience to reinforce racial and social stereotypes, holding Malaga and other isolated Maine communities up to ridicule in the national press, including the sensational "Queer Folk of the Maine Coast" in Harper's magazine in 1909; and

**WHEREAS**, in that era, prime island real estate, including Malaga, suddenly caught the eye of speculators and developers eager to build resort hotels for Maine's booming tourist trade; and

**WHEREAS**, in 1911, amid such tensions, Maine's Governor Frederick Plaisted and his Executive Council personally led an expedition to investigate conditions on Malaga and thereafter paid $417 to clear title to the island in the name of the State of Maine, which took possession; and

**WHEREAS**, in 1912, as public policy, the State of Maine evicted all Malaga islanders from their homes, paying token sums for the structures, ordered the Malaga schoolhouse, wharves and houses removed or destroyed, dug up the island graveyard, jumbling all remains into common caskets, and forcibly relocated many islanders to the Maine School for the Feeble Minded at Pownal, where some spent the rest of their lives and where the deceased of Malaga lie in mixed graves to this day; and

**WHEREAS**, in 1925, the State of Maine by law allowed forced eugenic sterilization of many residents of the Maine School for the Feeble Minded in order to, in the words of one Maine State Senator, "permanently improve the human race … and enforce sound, decent and efficient human beings"; and

299

**WHEREAS**, with Malaga deserted and the islanders dispersed or institutionalized, for almost 100 years the true story of Malaga disappeared into mystery and myth, a half-remembered legend deeply tinged with heartbreak, loss and shame, rarely referred to openly even by the scattered descendants of the Malaga islanders themselves; and

**WHEREAS**, the last known living former Malaga islander died in 1997 at the age of 103; and

**WHEREAS**, in recent years the story of Malaga has been rediscovered and has been the subject of books, national publications, television productions, university studies and a prominent Maine Public Radio production, "Malaga Island: A Story Best Left Untold," and will be the subject of a Maine State Museum special exhibition for the centennial in 2012; and

**WHEREAS**, in 2001, the Maine Coast Heritage Trust purchased Malaga Island, which now serves as a nature preserve, a University of Maine archeological site, a landmark on the Maine Underground Railroad and a place of education, reflection and renewal; now, therefore, be it

**RESOLVED:** That We, the Members of the One Hundred and Twenty-fourth Legislature now assembled in the Second Regular Session, on behalf of the people we represent, do recognize with profound regret the tragic displacement of the Malaga islanders in 1912, in the name of the disgraced Eugenics Movement, with its overtones of prejudice against poverty, racism and stereotyping; and, while rebuking this past, rededicate the future to the ideals of tolerance, independence and equality of all peoples in our ever-changing world, which are the birthright and heritage of all proud Mainers; and rededicate ourselves as lawmakers to the social and economic justice that is the right of all peoples; and be it further

**RESOLVED:** That suitable copies of this resolution, duly authenticated by the Secretary of State, be transmitted to the Maine Coast Heritage Trust, the Maine Historic Preservation Commission, the Maine Historical Society and the NAACP.

**TAMARA MERRILL** is the author of the award winning Augustus Family trilogy– Family Lies, Family Matters and Family Myths. A historical fiction series that follows the lives of one family through love, loss, adventure and misadventure. Her short stories, which are usually about family relationships, murder or mystery, are published in magazines and in four anthologies. In addition to fiction, she writes business articles related to Information Technology and how-to blog posts for DIY websites. She frequently speaks at book clubs and other book-related events. Tamara resides in Coronado, CA.

Website: www.TamaraMerrill.com

Facebook: TamaraMerrillAuthor

Instagram: tmerrillauthor

Email: Tamara@TamaraMerrill.com

www.ingramcontent.com/pod-product-compliance
Lightning Source LLC
Chambersburg PA
CBHW031643100726
47898CB00006B/1960